THE NEXT MINUTE

First Published in 2022

Beyond The Vale Publishing

Eric Kalume Mutshipayi

THE NEXT MINUTE

I dedicate this book to my wife, Angela Mbiya Kalume. children, late parents Kalume Lushikwa Mulamba and Mbiye Kazadi and family.

I thank God Almighty for making it possible, my wife, Angela Mbiya Kalume, Oliver Kalume, the late Pastor Kgosi Mogorosi and brother Thabiso Ntjepela for their prayers and encouragements.

Chapter 1

Colonel Themba suddenly entered his office full of worries, busy checking if his cell phone was in the pocket of his trousers. But he found nothing and he cried out loud, "Where is my cell phone?" He looked worried and regretted the mistake when he saw his wife entering the same hotel he frequently visited in the north of Johannesburg. But where was his cell phone?

All of a sudden his fixed-line rang and he rushed to respond. What he heard was a voice he knew like the fingers of his hands that could help him to get out of his embarrassing state of affairs; his cell phone was worth millions if any underworld criminal managed to browse through the data on it.

"Yes baby, are you better now?"

"What do you mean by baby? You know I don't like being called a baby."

"I need my money as quickly as promised; I know you always pay me on time."

"So why do you complain to me?"

She said nought and hung up. "This lady knows my fixed line and she probably has my cell phone with her and she can contact anyone to destroy my career". The truth is that he couldn't trust anyone with what he was doing. He started pacing up and down in his office seeking a possible solution on how to eliminate a disturbing witness but he still needed her. She was keen for the filthy works he was paying her for.

Last night was one of the best of his life but crazy for he forgot that everyone could see him enjoying one of the best moments of his life. Nthabiseng who knew too much about his life was there making no doubt that the plan was achieved as designed and it happened just the way he wanted. The last cargo was sold with a profit margin he never expected.

The fixed-line rang once more but he refused to act in response. Holding his chin he waited until it stopped ringing and it restarted again. This time he decided to respond.

"Colonel Themba is on the line," he said.

"You left your cell phone in the hotel room we were in last night."

"I beg your pardon? Do you have it?"

"Didn't you hear me?"

"Make sure that I have it by tonight."

"You know I always keep your stuff in safe hands and also clear up your mess with care, boss. What is the matter with you this morning, Colonel? And I urgently need an advance on my money by tonight, please make it happen. You are the best boss around."

"You will get half of the money tonight and don't forget that I feed you every day Nthabiseng and never call me on my fixed-line again."

And she hung up.

Unexpectedly the door was opened by his wife Siphokazi. The Colonel sometimes enjoyed calling her Sipho. She was a tall and pleasing to the eye woman working for the secret service of the South African government as a well-trained agent.

"Of which money are you talking about?" She asked. "Are you playing some dangerous games?" She said joking.

Colonel Themba said nothing but rather smiled at her for she was elegant and wearing an outfit that she knew he liked. And he welcomed her as a husband should welcome his wife in his office. He held her in his strong arms of a colonel who did Para-commando training about the first generation of the commandos who went for formation in Israel after the 1994 presidential elections. He was a well-trained soldier able to execute any fatal assault on the enemy and she knew that.

Colonel Themba saw his wife entering the prominent hotel of Sandton City with a secret agent he knew very well, and to see him around meant to look for something suspicious. Maybe he was the suspect they were looking for.

"How are you Sipho? You are gorgeous today."

"Thanks for noticing, and you? I tried to call you on your cell but no response."

"I can't find it," he said busy serving her a glass of wine.

She walked around the office to finally say, "Where were you last night? You're stressing me Themba because someone saw you in Sandton yesterday."

He almost swallowed a portion of his wine the wrong way, and then he responded.

"Yesterday? Doing what?"

"You know people talk, please I have prepared for you your preferred recipe, don't miss it."

"I will not darling." and she left after hugging him.

Themba's father was a retired former MK soldier. His mother, who was still living with his father, enjoyed her old age by travelling around all provinces, visiting her family members. She was incredibly attached to her family with loads of grandchildren to spoil.

Themba went through a difficult childhood simply because his father as an MK soldier was all the time gone to serve and that made him miss a father that seemed distant to him but his mother was always with him guiding his steps. She knew he was intelligent and wanted him to complete his undergraduate studies that he managed to complete in the University of South Africa (UNISA) but his dream was to become a soldier and a well trained one able to face the enemy without fear.

Physically apt he managed to qualify for a well-planned formation in Israel in the year 1995 with 49 others that he had never met before. Three years later he came back to South Africa with the title of a Para-commando. He was immediately nominated Lieutenant Commando mayor by the first democratic government, and three years later because of good commitment and dedication, he got promoted to Colonel Lieutenant.

As a civil servant working for the minister of national defence, enjoying working for the national colours of his nation, Themba realized that there were more profitable opportunities than just sitting in an office, taking important decisions and waiting for his monthly remuneration. He wanted more and quick money that could make him a multi-millionaire but he didn't know how much was going to come about.

He could meet very influential people he couldn't previously have envisaged meeting and that empowered him to connect with some evil of the city ready to sacrifice anything for their next million. And he became one of them in the beginning years of 2000 when he met people famous in the business of drugs. They promised him millions of Rand if he could connect them to the best customers around and he had them.

Having well disciplined and educated parents is a gift from God and he had them. He sometimes looked at himself in the mirror and could not explain the root origin of his affiliations with the drug business. He had passed the point of no return now; he knew too much to easily turn his back to the drug lord. But the money he was already making was amazing and he was enjoying making that money with many risks.

Unfortunately, his beloved wife, Sipho, was unaware of all those millions her husband had. He was too malicious to let her know. He never wanted her to have a glimpse of what he was doing. Sometimes he was thinking about introducing her and working together and then fleeing the country but it was very difficult. He loved her too much to dust her hands and those of his children too. She rather wanted another baby, a daughter to just look like her and not to turn into a drug dealer; besides she was satisfied with what she was getting from the government.

He was grateful towards his nation for giving him the perfect opportunity to become the person he coveted to become, a man in uniform loved by his father-in-law and a civil servant trusted by the government. And the authority was not finished with him because they wanted him to go further with his military knowledge.

Siphokazi his wife was the daughter of a rich man who never hid his riches. Spoiled since she was a child, her father wanted her to marry someone in uniform that believes in discipline and order. And Themba was the perfect match. She married the choice of the father who lacked nothing that the world could offer except for a son-in-law in uniform.

Working as an undercover was courtesy of her husband who responded to her desire and she thanked God for that. She loved being a secret agent of the government for she had the brainpower. And she was right now working on a very serious case that was undermining the effort of the government to create a decent drug-free society.

They met during a function in Soweto on Vilakazi Street not far away from Mandela's house. Holding a glass of unfermented wine in her right hand and talking to nobody but seemingly thinking, Themba considered this moment as the perfect opportunity to introduce himself. She had a natural smile on her face that misguided many and Themba took it as a facilitator and everything started there. Her father was very happy and financed seventy per cent of the wedding.

He never stopped loving her, spoiling her with the best he could give to her for she was well mannered, adorable and loving the presence of the Lord. She gave him two sons that he loved so much and she wished to have another one; a daughter to cherish with all her heart. She wanted a daughter to just look like her and to whom to give the name of her mother-in-law.

A dirty hand wounds the soul, carelessly bruising your emotions, and Sipho, innocent she was, didn't know what was waiting for her. She considered herself as a fortunate woman among so many in occurrence a husband whose father-in-law adores and respected but something was missing that she always kept for herself. A condom was found two months ago in his working bag.

"Are all men the same? Liars and unfaithful? Should I expect my husband to be completely faithful to me? He brings me beautiful flowers that cost thousands of rand and I like them but why a condom that we never used? What would my mother say hearing such a disgrace because as a couple we don't use a preservative? How do I talk to my mother about something like this?" A decision had to be made and she decided to keep quiet until she collected more information.

But on the other side, the money was flowing into his secret accounts. He had multiple accounts in his children's names that she didn't know about. And they were not his only children; he had two others with Nthabiseng.

Nthabiseng had a dream one day to become a chartered accountant but her gluttony couldn't let her get there but was rather carrying around her a charming attitude that Colonel Themba five years ago fell in love with while browsing the multitude of shops in the big mall of Sandton City. She wasn't far away from where he was when he got nearer to the restaurant area.

She was in one of the restaurants shouting at a waitress with such an authoritative voice, it made Themba think about his military training. Surprised by her authoritative voice he decided to fix his eyes in hers to give birth to a new relationship. And as she was interested in those strong eyes she decided to fix him too. The moment was favourable because he got close to her and said to her, "I have a better restaurant to take you to tonight". And everything started there.

"But I am a student," she said when he decided to take her out of the big mall.

"A greedy beautiful student deserves more than just passing her subjects". And she expressed the smile of a lifetime that stuck with Themba until today. But she realized later on that Themba was a dangerous man with an exceptional acquisitiveness.

"But you have a very beautiful wife?" She asked.

"You are right and she is more beautiful inside and I don't deserve her," he said. I am a man in uniform that her father likes. "I am her father's choice and she is an exceptional woman but she met the wrong one."

"Am I the right one?" She asked with sensuality.

"I enjoy the presence of mystifying women; I am the game that many hate except you." And they came together that night and she also disappeared from the university until today.

The children were already asleep and the dinner was already set on the table. She cooked his preferred recipe; she truly wanted the evening to be only one of its kind. She dressed traditionally with the intent to cast his mind back nine years in the past when they got married before four hundred guests including the vice-president of the republic.

But it was getting late and discouraging for she had no signs of her husband coming home. She made sure to keep the food hot but the hour was getting late and heartbreaking, and he was not even calling. What was keeping him so late at night?

Tears of deception started running down her face, wiping away the beautiful make-up she made for him; hating this moment of loneliness caused by the man in uniform she loved so much.

And suddenly she heard the car door banging. "It is him," she said wiping her tears but it was too late because he was already behind her calling her name.

"Sipho darling I'm repentant."

She turns around to see a man holding his suitcase with his tie unknotted and with sadness in his eyes.

"It's not too late my king," she said.

He got closer to her and began wiping her face of those tears that erased her beautiful makeup and she swiftly said, "There is a time for everything Themba. Don't do that again."

"You are so fine-looking Sipho and look at the layout on the table."

What an evening it was and once a month she made sure to experience such an encounter with her husband and Themba knew and liked it with all his heart. She had an infectious laugh every time they danced together to very soft South African Jazz music. After all, it was a well-to-do family with the best paying jobs out there and she made sure to turn the extravagance on that evening. And while dancing she noticed an unfamiliar perfume coming from her husband's clothes. It was a delicate perfume that could have cost thousands of Rands.

"What beautiful perfume you're wearing," she said with a soft eye in his eyes.

15

Expressing a meticulous smile, realizing the poison he turned into for he spent the whole afternoon with his secret personal assistant Nthabiseng.

"Yes, I entered a very expensive perfume shop in the mall and this is the next perfume you will buy for me."

She said nothing as if she was not bothered about what he said and while dancing she asked, "Then how was your day?"

"As usual."

"But you were not at the office when I suddenly popped in?"

"Come on," he was about to swallow his tongue and suffocate when she said smiling, "Let's not talk about it; I don't want to spoil the evening."

It was imminent that he was getting moneyed for he was in one of the best deals out there and no mistakes had to be made. It wasn't drugs this time but a more powerful deal than anything anybody could think of.

Like anybody else he dreads failure, taking the wrong decision was intolerable but he knew he was on the right path for he was a strategist. Nobody should try to double-cross him for he will kill and leave no traces. He was determined to become a multi-millionaire and to create an empire that nobody could even try to rupture.

They dashed upstairs holding each other, concluding the way a happily married couple should end the evening, in each other's arms.

"I love you," he said happy to be his wife.

Two days later at nine o'clock in the evening, Johannesburg downtown was shining from its lights, exposing a picturesque city that sometimes turns very unsafe. And Sipho at the steering wheel of her car followed by secret agent Dumisane was driving towards Gandhi square bus station. They were going not far away from Gandhi square bus station. A well known abandoned building where most of the illegal dealings were happening was under surveillance by the police. And once they arrived there detective Naidoo saw two cars arriving he knew very well and he didn't want them there. Once the occupants were out of their car, he asked them, "What are you doing here Dumisane?"

With a gun in his hand and followed by dozens of policemen, they entered the structure and headed in the direction of the second floor. Without hesitation Sipho and Dumisane followed the contingent with pistols in their hands, ready to surprise any assailant.

As they were following the police it wasn't long that gunshots surprised those following them behind, followed by dreadful screams of women and children. There was blood everywhere along the corridor of the second floor that was mostly occupied by drug smugglers.

Siphokazi and Dumisane made sure to lie on the floor when unexpectedly behind them gunshots hit mercilessly two chests of two policemen, who died on the spot. But in a quick move, Sipho managed to execute the perfect shot that hit the assailant right in the stomach, making him bleed to death.

The police managed to neutralize the outlaws. They were about to exchange a big quantity of drugs for money and the police managed to keep some alive who they arrested, and took to the police station along with drugs worth millions of Rands.

At the police station, detective Naidoo approached the two secret agents. "Why follow me everywhere?"

"We also have to cross-examine them," said Siphokazi.

"They won't talk and you know it very well, and maybe you won't find them tomorrow morning because they are well connected," said Naidoo.

"Don't worry Naidoo; they won't leave until they are thoroughly interrogated," said Dumisane.

"And how do you know I was getting there?"

"We are the secret agents," said Dumisane, "We listen to everyone. And don't worry for they won't leave this place until we say so."

Naidoo left to go to his office followed by the two secret agents and after sitting on his desk he said. "What are you up to?"

"There is more than drugs," said Dumisane.

"We need as much information's as possible to uncover what is happening underneath but it's very dangerous," said Sipho.

"We need your help, Naidoo," said Dumi. "We are secret agents and we can't expose ourselves all the time but someone who can feed us in any possible way."

"What do you mean by, more than drugs? Is there worse than these drugs?"

"Prohibited gold leaves South Africa for unknown destinations and this is costing the country millions of Rands. Some are getting very rich behind the government's and especially the nation's back and we need to unite to stop these illicit transactions."

Naidoo held his chin to say, "You can count on me, for my nation I will do so."

"Thank you," said Dumisane shaking his hand. First thing tomorrow morning we will come to question them.

"You are welcome."

Before leaving the police station, while Sipho was getting into her car, Dumisane approached her to tell her, "Mr Themba is very often accompanied by a woman. I knew her many years ago in high school. A gambling lady I've never trusted while studying with her."

"My husband Themba?" She asked.

"Check on him very well, he might be hiding something from you."

And she left without saying a word.

What an attractive restaurant it was in the middle of Midrand City, North of Johannesburg. It was a discreet restaurant twelve kilometres away from the big Mall of Africa where a mysterious couple was dining but at the same time sharing their daily activities.

Colonel Themba faced Nthabiseng and they were sharing a delicious meal as they had done many times before. They always made sure to never behave as a dating couple in public for Themba was a man of many relations and his wife knew it.

And from a reasonable distance on the first floor of the restaurant his wife Sipho's own assistant, another state secret agent was busy following their moves for quite a time. The agent was in direct contact with Sipho confirming the identity of the woman; an alleged suspect in many crimes happening in the city. Her assistant even made sure to send her a shot of their dinner but there was no evidence they were a dating couple because their behaviour was professional.

But Siphokazi received the news as a terrible blow for that lady was a suspect in many crimes happening in the city of Johannesburg. Still, the police were in search of evidence relating to her. Why would this man have a meal with such a person? She stood up paralyzed because that was her husband, the father of her children.

There was already a ray of brilliant sunshine in the city but it wasn't brilliant for her. She was troubled and disappointed, but she realized she had to be patient for this was going to take them somewhere. She hoped her husband was innocent of any crime committed by Nthabiseng.

"Be careful, Carol, make sure they don't see you following them everywhere, we need to get to the bottom of this, there's something fishy."

"Don't worry, Sipho my eyes are on them."

"Any kiss?" She asked.

"You know I would have told you."

"Thank you."

It wasn't a brief meeting for the conversation was long. They were talking a lot and both of them had concerned faces, noticed carol. She regretted not being able to record the conversation and put a final point to the wrong happening in the big city. But the way they talked proved that something certainly went wrong somewhere.

Carol had also gone through rigorous military training in Pretoria. She did it voluntarily for two years to appropriate discipline. She was first-rate in what she was doing and with such beauty, it was going to be very difficult to suspect her as a secret agent following evil people like Colonel Themba. But still, she had to be very careful of Colonel Themba as he was not an amateur and he could smell danger like a shark noticing its prey still many meters away.

Nevertheless, the couple was talking but this time with more intensity, the lady seemed very unhappy about something and that made Carol categorically question, the relationship for she was talking in his face and then she calmed down.

Colonel Themba enjoying the exquisite taste of his red wine suddenly told Nthabiseng, "Losing millions of Rand is beyond me, what went wrong?"

"Don't blame me, Themba, I told them exactly what you instructed me. Have our conversations been listened to?"

"Have you noticed that we have been followed by the white woman upstairs? Don't turn your head to look at her. She has been glancing at us for a long time. I want you to take care of her."

"Come again? Do you want her to die? I will do so for you."

"These kinds of people are those making me lose millions of Rands and your commission too is gone."

"Consider it done, Colonel."

Chapter 2

While In the interrogation room at the John Foster police station in Johannesburg CBD, detective Naidoo with Siphokazi and Dumisane listened to one of the drug dealers putting in plain words his version of the event. The trio wanted him to tell them everything he knew about the origin of such a big amount of drugs confiscated, where it was going to and who was the mastermind behind it.

"You tell us everything and we guarantee you protection, but only if you take us to the big boss," said Naidoo.

"I have no clue about the big boss, I've never met him and I will never meet him. They don't meet people like us, they don't mind about us."

"Then you will spend the rest of your miserable life in prison," said Siphokazi between her lips. "Why carry on risking your life for some careless persons? Isn't the business providing you with a lot of money?"

"I'm out of here," said Dumisane, "Just keep him in jail forever."

"Ok," said Naidoo, "that's your pathetic fate."

"No, listen," said the drug dealer. "They truly don't care about us, but I bother about my family."

Naidoo smiled sarcastically.

"Do you know that you are a dead man once out of here without protection?" Said Naidoo between his broken teeth.

"You made them lose millions to spend on more crap," said Dumisane. "You'd better tell us what you know and that will appease your sentence. With such a quantity of drugs, you will spend all your youth in jail doing nothing while your wife will enjoy the courtesy of other men."

The drug dealer sighed and said, "What do you have for me that will protect my life and my family?"

"Nothing. Unless you tell us what we want to hear," said Sipho.

"I can't now."

"When will you be ready?" Said Sipho, "Come on Dumi I can't take this anymore, he is wasting our time."

And they left the office.

It was Sunday, 09h00 A.M. in the assembly of Pastor Thabiso and Tshepang

"Only the truth will set you free," said the Pastor. "And the truth is the word of God. Freedom will come when you don't just hear the word but when you're a doer of the word. It's poignant when I see so many young people getting into drugs and believe that drug will set them free because of the money they get out of it".

Colonel Themba and his wife Siphokazi listened to the preaching attentively from where they sat on the third row on the left-hand side of the Pastor.

"His Grace and Mercy is alive today and you can make the decision right now to change your heart and start serving him.

If not, it is going to be too late. Repent and welcome the Messiah in your life, open your heart and invite him in and He will transform you. It is His will to transform all areas of your lives. Amen."

Everybody applauded.

"What a sermon it was," said Sipho to her husband.

"Yes indeed."

Minutes later the service was finished and the couple, as always, went to greet the pastoral couple. Thabiso and Tshepang greeted other members of the congregation. And when they saw them they gave the couple a warm hold close; hugging them and at the same time praying for them. And after the prayer, they left holding each other's hands.

Dumisane seated with the drug dealer was waiting for the arrival of his colleague Siphokazi who was on her way. She was a bit late because of the traffic and Dumisane was patiently waiting for her with Naidoo busy smoking his cigarette. They were all ready for about ten minutes, for this was the last time in the interrogation room to cross-examine the drug dealer before transferring him to the big Soweto prison called Sun City, to wait for his appearance in court.

And six minutes later she made her entry into the room, dressed and smelling very nice.

"Finally, here you are."

"I'm really sorry for being late. What terrible traffic on the M1 North. So are we winning?"

"We were waiting for you," said Naidoo busy extinguishing his cigarette. After that, he came and sat on his desk in front of the smuggler who looked tired.

"Yes body," said Dumisane between his thick lips. "What do you have for us?"

"As much as I want to be free I don't have much to tell you because the deciders are using people like us to make their millions. They've never shown up but in the past, I've met a very influential woman from the cartel, dark in completion and good-looking and she used to bring us the goods to sell and some money, and she used to do that when we were operating from Kwazulu Natal."

"Do you mean your headquarters used to be in Kwazulu Natal?" Demanded Sipho.

"No, just operating from there."

"So you no longer operate from there?" Asked Naidoo.

"No, we move from one place to another one after messing up."

The trio looked at each other without saying anything and detective Naidoo left his desk and lit another cigarette. He was getting nervous.

"What you are telling us is not enough," he said.

"Can you recognize that woman if I show you the photo?" Said Sipho under the observance of Dumisane who was in love with her.

"I don't know because it has been two years."

Siphokazi opened up her purse and took an A4 photo that she gave to Naidoo to show the smuggler. It was among the photos she received from her assistant Carol; it was the lady her husband had dinner with, and she gave the photo hoping it wasn't the woman he was talking about. She also made sure to give a photo where her husband was not appearing.

The smuggler with care took the photo and without hesitation confirmed that it was her.

"She is a very dangerous lady," said the smuggler.

Siphokazi dissimulated her disappointment and her big surprise that her husband could have dinner with such a person and concentrated on what was going on.

"Just like you, can I see the photo?" Requested Dumisane.

Dumisane took the photo and focussed on it for a while. He was surprised by what he saw. He said nothing because he knew the lady in the photo but avoided expressing it in the presence of detective Naidoo that this is the woman he saw with Siphokazi's husband. The trio decided to leave the room after calling two policemen to take the smuggler back to the prison.

"But what about my situation?" Demanded the smuggler.

"We are going to think about it. Nothing else to tell us?" Said Naidoo.

"I've told you everything."

"But your story is not enough," responded Sipho.

Once outside of the police station, Dumisane asked Siphokazi where she found the picture.

"I received this picture from Carol."

"And how does Carol have this information? I went to primary school up to grade 9 with this woman and I also saw her with Colonel Themba."

"Carol saw this woman with my husband dining together and it smells very bad Dumisane; I'm so confused."

"Dining jointly!"

They both entered her car and started conversing together.

"What do you want to do now? I'm a confused woman."

"I'm truly sorry for such bad news, maybe there are just friends."

"Come on Dumisane, you know there is no such coincidence in our job."

"Don't tell your husband anything yet and you need to keep these pictures very far from him for they can turn into a snare against you."

Siphokazi started crying for she was so disheartened by the man in uniform that her father held in such high esteem.

"What am I going to tell my children and my parents?"

"Just face it courageously. Don't allow your emotions to take hold of you; keep on acting professionally until we get the pieces of evidence we need and if he is involved, he will face the law."

"But I want you, Dumisane, to keep it for yourself pending we have more evidence; he is the father of my children. Please, God, help me."

"I will, Sipho. I will," said her colleague.

She started the car and left. Soon after, she received a phone call

"Hello!"

"Sipho it is me, Carol, I'm driving along Louis Botha Avenue and I'm being followed." Out of the blue, the connection went off.

"Hello! Hello!" Said Siphokazi unsuccessful. "What is going on?"

Carol made sure to cut the communication with Sipho to focus on saving her life. She accelerated so that she could overtake many cars in front of her. A blue fast car had been following her since Grayston Avenue, Sandton and that seemed unsafe. And on Louis Botha Avenue where the traffic was getting intense taking into account the hour of the day, anything against her life could happen, when suddenly another car, difficult to identify, brutally crossed in front of hers; but before completely crossing, one aggressive man shot twice in her direction, breaking the windscreen.

She braked hard, but the move was fatal, for the car behind smashed hers with such violence that she viciously hit her chest against the steering wheel, causing her to stop breathing instantly.

Siphokazi after communicating with Carol quickly returned to meet Dumisane who was still busy at the police station.

"What are you saying?"

"Carol is under attack on Louis Botha, we need to find her because she is in danger."

Without wasting time and like a rocket, Dumisane like never before ran to his car and accelerated hard. They needed to find her alive but first, she had to escape them, but how for she was alone and without help.

Unexpectedly Sipho's cell phone rang and it was a woman's voice talking.

"Good day," greeted a woman's voice. "I'm calling you because you are the last person Carol spoke to. She has been shot."

"Oh my God, she got shot! Is she dead?"

"I'm sorry madam but yes."

Sipho started weeping.

"We are going there now, oh Carol my good friend!"

When they arrived on the scene of the murder, the police and the ambulances were already cleaning up the mess, for it caused a terrible accident involving multiple cars.

Sipho approached the scene calmly, crossing her fingers but unhelpful because Carol was already in the mortuary car waiting to be taken to the mortuary. She approached her body that was completely covered, already far away from the physical existence. Sipho uncovered her face with tears welling in her eyes, and it was her, Carol, gone forever looking like an innocent child sleeping.

She cried, "Why? Why Carol was so young? Ooh!"

"Yes, there's a day to get born and a day to die." Dumisane came and hugged her. "I'm truly sorry for this loss."

Driving into her compound after being dropped at the gate by her in love colleague Dumisane; she got out of her car very discouraged. It was still early to expect the kids home. She had requested an early day at work to have some rest for her world was falling apart. The man she loved was involved with criminals and seemed to be a criminal himself.

She went inside the house thinking about her mother who was far away from her and expecting the best for her. But suddenly she felt a strong urge to vomit and she rushed into the bathroom to release what wanted to come out of her. Perhaps it was the bad news about her husband or perhaps seeing the dead body of her friend Carol caused the vomit. Everything was certainly falling apart.

In addition, the weather on that day was nice reflecting a good beginning of summer, and looking through the windows the flowers in her garden were being blown left and right, waiting to fade away like the glories of men as if they've never existed. She just wanted to never care any longer for she was deceived by a person who should never let down.

Turning around with tears streaming down her face, she put on soft music at the same time holding in her hand the family album that she began paging through but with regret. She managed to look at some beautiful family pictures where they were holding each other like forever. But suddenly she felt like vomiting for a second time. And this time she wondered if she wasn't pregnant. Maybe the daughter she wanted was on the way, the daughter of the man she loved with all her heart.

She thought about the condom she once found in the pocket of one of his trousers and realized that it was perhaps connected; her husband was busy playing some very treacherous games, but she had to keep her temper under control for he could violently turn against her if he realized that she knew everything. She was busy looking at the pictures in the album; crying at the same time as if it was the end of the whole thing. She started thinking about how life will be with her children and without him around them; a daughter on the way without the man of her life to father her.

Her cell phone started ringing and when she checked it was her husband calling, but she refused to pick up the call. He insisted but still nothing, she couldn't, it was too early to play cinema. Her tears were still pouring down her face, deeply regretting what could be the truth.

"I hate you, Colonel Themba," she murmured, "I hate you. Why did you do this to our family?" With the family pictures in her hands and with one picture showing her father hugging him like a father hugs a son; it was a very stunning picture drowning in the water to disappear forever.

He sent her a message this time and the message said, "my wife I want you to make the recipe I like for tonight, I love you". But her cries intensified, he was just an obscure husband who was about to kill her from stress.

Siphokazi left the sofa to stand in front of the open window that was exposing a peaceful view that never deceives. The branches of the trees of her garden were moving according to the direction of the wind for they had no choice but to do so. They were forced to do so to express the existence of the wind that no one has ever seen, a wind that will harm the tree the day it will get violent. And her husband was like that wind that she followed for many years to get deceived today.

However she could choose to stay and carry on being harmed by the wind or walk away forever, but it wasn't easy because she loved her family and wanted it united. And she had the forewarning that it would end badly. People were dying around them and her husband seemed to be playing a major role in the setting.

She took the Holy Bible in her hand and her thoughts turned towards Ps Thabiso, for she needed to hear a hopeful message that could ease her irritation. She started paging the Bible until she got to the book of Ecclesiastes 3:4 that says "there's a time to weep and a time to laugh" and she closed the book unable to say anything.

She right away decided to call the maid to tell her she was going out for a while and that she had to carefully take care of the kids after school, and then she left in the direction of Edenvale going to the East of Johannesburg. She needed to see her pastor and tell the whole thing; she needed to do it before any meeting with her husband, since facing an enigma was not going to help her for Colonel Themba was going to impose his will on her.

Driving at hundreds of kilometres per hour was safe on R21. She managed to inform pastor Tshepang about her coming, insisting it was an emergency. The off-ramp on Barbara Street was going to be her next turn on the left, which she did and she started going down facing a red light, but she turned left again and the assembly of pastor Thabiso was just one kilometre away.

Ten minutes later the pastoral couple saw one of their faithful members entering the church with a face expressing appalling disappointment.

"Good afternoon pastors," she greeted.

A hug was enough to start the conversation.

"I know you will be surprised by what I'm going to tell you."

"What is it that our Master cannot solve?"

"I've spent a great deal of time taking care of my family despite my dangerous job but what is happening right now is terrifying and I'm so confused."

"What is it Sipho?" Asked the pastor.

"I have discovered the dark side of my husband, he's involved with drugs and I don't know what else."

The pastoral couple were shocked by the news for they knew Colonel Themba as a qualified civil servant loyal to his government.

"Do you have proof?"

"I'm a secret agent working for my government and we have connections."

Pastor Thabiso and his wife Tshepang looked at each other and realized that vigilant consideration had to be prioritized for justice had to prevail.

"We are going, to be honest with you Sipho," said pastor Thabiso. The Bible tells us that whoever loves discipline loves knowledge, but whoever hates correction is stupid. We are very disappointed by such news from a man like Colonel Themba who has all our respect. But justice must prevail and you represent the law. He's your husband and you know him better than us. Is he the big boss?"

Siphokazi began crying before responding.

"Yes, pastor I believe he is."

The pastoral couple again looked at each other very sorry.

"You have to be strong Sipho," said pastor Tshepang.

"But how?"

"Sipho, the word says do not think that I have come to bring peace on earth but a sword. You must decide in favour of peace in your life and your children. We are not there to separate what God has put together. You should talk with your husband and don't tell him we know."

"I understand," she said. "But how to tell him?"

"Don't rush to your parents," said pastor Thabiso. "Find a peaceful way to talk to him, we know he loves you."

"I don't want him to consider me as a dangerous witness."

"What evidence do you have against him?" Asked pastor Tshepang.

"He's very connected to a prime suspect that has been identified by one of their men we arrested last week and they had dinner in one of the Midrand expensive restaurants and the agent who followed them got shot a few days later."

"Do you think it is a good idea to confront him?" Demanded pastor Thabiso. "You know your husband."

"He's my husband and I have to, don't worry I know how to react to dangerous situations. He's the father of my children and..."

She couldn't continue, she was about to vomit.

"What's wrong Sipho?" Asked pastor Tshepang. "Are you pregnant?"

"I think so."

"Congratulations."

The pastoral couple prayed for her for a couple of minutes, encouraging her to be soft on her husband.

"You don't have to fight him, just be patient with him to get to the bottom of the situation."

"Thank you pastor Tshepang."

"You're welcome sister Siphokazi."

Chapter 3

Wearing flamboyant clothes, Nthabiseng was walking elegantly amid dignitaries. She was used to talking to and entertaining with her strong female voice. She was impressive when talking and that was one of her potencies that attracted Colonel Themba.

That evening in one of the grand halls of the sumptuous Rosebank hotel had been set up by the well-known catering company called "Event" and most of the guests were from the national army. Some awards had to be given to those with excellent records for the last two years. And what a great atmosphere it was. Even the vice-president of the republic was one of the guests to hand over an award as the head of state was out of the country.

Everyone was well dressed and most of the guests were accompanied by their spouses. The soft music playing was perfectly matching the different conversations engaged with one another and they could hear each other talking very well. Elegant ball gowns in the very latest styles, fashionable tuxedos and military uniforms were everywhere.

Colonel Themba was already there but without his wife, Siphokazi, and he looked awesome in his colonel's uniform. He was busy chatting with one of his colleagues when he felt a tender hand landing on his left shoulder, and when he turned around he realized that it was Nthabiseng in a stunning dress smiling at him with her knowing smile. He first responded to her with a smile and then decided to introduce her to his colleague.

His colleague gave her a warm greeting acknowledging the natural beauty standing in front of him.

"Give me five minutes, Nthabiseng."

"Don't worry about me."

With a sign of the hand, Colonel Themba excused himself to his colleague and then got closer to Nthabiseng.

"Where are you going?"

"Remember you didn't invite me."

"Who invited you?"

"I invited myself, don't worry I won't mess up. I want to make some new friends."

The colonel was surprised for he never pictured her doing such a thing. This was a very organized evening and he wondered how she got in the midst of them in the first place. She disappeared into the crowd, attracting the attention of those around her.

On the other side of Johannesburg from the sumptuous hotel of Rosebank was a woman still waiting for her husband despite his early call to make him his preferred recipe. Yes, this was the kind of man she didn't wish to marry. Such behaviour was never expressed at the beginning of their relationship but now that the dog has his bone within reach he can start playing with it.

She had to confront him with all the risks attached to it. She sat on the couch contemplating her future, becoming despondent; this was an unexpected dilemma that she had to face with strength of mind. For what the pastors said to her was the choice of a wise person that should walk in the spirit to overcome the desires of the flesh. And she understood that without wisdom nothing good was going to come out of her but only more remorse; the bruise was devastating.

An hour later with no sign of her husband, she decided to lie in bed, wondering if she was actually going to find some sleep. The children about twenty minutes ago went to sleep after waiting for the return of their father.

She thought that her husband was well cultured and well-read to avoid integrating himself with the under-world but what went through his mind? Who was the mastermind behind such courage? All those questions without answers could drive her crazy. This was going to be the longest night she has ever experienced.

A very expensive fashionable wine was being served in the hall and Colonel Themba glancing around noticed that many dignitaries were not alone but accompanied by their partners. Nthabiseng was nowhere to be found; she disappeared like a cloud of smoke in the air. He started missing his wife who was not by his side. The master of ceremonies was already speaking busy introducing some dignitaries including the vice-president of the Republic of South Africa.

He thought about calling her and then finally decided to give her a call and see how she was doing. But no one picked up the call. Unfortunately, he received his invitation at the last minute and luckily he was wearing his uniform, so he never got the time to inform and prepare his wife for the event. But he knew that she was not going to be happy about the whole situation.

The colonel trod carefully amongst the guests hoping to see Nthabiseng who was undetectable. Then he took a walk outside the hall, finding a peaceful area where no one was but he heard some strange noises. Then he tiptoed to see what was going on and in his big surprise he saw a man holding Nthabiseng with both hands and he knew that man. He was high profile in the security world working undercover called Peter, very influential with a great reputation. What was Nthabiseng's plan? A crazy mind like hers was helpful for their kind of business.

He decided to leave them alone and to wait for her to come back. First of all, he had no idea how she got in but above and beyond it was getting late and he had to return inside for the ceremony had already started. Ten minutes later while enjoying his glass of wine he felt once more a hand falling on his left shoulder and the hand was softer and when he turned his face he saw it was again Nthabiseng with her mysterious smile.

"Where have you been, lady?"

"Always working for you, Colonel."

"Working!" He said.

"Look at this."

She presented to him a picture in which the boss of the national security was kissing her.

"Where did you get this?" He asked.

38

"Just now. Come on, we need this to shut them up. A faithful husband like him will never dare risk his name for anything."

"Keep it well until we need this. They are digging too deep so we need something strong to counter-attack. What a great kiss, lady."

She laughed knowing the impact of such a picture in case a rough decision was made against them and they had to negotiate. And she knew that her boss was happy and was going to recompense her with a lot of money because it was a good, clean job.

After two hours of prizes being awarded, the colonel decided to leave the premises, direction home. It was late and he was missing his wife and children. He loved wishing them a good night before going to sleep. He had a fervent hope that she will one day stop her precarious undercover job and join his underworld one. Besides his wife had nothing of Nthabiseng and that's why he married her, and the only reason she was into secret agent was that she loved it and they had less money then. But he had to convince her to join the cartel and enjoy the money together despite her intense dislike of illegal activities. Fifteen minutes later he entered his premises and the house was quiet, everyone was sleeping. So he decided to spend the night on the couch, in his sumptuous sitting room. He didn't want to disturb her sleep.

While he was about to go to sleep he suddenly heard the voice of his wife snapping at him, followed by the light being switched on. He realized that he was in trouble.

"Yes, darling I'm here."

Siphokazi instantly remembered the pastoral couple's words of wisdom and decided to suspend the discussion until the following morning before he leaves for work. She had the opportunity to wallop him over the head while sleeping and never wake up. But turning emotional was not going to solve the problem she was facing. She had to decide on continuing living with him or leaving him and fighting him.

"Finally, you're home? You're welcome to sleep on the couch, don't come upstairs."

And she left.

She had difficulty finding sleep. She couldn't stop thinking about the betrayal by the man she loved with all her heart; the man in uniform her father admired so much. She also thought about all the cash he made that she had never seen. What a terrible mess it was.

She looked at her watch and it was indicating five-twenty in the morning and she could hear the heavy snoring of her husband while coming down the stairs. She needed a glass of water so she had to pass through the living room because their small fridge in the bedroom had no water to drink. And sleeping like a baby, watching like a deceived woman, searching for an answer that she couldn't find.

After drinking the water she made sure to go back to the bedroom and find some vital sleep and avoid developing a headache. And she found some sleep until her husband woke her up around half-past seven. It was Friday morning and a public holiday for all private schools so the kids were still asleep.

"Thank you for waking me up, it was a good sleep I had."

"I need to bathe and go to work," he said.

"Wait a minute," she said calmly, "I have to speak to you."

Like a considerate man, Colonel Themba took the position of a good listener.

"I feel like I'm alone in a strange country right now," she said.

"Why say something like that, Sipho?"

"Like you don't know, Colonel."

That shook him.

"If I'm your wife, please tell me the whole truth."

"I couldn't help it yesterday, I received the invitation yesterday while in my office and…"

"I don't care about yesterday."

Colonel Themba noticed that his wife's face features were deep with grief.

"But if it isn't about yesterday then what is it?" The Colonel could feel his heart beating quicker.

Without wavering, she put some photos on the table, in which he was with Nthabiseng dining and talking. And when he saw that he took them in his right hand surprised by the unexpected.

"I need you to tell all the truth."

Trying to escape, he said, "She's part of the department, that's all."

"She is a very dangerous person, Themba, please tell me the truth."

Themba left his seat to start pacing up and down. "Are you able to handle the truth?"

"I need to know. Why are you breaking the law?"

"Which law? Which law are you talking about? Who doesn't break the law?"

"I don't."

Hein!

"I don't, Themba."

He went to the window, opened the curtains and started watching outside.

"Themba, why my husband?"

"Because we love money Sipho."

"We? Not I, what I have is enough."

"Are you going to arrest me now? Arrest me now," he said turning around with his wrists joined together.

She held her head, expressing a symbol of depression.

"Why did you turn against your government and all your family?"

"All my family? Talk to your mother, she will tell you what."

"What! My mother? What does she have to do with all of this? Talk to me Themba."

"Sipho left the couch and came in front of him and slapped him on the face."

"Don't ever involve my mother in all of this."

"Go and talk to your mother, Sipho."

Siphokazi was completely confused and started crying like never before while Colonel Themba used the opportunity to leave the house. The situation was getting more complex than ever. What was the role of her mother in all of this? But with her job all surprises were possible. She took courage and decided to get ready and drive to the west of Johannesburg to meet head-on with her mother, for her husband never said this in vain but to help her to get to the very root of the bruise.

Pressing his right foot on the accelerator, and not yet bathed, Colonel Themba in seven minutes crossed the M1 North going to Midrand. He had to retire for a while. No sin can be hidden forever and his wife was on the right way with some prominent proof that something fishy was going on with her husband. Indeed she was right for Nthabiseng was a very dangerous woman who knew too much but was very instrumental. He didn't know anybody who could accomplish her kind of job with as much enjoyment as she took from it.

Siphokazi had to know the truth and decide for herself, he thought. She was unaware of what she was missing. She needed to know the truth and take the right decision to join them in what they enjoyed, and when thinking like that he smiled. But he felt some remorse because she was his beloved wife and the mother of his children and she was in pain for discovering the worse truth of her entire life; she had just discovered the worst side of the man she loved and married.

Colonel Themba decided not to meet Nthabiseng who had an incredibly evil sixth sense. Staying away from her was going to settle him down for a while. His marriage was in jeopardy, and he was not ready to divorce her and let her go into another man's arms.

Sipho arrived in Roodepoort at 09h20 a.m

Always impressed by the extravagant domain of her parents, but this time she was going in with regrets and thousand of questions without answers. It was the beginning of a thorny season in her life, and her faith was tested to the extreme for she never imagined crossing a crisis this big in her marriage.

Her mother and the rest of the family seemed to be there. She was surprised to see Sipho's car entering the premises on a Friday morning. She was supposed to be at work dealing with crime issues. And when she entered the house her mother realized that her daughter didn't have a brave face. She received a warm welcome from her mother who suddenly said, "Are you pregnant?"

"Mum, how do you know?"

"Come on my daughter, I went through this before you, I have five of you, but you seemed depressed."

"I am a mother."

"Let me give you some water before your talk, come and sit down. Your daddy just went out now."

Siphokazi sat on the couch watching the floor, searching for the right words to ask her mother, Helena, who was always ready to listen to her daughter.

"I'm listening to Sipho, what's wrong? Is it your husband again?"

"Mum, what is going on in the family that I'm not aware of? I need to know?"

"I don't get you."

"I have discovered that my husband goes around with people involved in smuggling drugs."

"Yes, yes," said her mother.

"And he said to me, 'talk to your mother'."

Her mother sighed, nodded her head and then crossed her arms against her chest while her daughter started crying.

"Please don't cry and listen to me."

"I am listening, mum."

"You need to know the truth and be strong because it is going to hurt you the way I got hurt many years ago."

Siphokazi with a face full of tears decided to pay heed to her mother.

"My daughter everything started in the early nineties with your father when he turned into the drug business. I don't know how you call it; smuggling or what."

"What! Dad?"

"Please Sipho my daughter; it is time for you to know what your family is all about because I was already prepared for such a day like this one."

"Dad?"

"It is your father who introduced your husband to the drug business."

"Oh my God! Why heavenly father? Why?"

"The day I married your father and before so many witnesses I swore to love your father no matter what. Not because I could imagine him involved in such activity but because we got married for good and for worst. But I couldn't imagine such a dilemma coming to light and coping with it until today. It is difficult to stay with a man you love my daughter."

"Are you happy with daddy?"

"I don't want to focus on the dark side of your father because if I do, I will die early and leave you alone my children."

"Is it the reason why Bongani never returned home after so many years?"

"Your big brother could not handle this and left until today."

"Mum, I've never been this confused in my life. I am so disappointed by the men I love the most. And I don't know where to go, what to do right now."

Her mother left her seat to hug her daughter, and both started crying endlessly in each other's arms.

"I need to talk to dad to know why he did such a thing to our family."

"I cannot stop you my daughter for sin doesn't pay off but just ashes."

Crying was necessary but was not going to solve anything. She certainly needed some support but from where? Those she loved so much were involved in lawlessness and wanted her to join them and die together. While in her car she took some time to page her Bible and fell on the scripture that says "cursed is the man who trusts in man and makes flesh his arm, and whose heart turns away from God".

Only God could help her out of this circumstance for it was too much to handle alone. Her father was the author of the business and he was the one who carried away her husband with him, becoming two powerful smugglers in the country. How to stop them and how to protect those she loved with all her heart?

Thinking about the children, she hurried along the road, driving beyond a hundred and twenty kilometres per hour. Her thoughts were going all directions not knowing how to stop the two men so dear to her. What she experienced with her father while a child blessed her life for he was a loving father with wings of protection and he made sure he provided his children with the best education. But what went wrong with him?

Chapter 4

Dr Khumalo entered the room holding a file with a smile on his face while Colonel Themba with Siphokazi was calmly waiting for the result from him. Without talking to each other, Colonel Themba in vain was seeking to hold his wife's hand. She kept pushing him away. She truly had a hard time since the unveiling of the lawless family business that her father created. The truth came to her like a violent storm, and since then she has been silent and distant towards her husband, and her husband understood that her silence was a sign of deception.

And her husband noticed how regularly she was vomiting, he calmly came and convinced her to take a ride to the hospital and hear from the doctor who was already in front of them reading the result.

"I have great news for you, he said. Your wife is already two months pregnant and do you want to know the sex of the child?"

"Please doctor," said the colonel with excitement.

"A baby girl."

"Thank God!" Exclaimed Colonel Themba.

As he looked at his wife he saw one of her best smiles, that smile he fell in love with on the first day he met her.

"Thank you doctor for everything, we wanted a baby girl," said the colonel.

"Thank you, doctor."

While driving home, weaving his way through intense traffic, she said, "Have you heard about the Cobra's deadly venom?"

Colonel Themba kept silent.

"Have you heard about it? It kills. You must leave this business if you truly want your daughter by your side all the time."

"They will kill me, Sipho."

After parking the car the couple went inside the house and continued the conversation, and Colonel Themba, dressed in his colonel's uniform. sighed.

"The devil here is your father. The man in uniform he wanted by his side was because of the influence of it for the protection of his fortune. He got me because I received my first ever million from him without knowing it was from the illegal smuggling of drugs in South Africa. What do you want me to do Sipho? I know I wanted to get rich but not this way."

"You could have chosen."

"What? To run away from South Africa my beautiful country because I already accepted the money. I love this country."

"Not by poisoning it with drugs."

Colonel Themba left the sofa and sat beside her.

"You must join us for I'm aware of too much to be kept alive."

"I hate all of you; you're so disgusting in my eyes. What about the word of God? It was just a big lie. A way to divert my attention and those surrounding us."

Colonel Themba was about to wipe her face when she refused, turning her face aside.

"My life was never going to be like this if I haven't met you Sipho, you have your father's blood."

"But I'm not doing what he does, Themba. You could choose. You betrayed your family. I am so confused and bleeding in my heart. And I can see you don't want to give up because of your greed. How many millions do you have that I don't know?"

Suddenly colonel Themba's cell phone rang and he looked at the screen and saw that it was his father-in-law.

"It's your father, hallo daddy!"

"Are you with my daughter?"

"Yes, she is here with me."

"I need to see both of you now," he ordered.

"I heard and I don't want to see him, dad I don't want to see you," Sipho screamed.

"You are going to wake up the kids."

"I don't care anymore."

Colonel Themba retreated for a while to let her cool down. He took some time with the kids playing outside and after decided to meet his wife who was laid on the couch in the TV room. Surely we all got on her nerves, he thought.

"Sipho we are the upper classes of the city."

"Please shut up, you are not ashamed of yourself talking like that."

"You are pregnant and you need rest," he said kindly.

"I don't want your dirty hands to touch me anymore."

Her telephone rang and noticed that it was her father calling her, but she declined the call.

"Tell my father I don't want to get near him," and immediately after saying that she fell asleep on the couch.

"You know I won't tell Malume that."

The colonel decided to leave the premises; he had to meet his father-in-law.

It was 17h00 p.m. in the south of Johannesburg and raining.

Every car was moving at a moderate speed. Nthabiseng was seated at the front of a car driven by General Peter the number two of South African national security. He was influential and to the cartel, he could become very instrumental and enable them to allow any merchandise to leave the territory without suspicion, really the cartel was very ambitious. He was a trustworthy person to the government that the cartel wished to enslave, and he didn't know that the beautiful lady seated beside him was a very dangerous instigator who had enough attributes to fool him around and make him a component of the team that imports and exports illegal goods.

While driving on National 1 South, going toward Roodepoort, an ambush that seemed like a carjacking to Peter happened to their car without him having the time to react with his firearm for he didn't have one. Nthabiseng took care of it by telling him she hates men carrying firearms all over the city.

And without harming the high-profile security man, he was transferred to another car that took him to an unknown destination with Nthabiseng next to him screaming like hell.

The kidnappers, without wasting time, deprived him of his cell phone, covered his face with a black cloth while disappearing at a staggering speed toward Roodepoort. Peter overwhelmed by fear remained calm and avoided fighting against his kidnappers. To cover his face meant for him to hide something until destination.

Twenty minutes after travelling at high speed the car slowed down and that increased his blood pressure. As a high-profile security man, he had enemies unknown to him and he wasn't surprised about it. He also noticed that for a moment the lady that accompanied him was silent and that truly worried him. What could have happened to her?

Finally, the car stopped after entering a compound in an unknown area to him, and very quickly one of the kidnappers uncovered his face and everything became bright and scarier for he found himself in front of some folks amongst which he recognized two of them; Nthabiseng and Colonel Themba. And that surprised him but they smiled at him.

"Colonel!" Peter exclaimed, "What is all of this? Nthabiseng, what's wrong?"

"There's nothing wrong unless you turn it wrong," said the lady.

"Is it a set-up?"

Colonel Themba expressed an additional smile while approaching him to say, "You know I have a lot of respect for you."

"It doesn't seem like one right now, responding with authority."

"Calm down, general. We want someone like you to join us and be part of the cartel, and we would like you to know a whole lot about us. We also intend to make you rich, more than what the government can do for you in forty years of faithful service; and sorry for the scenario of kidnapping and don't worry about your car, we took it to someplace safe."

The staff that was there brought two chairs on which Peter and Colonel Themba sat with his cigar in his mouth. Nthabiseng also was given a seat.

"We need the influence you have to help us to export some items to Brazil," said the colonel.

General Peter looked angrily at the lady who set him up, but she responded with a smile.

"I'm surprised, Colonel, that after what this country has done for you, you dare steal from it."

"I'm a tax-payer, General. We urgently need gold out of this country by next Wednesday."

"You're asking me too much, Colonel."

"The parcel will provide you with enough cash for your retirement; think about what you will be in two years."

"I'm sorry, Colonel but I can't partake in such a fraud."

"Fraud!" brutally responded the colonel.

Colonel Themba signed to Nthabiseng and without delay, she exposed a photo in which the general was kissing her.

"You're well-behaved to your family, General," said the colonel between his teeth.

"Where did you get this? Anyone can create this?"

"We have more than that, General," said Nthabiseng at the same time exposing a worse picture than the first.

"Don't you recognize the lady beside you? Isn't what you are doing deceitfully general?"

General Peter was reduced to nothing. He nodded his head and expressed some words that they couldn't understand.

"What do you want me to do?"

"Now we can talk in general because your wife and children as well as your grandchildren and of course our government won't appreciate such a dishonour."

"I hate you," he said.

"Don't hate me, General; learn to make more money in silence."

24 hours later; west of Johannesburg

What a shining and beautiful day it was in Johannesburg. Being driven by a friend of hers to where her husband and father were waiting, Siphokazi was enjoying the beautiful day with thousand unanswered questions. The friend was just going to drop her at the gate of the hotel and continue her way. She declined driving on that particular day, looking for a way to take pleasure in the company of a good childhood friend. She needed good company for survival for the dark cloud was merciless.

Why meet them at the hotel? Anyway, she was determined to lash out everything she had in store in her heart to them. A tough and dangerous decision had to be made by her, and shame lawlessness for she was no longer that little girl to be left alone without knowledge of the truth.

There was a lot about the family that she was unaware of and her father was about to tell more family secrets. She never thought probing deep into her family despite the disappearance of her elder brother. But there was now an explanation to all of that; her brother left the family business and kept his mouth shut. She had to come up with a way to distance herself from the family trade and see some justice be done if possible because of her affiliation to the government.

Sifting the evidence for a conclusion had to be reached, but not with her on board for she loved her family so much to be the one to make an end to such illegal activities by arresting her father and her husband, the father of her children. Being pregnant also in such circumstances was very difficult and she thoughts of taking many days off or just resigning from her duties and focusing on something else less demanding and dodgy.

Twenty minutes later with the help of the GPS, her kind friend dropped her in front of a sumptuous hotel hidden in Roodepoort. It was six floors tall with a magnificent front view; a five-star hotel that could accommodate government dignitaries.

Siphokazi without wasting time entered the sumptuous hotel led by a kind administrator with a badge on which read 'manager'. With a kind smile, he said to her, "They are all waiting for you."

Siphokazi didn't know how to react and just followed him. They were already crossing a beautiful corridor while quite surprised by the venue to talk about family matters; surely they wanted to impress her, she thought. And with care the caretaker opened the door for her that was in front of them; allowing her to enter and then he disappeared.

Left unaccompanied by the manager didn't mean she was left alone in what seemed like a hall for venues. To her big surprise her mother, husband and father with other people she had never met in the past were there watching in her direction, smiling at her like they had been waiting for her all along. But she was happy to see her father whom she loved so much, and he was the first one to approach her with his arms widely opened. He was in high spirits to see his baby girl who he never met before.

Siphokazi finally called her father, what a moment I've been waiting, for many years.

He hugged her with passion and invited her to join the rest of the guests. Her husband came after her and introduced her to the well-dressed guests. They were all smiling at her, happy to discover another family member of Mr Malume.

"I've got the honour to present to you my beloved wife Siphokazi," said Colonel Themba.

She responded with a surprised smile and took a seat where her husband took her, and the move was followed by the rest with music that had already started playing. Her mother joined her and she was superbly dressed up.

"Mum what an outfit; I've never seen you dressed like this, you look so different."

Everything was just a bombshell to her for the reason that she never saw her family surrounded by such riches.

"Mum, why are you showing me this now?"

"You are part of this family, but understand that we couldn't before and we were waiting for the right moment to introduce everything to you."

"The right moment? Can I leave mum because I've seen enough?"

"You can't my daughter."

"You're like them, mum. You all don't care."

The music stopped playing and her father began to speak.

"Sipho my beloved daughter, we're all here for you and we welcome you among us and start enjoying what your family is all about."

Siphokazi contemplating in silence decided within her to obtain as much information as possible about her family. Her father was the architect and also the deceiver's instrument that the government was coming after to neutralize.

"Sipho we would like you to watch this video about your family," said her father. Colonel Themba, her husband, held a remote control in his hand.

The brightness of light in the hall got reduced and right away the video started running. It started showing her in her mother's arms when she was fifteen years old in uniform laughing together and her father was also there holding her chin, expressing happiness.

Sipho couldn't retain herself to let some tears go along her face. Soft music from the video was playing at the same time showing her sleeping in her father's arms when she was still a baby, and suddenly a documentary started concerning the family business.

What an interesting documentary it was for it showed a not for profit organization attending to very serious HIV cases at different locations of the Republic of South Africa. She even remembered the broadcasting of the documentary on one of the national television channels. And none of the family members participated in that documentary.

The video also showed a textile manufacturing company employing so many people with branches nationwide. In the video, she was very surprised to see her father and mother speaking to their subordinates. She never saw her mother playing such a role in the community. Still, the video was showing a certain number of hotels nationwide with her father as the CEO, speaking concerning all those hotels having quality conference venues. And then appeared on the screen a door upon which her name was written on, and someone opened the door into a sumptuous office so well decorated, and one of her pictures appeared on the desk of the office.

Siphokazi smiled, covered her face with both hands, shaking her head and that was the end of the video.

"This is the family empire, Sipho," said her father, "The one you've always belonged to. Besides, we already have an office for you to be one of the directors of our Not-for-profit organization. Everyone that you see here is a director of the family you belong to."

"Dad, can I speak to you in private?" She said with everyone watching.

"Why not, my daughter."

"I want mum there and Themba too."

The hall was cleaned up and just the family remained with her. But she was crying regretting the truth that was untold by her father.

And once those she wanted to listen to her were gathered, she first wiped her face with her handkerchief.

"Is it the all truth dad?"

Her father replied with just a smile.

"I need an answer dad and I need to hear that from you, the whole truth."

"I'm a businessman my daughter, I sell what comes into my way and at a profit."

"Anything? You, mean anything dad?"

"Why do you worry about anything? The way I amass my fortune is my business and every entity you saw on the video are registered companies, and we're tax-payers. Come on Siphokazi, my daughter, don't go away from me as your big brother did. And you're doing a very dangerous job that can kill you any time. Please be one of my directors."

Colonel Themba her husband looked on sadly.

"You have destroyed my career dad, she said. I can't be the one investigating my family. It will kill me."

"Become one of my directors, simple."

"I don't want that either. I want to rest and forget about all of this. I need some time off."

"Sipho!" called her father.

"Enough," said her mother, "all of you out and leave us alone."

Her husband and father looked at each other and left the hall leaving them alone. Her father also realized that he wasn't completely candid with her. Maybe his wife Helena could do a better job than him.

"My daughter," Helena called with some tears running down her face.

"Mum you suck. I can't even look at you."

"Please my daughter, take it easy, don't destroy your life because of this."

"But I don't want to be part of it. I'm quitting my job to stay away from your business. I don't want to be part of those who will one day arrest you. Please, Mum, I need someone to take me home, I miss my children and some good times of relaxation."

Secret agent Dumisane was at work and work responded to a phone call from his superior Lieutenant Keegan telling him to come to his office in the next ten minutes. And after finishing his cup of coffee, he took a look at his watch that indicated 14h20. It was time to go and see his superior Lieutenant Keegan, and once in his office, he met a man rather disappointed by something.

"Have you talked to secret agent Sipho lately?"

"I've tried but in vain, Lieutenant."

"She resigned."

"Why?" Said Dumisane surprised by the news.

"She's pregnant and needs to sort out some family problems."

"That's all she said?"

"Talk to her maybe she will tell you more. You need a partner to start working with."

"The only way to talk to her is if she calls me, chief."

"You're dismissed.

Thank you, Lieutenant."

Not knowing what to do to get hold of her, Dumisane calmly left his workplace for a meeting he had with some of his colleagues working in the city of Tshwane. But he knew what was going on with his colleague. Her husband was connected to the most dangerous woman in the city. The only thing that the police needed was more evidence to lock her in a cell. But he had to find a way to talk to her and encourage her for she was surely very confused.

On that same day while at home, Siphokazi, busy feeding her children, saw the door of the main entrance to the house being opened by her husband. And without telling her anything he went straight upstairs into the bedroom. She also kept quiet and continued feeding the children. Trying hard to persuade him to stop with the dangerous business was not going to work out, but showing some jealousy toward his relationship with the dangerous lady was going to help her to take the right decision.

A few minutes later her husband came back holding some toys for the kids. And that excited the kids. Instantly they turned their attention towards their father as he put those toys on the living room table.

"Please finish your food first," he said.

"Finish your food first," repeated their mother. "Do you want to eat also?" she said nicely.

"Yes, I would like to, Sipho, thank you," he said surprised by her tone towards him that seemed reconciliatory.

She quickly went to the kitchen after receiving a shocked look from her husband because he was expecting her very distant from him. And a few minutes later she came back with what he enjoyed eating every day in his home.

"Enjoy your food," she said.

"Thank you, Sipho," marvelling.

Just when he started eating she said, "The paperwork for our divorce will be ready in a week."

Colonel Themba received it as a bombshell.

"I'm going for a divorce, Colonel."

"Why Sipho?"

"Why? Why? Tell me the truth; did you sleep with that woman called Nthabiseng? I know her name."

Colonel Themba remained calm and did his best to continue enjoying his food.

"I've also resigned from my duties as a secret agent of our government because I don't want to be the one to arrest you with my father."

"Nhlakanipho Empire is yours, Sipho. Your father can't stop talking about her child who will take over, and that child is you."

"Did you sleep with Nthabiseng? That's why I'm divorcing you."

But the colonel said nothing and decided to take the children outside to play when his phone rang.

"Colonel Themba," called the voice talking to him on the other side.

"Who is speaking?"

"It's me, Mboxela."

"What's wrong?"

"Nthabiseng has been shot dead!"

Chapter 5

Three days later

Secret agent Dumisane was far away inside the West Park cemetery, busy taking pictures of Colonel Themba standing in front of Nthabiseng's grave. He noticed that the colonel loved that woman who was wanted for trafficking drugs and other valuables of the state. She was found dead in a hotel room in Kempton Park, east of Johannesburg, and the motive of the murder was still unknown.

After taking those pictures, he left quickly to meet his former colleague; who he loved working with, Siphokazi. She was waiting for him for a brief conversation in one of the restaurants in Rosebank, north of Johannesburg. After a thirty-five minute drive, he finally arrived where she was and she looked radiant.

"So happy to see you, Sipho."

"I am too, Dumisane."

After hugging each other they sat. Dumisane held her left hand that she had rested on the table. It was a way to comfort her, and she welcomed the move.

"I missed you so much," he softly said to her.

"I missed you too, especially my job."

"So why resign?"

"Understand me, I can't be the one arresting my husband, but I'm filing for divorce."

"You're joking, right?"

"I'm not."

"Do you know that Nthabiseng was murdered?"

"I didn't know," she said surprised. "What happened to her?"

"She was found shot dead in one of the hotel rooms in Kempton Park."

"Maybe she knew too much, and I can understand his grief lately."

"But you're pregnant, Sipho."

"I'm a deceived woman, Dumisane."

"But you know I've always loved you Sipho, I don't care if you're divorced, have children, and I can make you a very happy woman."

"Siphokazi expressed a joyful smile, but said, "I have to go."

"Already! And are you saying nothing?"

"I'm sure you don't want a deceived woman cooking for you and crying late at night at your side."

Dumisane smiled, and she stood up, took her purse, and Dumisane did the same and gently held her left hand and said, "I'm wishing you all the best and don't make a decision you may regret again; especially don't take long to see me again, I'm here for you."

In an unthinkable move, he kissed her on her left cheek; it was a gesture he had never done before. She accepted it with enthusiasm and left without looking behind her for she was crying.

Colonel Themba, at his desk in his office, was watching two photos of those suspected to have gunned down Nthabiseng. He felt very bad since the whole thing was crumbling around him. His marriage was on the edge of a divorce and Nthabiseng's death was worsening the whole situation. He knew she had many enemies in the city but being murdered was the last thing he thought about. Even he had to watch before making any step. She had many enemies because she hurt so many people that she has even forgotten. What happened to her was not a surprise to him as she knew too much to be arrested and tortured to divulge the truth but why kill her?

Nothing seemed possible to change his wife's mind, except if he turned his back on his father-in-law. She rejected working for the family business, hurting both parents; but she was a woman of character, up to resigning from her duties because of the dignity of her family, and even being able to turn her back on the fortune of her family. He knew it would never be the same again.

He thought about how wonderful their marriage's early years were. Walking hand by hand as if nothing could separate them one day. Now, he felt alone and lost, incomplete without his wife next to him; truly money is not everything in life. Nthabiseng was gone and gone forever, and telling his father-in-law about a possible divorce with his daughter was not going to help the situation because his old father-in-law was getting very fragile.

But he had a wonderful mother-in-law; no matter what she remained faithful to her husband. Malume was evil, enjoying

66

manipulating people and Themba became one of his best victims. He was that man in uniform he dreamed of having by his side for his interest. The deceiver truly is just around the corner.

Deep in his heart, he hated Nhlakanipho, his father-in-law, but a man full of strategies and a great remunerator. The people surrounding him had nothing to complain about, all of them with the best salary of the Republic of South Africa. He was a cunning man with a terrible positive attitude towards money.

Still with those photos in front of him he wanted those killers of Nthabiseng dead. Retaliation was inevitable. They killed his best friend who was faithful towards him. She was the mindset that worked against his enemies.

Wearing his P38 pistol and his uniform with tears streaming down his cheeks, Colonel Themba looked at his watch that was indicating 07h00 p.m. and he was determined to put an end to their lives by himself. He knew them very well for there was fierce competition within the smuggling business and Nthabiseng made sure to expose their weaknesses to Malume (Pty) Ltd. Because of that, Nhlakanipho's business absorbed theirs and they never forgot that. She should have been more careful.

Colonel Themba made sure he had enough bullets in his P38 pistol. Regretfully and sweating he left his office and took the lift. But when the lift door was about to close and leave the floor, two unknown individuals invaded the lift, squeezing him in the middle. His reaction was of a professional; truly he was a Para-commando. Fear has never been part of his agenda for he made sure with a quick move to avoid being squeezed in the middle by brutally pushing both guys in front of him, and to accompany the move with two simultaneous powerful punches to both their necks causing the guys to strongly hit their faces against the metal of the side of the lift, loosing for a while the control of their memories. But suddenly the lift started descending and without wasting time he took his pistol from the back of his trousers and pointed it to both of them at the same time pressing the button for the ground floor bottom, avoiding landing with them at the parking floor.

And when he paid more attention he realized without mistake that they were those who shot dead Nthabiseng. Meaning they were after him to kill him too.

"Who are you? Are you after me to kill me too?"

But they remained silent holding both their faces and necks. He could hit hard. But he found himself in a dilemma; should he kill them while they're in the lift because that was what he felt like doing or should he escort them by force to an unknown remote area. That was also too risky for they were merciless and ready to capitalize on any opportunity.

Realizing the advantage he had of wearing his colonel uniform, colonel Themba once the lift stopped at the ground floor and with his pistol still pointed at them, screamed out calling the security. The building was the department of defence and killing two suspects in the lift was going to make the best news of the month with the broadcasters, so he had to do the right thing.

Quickly the security arrived on the scene and handcuffed them.

"Call the police immediately, these two guys were about to rob me, I want them to be interrogated and their fingerprints to be taken."

Ten minutes later the police arrived.

"These two guys were after me to either kill me or rob me but I was quicker than them. Interrogate them and take their fingerprints and they can only be released on my authorisation. I had to fight them to be safe.

Without wasting time the police disappeared with them. He was about to shoot, he thought and that was going to be his worst mistake. Tired, he quickly left the ground floor, took the lift with the help of one of the security guards, escorting him to his car. From now on even after hours he needed some bodyguards.

48 hours later at the John Foster police station:

For the first time, secret agent Dumisane was in front of Colonel Themba who had paid him a visit regarding the two suspects that attacked him in the lift. The interrogation had to occur behind closed doors by those secretly working for the government. This was a very serious matter to the colonel, and he needed feedback to take a decisive course. The two were the prime suspects in the killing of Nthabiseng so he wanted to uncover the sad truth. He wanted to know if it was them and under what circumstance it happened. Was she alone or accompanied?

Of course, the colonel didn't know that his wife used to co-work with Dumisane the man beside him interrogating the two suspects; besides Dumisane didn't want him to know that.

"Why did you try to attack this man?"

The two suspects were put under very uncomfortable circumstances to feel the pressure.

"Why do you attack a colonel? Who sent you?"

The two suspects sweated and realized that the situation was not in their favour.

"Attacking a civil servant, such as a colonel represents an infringement that can cost you many years in prison unless you cooperate," said Colonel Themba. Secret agent Dumisane looked at him, worried.

"We were sent to kill you, sir."

Secret agent Dumisane received the news like a storm hitting his face with dust. Colonel Themba expressed a sadistic smile.

"Why?" Asked Dumisane.

"Because I've got enemies, jealous people without visions."

Secret agent Dumisane made sure to speak less and especially to not say anything about Nthabiseng. To his surprise, he saw Colonel Themba taking a picture out of his suitcase with Nthabiseng on it. He remained silent and observed.

"Who killed this woman?"Themba showed the picture to the two suspects.

The two after looking at the picture looked at each other and then looked at the colonel.

"We don't know this woman."

"This woman was killed by you not long time ago."

Secret agent Dumisane was listening attentively, behaving as if he knew nothing about the case.

"Who killed this woman? I'm asking for the last time."

"We were sent to kill her."

"Shut up," said his colleague surprised by the reply of his co-worker.

"Agent Dumisane, transfer them to the right authorities for their immediate arrest. I have registered this conversation held today. Take good care of them. But before I go you have to tell me who ordered such a murder. Maybe you don't know secret agent Dumisane, Nthabiseng was a diligent civil servant working secretly like you."

"I'm truly sorry, Colonel for such a loss."

Who ordered such a murder because by cooperating with us your sentence will be reduced?

Dumisane suddenly received a phone call and left the interrogation room to answer it, and once out of the room one of the suspects responded in two words.

"Mr Nhlakanipho, we believe you know him, Colonel."

Colonel Themba expressed a horrific grimace for he could not believe what he just heard.

"And our mission in the lift was never to kill you, Colonel but to protect you against your enemies that worked in connivance with miss Nthabiseng, but you were just too quick for us colonel. We couldn't tell you that in the presence of this man. Nthabiseng was about to kill you."

"What!?" And before Dumisane came back in he said, "don't say anything to this man, just follow him until your release."

Suddenly secret agent Dumisane came back into the room.

"These suspects confirm they know nothing about the murder of this woman but take them to prison before the court settles this matter."

"As you say, Colonel."

Colonel Themba frightened observed agent Dumisane leaving with the two suspects. What was going on that he didn't know? He hurriedly had to meet his father-in-law who certainly had more to tell him about Nthabiseng's murder.

A family function was being held at the main mansion of Mr Nhlakanipho in Roodepoort and Colonel Themba, lonely but very well dressed, made his entrance to the premises that he knew so well. Much to his amazement, his mother was presently talking to his mother-in-law. But he did his best to avoid her for he wasn't ready to answer any questions concerning his wife who was not with him. So he made sure to quickly join the guests that were with his father-in-law.

The whole situation was about to turn him eccentric. He never experienced such a dilemma in his life. With his wife requesting him to turn his back on the cartel and follow the truth and him declining the extreme burden had put his marriage in jeopardy.

He refused to consider what his wife requested of him. To do for the price to pay was going to be too high; he could lose his life just the way Nthabiseng lost hers even after many years of loyal service. Mercy was not part of the agenda; the covenant was made in such a way that the covenant head and his members perished in cases of betrayal, and beginning to behave strangely was never an opportunity to find love. As for the cartel behaving strangely, that was the beginning of the end for one or many. No gaffe had to be made; all your senses had to labour perfectly to avoid any bad decision that could harm the whole organization that was counting millions of South African Rand that had to be redistributed among them.

Very expensive Champagne was being served in the moment of great happiness. He started greeting those who were close to the entrance and continued until he shook Mr Nhlakanipho hand.

"Nice to see you, son," he said with a cigar in his mouth. Why are you alone? Where is Sipho?

"I'm sorry, sir but she is not with me because she is busy filing for divorce."

"You better tell her to stop that nonsense. I'm still her father even if she disagrees with my methods. Listen you're the man in the house and she must obey you," and Malume left the place to join his wife who was outside with his mother.

Colonel Themba saw his father-in-law disappearing with his wife Helena and his mother to one of the TV rooms of the big house. They remained there for about fifteen minutes surely discussing the problem their children were facing and Mr Nhlakanipho reappeared with a stretched face and called Colonel Themba to his office.

"We are going to visit her, son, what do you think about it?"

"That will probably help."

"Let's hope but I blame you for this because you took too long to let her know, son."

The colonel sighed. "Are you aware that Nthabiseng has been assassinated?"

"Nthabiseng betrayed the cartel."

73

"How? I don't understand."

"Nthabiseng because of her voracity, enjoyed filling up her pockets using our competitors and she had friends throughout South Africa talking too much. And you couldn't see that because you were busy sleeping with her. Let me show you this video about Nthabiseng."

Colonel Themba dreaded what was coming out of his father-in-law's mouth sat down to know what he was unaware of.

"Watch this son and you'll tell me what."

The first image that appeared on the LCD screen was of the main rival of the organization, and that big-time surprised the colonel. They were in Sun City enjoying the sun, holding each other as a dating couple unafraid of the crowd.

"I know this guy," said the colonel.

"Did you give her such a mission?" Demanded Mr Nhlakanipho after stopping the video.

"Never, Pap."

"This is very dangerous for our business because Moloto is as ravenous as we are. We don't know what she told him of what we do and you're aware that this is against our code of conduct."

And he let run the video. This time she was dining with one of the top-ranked officers of the national police force and seemed to be having a very long conversation. The colonel couldn't believe what he was watching.

"When accelerating these images they are eating, drinking and mostly talking for more than forty-five minutes, son. Tell me, talking about what? Was she not under your authority and

74

could only meet those mandated to her? This is the commissioner of the police and he's a lawful man and talking to someone like Nthabiseng is like digging deep into our commerce."

"I was unaware of all of this, Pap."

"You must know son that the next minute is dangerous with this kind of business. Dangerous, indeed. We don't take risks. I know how much you appreciated her but she was only around you for the money and you around her for the comfort of a woman beside you."

"Thank you, pap," and they hugged each other.

"So Siphokazi still wants to divorce you?"

"Yes sir."

Mr Nhlakanipho opened the fridge that was in the left corner of the TV room and served himself a glass of red wine from the Cape.

"This is the problem I have with young women today. They think divorce is part of our tradition. Not at all. She's making a big mistake."

"She resigned from her work and stays home."

"While I have prepared for her one of the best jobs out there, rather than going after delinquents or staying home focusing on something she won't be able to solve. I will talk to her tomorrow afternoon; you are dismissed."

After thanking him Colonel Themba left the TV room to join his mother who was still talking to his mother-in-law. And while he stepped in their direction, he thanked God for having a mother for she saw him coming and then expressed her best smile towards his son. And he loved that for he could lean on her soft shoulders like a child seeking for her mother's comfort.

Chapter 6

Siphokazi whilst in the kitchen heard her phone ringing and after checking on the screen, it showed an unknown phone call so who possibly that could be, but she decided anyway to pick up the call, and the caller was Dumisane.

"Don't be surprised it is me. You've never bothered getting my private number."

"But how did you get mine?" She said, happy to hear his voice.

"You gave me it and you refused to get mine."

"Come on, how possible?"

"Anyway, how are you Sipho?"

"I'm missing my job, but this period of retirement is helping to focus on what is central."

"And what's important if I may ask?"

Dumisane heard her sigh on the other end of the line.

"My family, Dumi."

"Including your husband?"

"I'm divorcing him."

"He doesn't deserve you, Sipho."

She remained silent.

"Besides, I was with your husband on duty seeking who killed his beloved Nthabiseng."

"When?"

"Twenty-four hours ago. We were together interrogating two suspects of the murder. Don't tell him I told you that, he doesn't know I used to work with you."

"I am no longer interested in his miserable life; I'm divorcing him and that is the best way for me to live in tranquillity."

"What do you think about meeting tomorrow afternoon? I truly would like your company."

"I can," she said without hesitating.

"Don't worry about my behaviour; I'm a much-disciplined man."

"Where abouts?" She said laughing.

"Three o'clock at Connecto restaurant at Eastgate mall."

"Okay, see you then, but you know I won't take long."

Dumisane looked at the ceiling in a state of bliss; he was for the very first time going to date the most beautiful woman in South Africa. And Siphokazi was amazed that this unmarried adult male was willing to date a mother of two children with one on the way; men.

Just after her telephone call, amazingly her husband arrived home, entered the house followed by her father.

"Daddy!" She called surprised to see her father.

She walked to him with her arms opened to hug him, and in his turn he reciprocated, happy to see her smiling. But her husband was rather reserved, observing with amazement the joyfulness of a daughter meeting her father.

"Come sit down dad, what a good surprise. What good wind brings you here?"

"I'm missing my daughter," he said sitting at the same time.

Colonel Themba was happy to see them together and expected the best decision to come out of the meeting. So he decided to leave them for a while so that they could freely talk.

"I will be back, " he said.

"Don't go for too long," said his father-in-law.

He left to go to the TV room for a moment of relaxation.

"Would you like something to drink, Dad?"

"After my daughter, let's first talk."

"Okay., Dad."

"I'm not happy with your decision to divorce your husband," he said going straight into the matter.

She looked down and kept on listening.

"I'm devastated by such news that dishonours the entire family."

"I'm also devastated by this entire situation, Dad; I had to resign from my work because of your activities and on top of that my husband's infidelity."

"I'm the cause of all this, let me confess my daughter, I introduced your husband into my world. He was innocent."

"He's no longer, Dad."

"Don't make a decision that you might regret, and additionally, you refused my job proposal, why?"

"I need many days off, Dad. Everyone has disappointed me. Your greediness has spoiled everything."

Her father sighed and looked down, realizing that certain mistakes need big sacrifices to fix them.

"I want my husband to leave your business and concentrate on his colonel's duties. I have my life, Dad and you spoiled it for your millions."

He looked at his daughter again, stood up, calmly turned around and left the premises. And to his big surprise Colonel, Themba realized when he woke up from his twenty minutes sleep that his father-in-law was no longer around.

"What happened?" He said.

"He left without a goodbye."

"What did you tell him?"

To leave my marriage alone; I told him that I won't divorce you if you resign from his useless business and he left. Follow him if you want. Do you remember what you promised me?" She said, "Do you?"

Not knowing what to say Colonel Themba held his forehead looking down, realizing that he married the queen that's irreplaceable. He looked at her this time holding his chin; he had to make a decision.

"Why are you doing this to me Sipho?"

"I thought you loved me."

"Of course, I do."

"But you love your money more than me, Colonel. And you've already made up your mind. I'm nothing compared to your money, power—"

"Stop!" He cut her off.

"I will divorce you and make sure that I don't see you again."

The best thing to do at that particular moment was to leave for the nervousness was increasing towards a quarrel and he didn't want to harm his unborn daughter.

Wearing his best suit with a blue tie, following the walking steps of his boss's wife, Mboxela made sure to be unnoticed by the woman he was following around Eastgate mall. She was pretty well dressed and seemed jovial for she was from time to time greeting those she seemed knowing. Besides his boss's wife didn't know him, but if she felt like she was being followed that could create a very bad reaction from her. So what he just wanted was to know where she was going, who she was meeting and bring that information to his boss. The mall was multicolour and moderate in the number of people, so it was easy for him to follow her without losing her tracks.

Mboxela was happy that it wasn't the weekend, if it was his job was going to be very difficult. After a while, he saw her going in the direction of the restaurants, and once there he saw her going straight to a man sitting in one of the chairs of Connecto restaurant outside, and he knew that man. It was secret agent Dumisane. Quickly with his cell phone, he took some pictures. He had to be very careful for he was dealing with a man used to what he was doing.

Why was his wife's boss meeting such an individual? He wondered. What was she plotting against her husband? Many restaurants were around so he decided to occupy one of them and order something to eat and drink; positioning himself in such a way to have a good view of what was happening between his boss's wife and the state secret agent for he was bad news for his boss's kind of business.

Dumisane was very happy about his first date with the woman he loved. That crush on her started three years ago while working together. He was wounded after a bullet missed penetrating and breaking his left shoulder's bone; but while having a bit of pain on the shoulder and with a tenderness she took care of him, administering the kind of care he wanted from a woman. She was so close to him and he could nicely feel the softness of her hands on him. She was just naturally taking care of him, but he took it too personally.

Dumisane was 1.75 meters tall and had one of the best smiles, and he expressed it as she was entering the restaurant; standing up to welcome her with a hug that she honoured with great joy. He helped her to sit down and he also sat in front of her.

"You have a good restaurant taste," she said.

"Thank you, Sipho and I'm very glad that you have come."

"You're welcome, it is also a way for me to forget my past."

"Including your previous job? By the way, what can I offer you?"

"A mango juice will be enough for me.

"They cook very delicious food here also."

"Let's order some then."

They ordered the kind of foods and drinks that made the moment unforgettable. Dumisane looked at her for a while without saying anything.

"Why such a look?" She asked.

"How is the baby doing?"

She smiled and said, "I'm so happy to be pregnant, I'm going to have a baby girl and she will look exactly like her mother."

"Great! And still determined to divorce him?"

"Please Dumi, I am not here to talk about my used to be beloved husband."

"I know but do you think your children will forgive you for that? I care about you and you know it."

"I know you're a caring man, but we met before our children came. When the Bible talks about divorce because of adultery, children are not mentioned. God will take care of them."

Dumisane smiled interested in what she just said. "So you mean we should just do what the Holy Bible says."

"Yes, and it will flow."

"I didn't know, Siphokazi. But God hates divorce."

"Yes, of course, but he allows it in cases of adultery."

"What about forgiveness, Sipho? And I know you still love him. Why divorce someone you still love?"

"That's the worst part, I presume."

While Dumisane was talking, Siphokazi started thinking about one of the wonderful moments she spent with her husband. One day while she was cooking for her family, he came calmly from behind, holding some roses in his right hand; she felt his presence despite his inaudible footsteps and she made sure to quickly turn around and immediately hugged him, turning around as if their love will never end.

"Sipho, Sipho," called Dumisane.

"Oh sorry!"

"You see, you're already missing him."

"I don't know if I will trust a man again."

"Deception is part of life."

"Faithfulness is also part of life."

"You just married the wrong guy."

After ordering drinks and food, Mboxela the spy left the restaurant area and disappeared into the mall without being noticed by either of the experienced secret agents. Besides the food was delicious the moment was enjoyed by both secret agents.

Colonel Themba was not far from Eastgate mall waiting for his informer to bring him information about his wife dining with another man. Who was that man? His wife was slipping out of his hands and that was eating his soul alive. He loved her too much to let her go in another man's arms.

A little while later, Mboxela arrived, confident with what he was holding in his hands and without delay, he entered the car.

What do you have for me?

He handed over his cell phone.

The colonel with his heart beating faster in his chest began browsing all the photos taken by his man of action. Mboxela was a well-trained commando with the ability to live under very dangerous circumstances.

"But I know this man; he's one of the state secret agents."

"Yes, sir, I also know him."

"I interrogated a man with his help. I think he's the colleague my wife told me about. I don't like this. Did you manage to hear anything about their conversation?"

"Nothing, sir. What do you want me to do next sir?"

"Don't do anything until I tell you what to do. You're dismissed."

Immediately Mboxela disappeared like a cloud of smoke from the mall. And while in the car he decided to go to one of his friends who lived in the surrounding area. Integrity was unquestionably part of his wife's lifestyle and allowing another man to touch her was not her style. But for now, he had to see his green-fingered friend for some good advice about what was going on in his life. The business side was stable and his friend Radek was a prominent member of the anti-gang movement of South Africa who escaped so many times to be buried before his time. He was a genius of the happenings of the underworld activity. He understood their philosophies and was the author of so many arrests, and used to say to Colonel Themba that the day I will detain enough evidence against you, I will expose you on national television.

"Your daughter is very stubborn."

"You all need to give her some time; this has been a shock to her."

"But why divorce her husband?"

"She is accusing him of adultery."

"Are you going with that?"

Pacing up and down was not enough for Mr Nhlakanipho who was at the same time smoking his cigar. His one day trip to

Namibia was lucrative as usual but unfortunately, one of his best men got arrested and incarcerated in one of the prisons of the capital city, Windhoek; and bribery was his only way to take him out of jail otherwise the only solution would be to kill him.

While driving on the road of Windhoek and during the police roadblock, a small plastic bag of Cocaine was discovered in the boot of his car. He was Nhlakanipho's strong man in Namibia and the South African police were after him for illicit activities and to be in the hands of the Namibian National Police was dangerous. Extradition was possible and harmful for the business.

"Can't you relax my Malume, sit down."

"What is bothering me is what your daughter is trying to do. Talk to her before it's too late. I'm still her father even if what I'm doing according to her is dishonouring us."

"I will go see her; just give her some time and know also that we cannot change people. She has her own life now and can decide for herself, and she is accusing her husband of sleeping with other women."

"I have built this empire not only for myself but for my children too."

"Don't worry too much about them, they are adults now."

"So talk to her," and he left the premises.

"Listen to me Sipho, once you divorce him and if you don't have a place to go you're welcome to stay at my place for a while until everything gets to normal."

"It is so sweet of you."

"Don't forget that your pregnancy needs good care."

"But don't forget also that you represent a dangerous person to my husband, what about if we have been followed. Don't forget he knows you. Think also about your security. Look at what happened to Carol. He killed her."

"But think also about yours, Sipho."

She laughed and said, "I know he's fathering Nthabiseng's children, and they are his kids too."

Softly Dumisane approached his hand towards hers and said, "I admire your courage for justice and I will always be there for you."

"But why until now you aren't married Dumi? A caring man like you."

The man moved in his chair and said, "I once found myself so in love with a well educated Tshwane lady from a very distinguished family in Pretoria, but I never knew she had cancer."

"Really?"

"Yes, we dated for more than a year without telling me anything. A very humble and distinguished lady; and I loved her and was ready to marry her, but she passed away a few months later after I introduced her to my family. Sorry but every time I see you I remember her."

"Why?"

"You're a moderate person, it is easy to talk to you and I miss you so much. You used to be my partner and you are about to vanish just like her."

Siphokazi stood up and hugged him.

"You have to let it go my friend, but I'm here."

"Yep. Strange right."

"I knew you were hiding something that you are trying to forget. You've always been a good friend to me and I'm grateful to God to have met you Dumi."

"Thank you."

"I have to go now."

The day was getting to its final stage of existence; a unique day with its truth to be told and heard by those in love and deceived; by those willing to restart a new try with the hope to never go back. "I salute the day, this particular day of my life far away from my expectations."

"Oh Yahweh! Where are you taking me amid so many confusions? Look at me now I doubt a better tomorrow, I no longer know where to land my footsteps. I am far away from the man I've always loved, confused and disorientated, oh! You're the master of my life. Am I no longer the righteous daughter you help taking the next steps?"

Still walking in the mall, browsing where she could, smiling to whom she could, wishing it was never as it was, far away from each other, searching for what she thought she had already but sour like the news of the end of the world.

Father where is your peace? For you have promised me peace, the peace that never ends and incomparable. I am not the daughter of the world but the daughter of the highest one troubled by circumstances; please show me how to forgive my life and those of others.

And once in her car and before starting the car, her cell phone rang; and when checking who was calling her; it was her mother.

As usual and after several months without visiting each other, Colonel Themba found the same protocol before meeting him. Radek was the boss of all secret agents working under the government and he knew too much to be left unreached for a very long time. He also deserved being protected every single second while in his domain of Bedfordview and his movements were monitored through satellite surveillance for he was valuable to the government; so losing an asset like him was going to cost a lot to the government.

Obtaining a PhD in criminology from the University of Johannesburg almost at the same time when Colonel Themba came back from Russia after one-year specialization in armament; and while intervening in one of the complicated cases in the east of the Democratic Republic of Congo, Colonel Themba while wearing on him one of the most sophisticated AK 47; and while talking to his commandos, heard a voice telling him to never think the way the AK 47 thinks.

What he did was turn around and meet that person's eyes, and it was Mr Radek with his cold eyes speaking with assurance, and their friendship started there. He was around those militaries to tell them something about their job and to detect any criminal mind that will kill for pleasure. When Colonel Themba finished what he was showing with the AK 47 to the elite commandos of the South African defence force, he immediately came to talk to them and what he told them was much appreciated by the Colonel.

Colonel Themba, helped by Mr Radek's son, entered the house where silence reigned. And his son took him to the visitor's room where soft Afrikaans music was playing.

"Make yourself comfortable sir, he's on his way and you can serve yourself a drink, the bar has more than enough that you would like to have while waiting for him."

"Thanks a lot."

Left alone the colonel considered another minute to look at the photos taken for him by Mboxela. His wife was comfortable, speaking to his enemies who were after the dismantlement of their profitable business. After all, it was justice against fraud and one had to suffer loss but not his. He heard some noises behind him as he was facing the window showing a beautiful garden of course maintained by his friend who was a conserver of the environment.

The colonel turned around and what he saw displeased him; his friend was in a wheelchair unable to walk by himself.

"Radek nice to see you fellow, what went wrong?"

"Nice to see you too, Colonel Themba, what a good surprise. Don't worry about me in the wheelchair."

"How can you say something like that?"

"I got shot three months ago in front of the gate of my house. I was followed but I'm still alive and improving."

"Sorry for what happened."

"Are you not taking anything to drink? Serve yourself; the bar is full of what you like."

"Why not?"

The colonel without wasting time poured himself a red wine from the Cape.

"How is the department of justice?"

"Doing well," he said walking at a leisurely pace.

"Too busy not to see your friend anymore?"

"I've been sluggish lately; my marriage is not doing well."

"Why?"

"Committing adultery."

"Are you?"

"She's right."

Mr Radek directed himself to the bar and also poured himself some red wine from the Cape.

"What do you intend to do?"

"I'm a crafty villain in my wife's eyes."

The criminologist laughed when he heard what he said.

"Are you becoming a devious man Colonel? Be watchful with your surrounding."

Surprised by what the criminologist expert said, Colonel Themba gave him a confused smile.

"Why are you hiding a lot from me, Colonel? Is it the reason why you've been isolated from your friend to whom you used to tell all?"

"Many things have changed, Radek."

"That's why your world is falling apart. Why does the secret service have many pictures of you with Mr Nhlakanipho?"

"Is it proving anything? You know he's my father-in-law and the secret service likes being after everyone, especially my fortunate father-in-law."

"He's also a prime suspect."

Colonel Themba in one sip finished drinking his glass of red wine.

"I cannot help you, Colonel, because people like you are the cause of my misfortune. Look at me, I'm in a wheelchair unable to make love to my wife but still, she loves me. You're full of guilt and you're killing this country. It is never too late."

Finding his friend conceited, arrogant; without saying more and without glancing behind him, Colonel Themba left the premises. But in the end, he was right and his prejudice was understandable. He was the son-in-law of the well known Nhlakanipho and nothing could change that. What the police needed against him was enough evidence to put him behind bars and close his file, but he was too meticulous to make it that easy for them.

Dealing with a morose wife was quasi-impossible, she despised him and he didn't know how to turn the hand of time whilst still involved with the family business. Leaving the business meant being on death row and only God could succeed to make it happen without danger and he didn't want to deal with God right now.

And while driving he thought about his pastor Thabiso, that he decided to give it a miss for it was a long time without being in the house of the Lord and he also thought about what he could tell him, and it came to the same conclusion as God. They were going to tell him to leave the business and start serving in the assembly as in the past. Yes, he served with commitment and never thought of turning his back on God until his father-in-law persuaded him to join the business. In the beginning, it was just to work for the family where he married but the size of his first gross income surprised him for it was exorbitant. Not everyone would easily accept working in the underworld; with all the risks attached to it, a lot of money must be put on the table.

Chapter 7

Taking copious notes of the state of affairs, detective Naidoo of the John Foster police station in Johannesburg CBD together with secret agent Dumisane had in front of them Mr Nhlakanipho's photos. And one of the photos was showing him holding his daughter, Siphokazi.

"Where did you get all these photos?" Dumisane was surprised to see him with so many pictures.

"We are working hard against the smuggling of drugs in our country. And I was surprised to notice that your colleague is the daughter of the big boss."

"This is the main reason she resigned, I presume."

"She took the right decision; I would have done the same thing if I was in her place. But these guys are very powerful and know how to cover their money. They have businesses throughout South Africa and employ thousands of people and no tax evasion. Can you imagine that?"

"Are you sure there's no tax evasion? Ask our revenue services but what proof does the South African police have against them?"

"Those you know, people that we have arrested and recognize them as their bosses."

"So what we need is to spot them where they deliver their merchandise or at their warehouses. Arresting one of the bosses while involved and put pressure on him to expose others."

"What about his wife?" Asked Dumisane.

"Be careful she will end up turning against us for she loves him."

"She knows a lot and if she can agree to testify against her husband by working for the business, we can arrest all of them."

"Including her father? It's a devastating decision."

"We don't care. We don't care because we need someone from the inside," said secret agent Dumisane.

"This is possible only if you can convince her to rejoin us in the force and put an end to those perpetrating those acts. She will need willpower but with a woman who is still in love with her husband!"

"Besides she is pregnant and they are about to divorce and that will be good news to us for she can rejoin us."

"This must be ultra-secret. If not you and I are dead agents of the state."

Detective Naidoo left his chair to serve himself a glass of water.

"I like your idea," he said after drinking some water.

"We should wait until she divorces him, then she will become open to us."

"What about her father?" Said Naidoo.

"Wait a minute, she signed to be loyal to her government, or we convince her, what do you think about this one? We make

94

sure that she does not divorce him and go into her father's business and help her government to get rid of such people.

"Did her husband already sign the papers?"

"Not yet detective."

"Is it possible to meet her privately and without being pursued? Those guys don't tolerate any threat to their businesses."

"That needs to be organized as quickly as possible for some lawyers are about to make some good money out of that divorce if we don't try this one," said the secret agent.

She had to conspire to acquire valuable evidence to arrest and dismantle the cartel, and this one was going to be a complicated feature to swallow for Siphokazi, thought secret agent Dumisane once in his car. Arresting smugglers was her strong point and this was going to be a significant step into the mystery if he could convince her to not divorce Themba, join them and finally join her father's business to put an end to the smuggling.

First of all, a private conversation with her was of necessity before taking her to detective Naidoo and on acceptance Lieutenant Keegan will be part of the process.

24 hours later:

Colonel Themba was reading his book in the TV room and at the same time observing his wife's movements and gestures. He was also under the impression that she was about to tell him something for she was busy in the kitchen, passing where he was without saying anything. He was missing his wife's cooking but he was determined to talk to her about her dinner with secret agent Dumisane. He was jealous and uncomfortable with the whole situation and he knew that she was not going to agree with him about spying on her, but he had to remind her that still, he was her husband, the father of her children and also the coming child in her womb.

Still in the kitchen at around 3 p.m., Siphokazi saw her husband entering where she was with a face expressing an attitude of self-control. She had never known him as a physical abuser of women. He was holding an envelope that he gave to her without saying anything, and she took it also without saying anything but curious to know what it was all about, and that made her think about the divorce papers. And once the envelope was in her hand he turned around and left; leaving her with the big surprise.

In the guise of response, she opened the envelope and saw what she couldn't imagine seeing. Four pictures were showing her with secret agent Dumisane dining at the restaurant. She just smiled without panicking. She admired the quality of those pictures for they were clear and put them where they belonged in the envelope. She sighed when all of a sudden her cell phone rang, and when checking the screen it was an unknown number and that gave her the confidence to take the call.

To her big surprise, it was secret agent Dumisane.

"Hello Siphokazi!" It's Dumisane.

Before responding she first went to check if her husband was not at the door listening. But no one was there.

"Hello, Dumisane! I cannot speak to you right now."

"I need to see you urgently."

"I can't now for my husband spies on me."

"Listen the intelligence is asking after you and don't forget that you signed the loyalty statement."

"I know."

"So they don't believe you resigned just for the fact you are pregnant. Listen, we need to meet and I will tell you more. Listen to this one, don't divorce your husband, and he cut the line."

"What!" She said.

Colonel Themba entered the kitchen, opened the fridge and he was about to make himself a sandwich when she suddenly said to him, "I will do that for you."

"Why?" He exclaimed.

"Because these pictures mean nothing," she said showing him the envelope. "You know Dumisane, he used to be my colleague and why do you spy on me?"

"Because you're still my wife and you have to respond to me."

She sighed and smiled. "What about your children with Nthabiseng?"

"What are you talking about?"

"You think I don't know about your immorality out there. Are they your children? Go for a DNA test and check really if they are your own because mine are yours."

Colonel Themba received the news with a big surprise for he couldn't imagine his wife going that far with her investigation about what he was doing outside the marriage. She cared about him. And without responding he left the kitchen and went walking in the garden.

Left alone in the kitchen Siphokazi immediately dialled secret agent Dumisane's cell phone number. Five seconds later her former colleague responded to the call.

"Your dreadful story stinks," she said straight away.

"I know that's why you have to see me if possible today."

"Where are you?"

"Come in half an hour to the Hillbrow police station on the second floor."

"You're crazy, I'm coming."

With her husband around she had to find a way to meet her colleague, but how? She thought. he wants some food right; let me give him what he wants. So with the care, she made him the sandwich he wanted to make for himself and she accompanied that with a glass of juice. Then she followed him in the garden and gave them to him saying nothing.

With surprise, the colonel took the food and the drink in both hands, and she left. While eating he heard her starting her car and saw her leaving the premises.

Hillbrow as usually was busy with people walking in all directions and she was to a great extent confused while driving. How could secret agent Dumisane could tell her not to divorce her husband? What were they busy preparing behind her back that it was time to let her know? Of course, I've signed the loyalty statement but not for me to be enslaved by it she thought.

Proceeding to the parking area, she realized that there was something fishy that she was going to decipher. The force was expecting more from her but how to deliver according to their expectations while pregnant and deceived by a husband?

Crossing her fingers, she went into the building up to the second floor where she found the secret agent busy drinking his cup of coffee.

Happy to see her, the secret agent stood up to welcome his former colleague.

"Very happy to see you, Sipho."

But she said nothing, she just sat.

"I know I was straight with you on the phone, but I had to convince you to come."

"What is it this time?"

"Can I offer you something to drink?"

"Give me a glass of water, please from the fridge."

"Sipho, our superiors are not happy and convinced that you left the force because of a pregnancy. South Africa has good laws that protect working pregnant women and that should be enough to still play a positive role in all the investigations we are busy with," he said whilst giving her the glass of water. "Our service detains a certain amount of evidence regarding Colonel Themba's activities with the underworld and their conclusion is based on that."

"What?"

"You left the force after discovering that your husband is part of the underworld and that you don't want to be the one arresting him one day, and it makes sense but they've insisted on your engagement with our government. If not it will be considered treason."

"What?"

"I'm sorry, Siphokazi."

Siphokazi with both of her hands held her head.

"I don't understand."

"They want you back into the force, but this time to get closer to your family business."

"You got to be kidding."

"It's no joke."

Dumisane saw some tears going down her face.

"That's why you said to me not to divorce Themba?"

"It is part of the plan; you no longer want this man anyway."

Wiping her tears with both hands, she sighed and said, "Is that all?"

"You should come on Monday morning at ten o'clock to our meeting in our Midrand office. Please take it easy, Sipho."

"So you want me to go undercover to have my family arrested?"

"All of this is because of your husband Sipho, he doesn't care but only about his money. Is it what you wanted for your life?"

"But not to the point of using me to facilitate their arrest."

"You know we have been trained for this, you cannot turn that emotional then this job has never been for you. If you don't they will press charge against you."

"I don't have to cry, there is no need to cry in this selfish world," she said angrily.

Allowing her to absorb the shock, secret agent Dumisane with both hands holding his waist, looked at the floor and then turned around and went stand in front of the open window. And after a while, he came to her, took the chair and sat in front of her.

"We all know that you're a strong woman and I love you so much. You don't deserve what is happening to you, but it will be over soon and for a good reason, for justice must prevail."

"I will come," she said desperately.

"Start playing the game, don't divorce him now; but on Monday more will be said to you."

"Goodbye, Dumisane."

"Goodbye, Sipho."

Sunday, 08h10am

While driving by herself, going to church, Siphokazi on her own managed to tolerate the pain she went through while in the Hillbrow police station. The stake was to apprehend the culprits, and her husband with her father was amongst those orchestrating everything. It was very difficult to bear this alone so she needed her pastor's influence. She needed to hear their voices and impressions about the whole matter. She was considering the pastoral couple as pre-eminent shepherds with the right advice and professionalism.

Arriving five minutes later with praise and worships already started, she made sure to occupy the back seat. She had difficulty concentrating but she finally made it by focusing on the work of the cross where every solution comes from. The moment became agreeable, forgetting the real world for a peaceful and awesome moment with the Lord while allowing some tears to go down her cheeks, searching for the ultimate boldness to carry out her job without failure.

After praise and worships and after welcoming the newcomers the sermon commenced and it was Pastor Thabiso preaching a touchy message. It seemed as if the Pastor was talking just to her saying that there's nothing impossible to the one who believes in God as our Messiah said in Mark 11:22. After the sermon as usual with his wife Ps Tshepang, they made sure to greet the congregation outside the church.

The pastoral couple marvelled when they saw Siphokazi. "Sipho!" Called Ps Tshepang, "How are you? You look, great, sister."

After hugging each other she said, "I would like to speak to you."

"Ok wait for us in our office; we will be with you in a short while."

"Thank you."

It was great to belong to a place that didn't disregard human rights. And deep in her heart, she knew she couldn't overrule the force's decision. That was the government and reinforcing the law against her was going to be detrimental not only to the family but also to her reputation.

The Pastoral couple were wearing clothes that suited them very well and she needed their optimistic view of the future, but hers seemed complicated with horns that nobody could break. Her marriage was in jeopardy because she married the man in uniform that her father loved and found suitable for her but it was rather for his business.

Her going back into the force was no longer going to be to surpass the achievement of any of her colleagues but the achievement of a wife betraying the whole family she loves for the interest of the nation.

The pastoral couple after a short while entered the office ready to hear the dilemma of the daughter of the assembly. They both were confident and ready to listen to her.

"Sipho," called Ps Tshepang, "It was nice to see you among us this morning."

"It is also nice to see you, pastor."

"What's bothering you?" Ps, Tshepang asked.

The Pastors and Siphokazi occupied the lounge for a good discussion.

"It is getting harder for me because the force wants me back; my resignation has been rejected because a pregnant woman doesn't just resign because she fell pregnant."

"Of course, Sipho," said Ps Thabiso.

"They are forcing me to go back and obtain evidence against my husband and family for a possible arrest and this is asking me too much now."

The Pastoral couple looked at each other while Sipho started weeping.

"Sipho, what is your intuition?" Demanded Ps Tshepang. "Is your husband involved in all of this? Please don't cry my daughter," and she gave me some serviettes.

"Yes, he is, including my father."

"Oh! Father in the heavenly places, help your daughter to go through this period as an overcomer," said Ps Thabiso.

"You suffer because you don't want to join them Sipho, and God will help you during this very difficult period of your life, but resigning shouldn't cause a problem if you don't want the job anymore," said Ps Tshepang.

"I have signed a loyalty statement with the government and overruling it will be treated as treason."

"To Caesars what belongs to Caesars and God what belongs to God," said Ps Thabiso. "I am confident that everything will come out right in time. The underworld is a resistance to good morality and the government will use any possible means to stop that oppression."

"They don't want me to divorce him now, they are controlling my life."

"What is your decision, Sipho?"

"Pastor Tshepang, I still love my husband, really this job sucks."

Both pastors remained calm.

"But he is a careless, bastard man without a future."

Still, the Pastoral couple remained calm.

"What's God's opinion?"

"To forgive and justice must be done," said Ps Tshepang.

This was a more sanguine view that she couldn't resist. Wiping her tears that she couldn't stop wiping; she stood up, sighing at the same time.

"Don't lean on your understanding, Sipho, but trust Him who gave you this responsibility to track wrongdoers, said Ps Thabiso.

Thank you Ps, I will.

There is a time to laugh; there is a time to cry.

Secret agent Dumisane was listening to some music through his earphone when he saw the office door being opened by Colonel Ramaphosa followed by Lieutenant Keegan. A third man followed a few minutes later with a facial impression of someone ready for any attack against Colonel Ramaphosa, his boss. He was a bodyguard ready for any brutal action; with a quick eye examined the office including the chair where his boss was sited. Satisfied he went and stood behind the Colonel.

A few minutes later it was secret agent Siphokazi's turn to enter the office. The air conditioner was allowing fresh air to cool down the office, so everyone sat comfortably. The day was hot and a little bit windy.

A bit intimidated by the presence of her superiors, secret agent Sipho went straight to sit behind her colleague Dumisane.

"Are you not greeting us," said secret agent Dumisane.

Immediately she stood up and said, "Good morning!"

"Good morning secret agent Siphokazi." responded the Colonel.

Her immediate superior Lieutenant Keegan dressed in uniform began to speak.

"A month ago you deposited on my desk your resignation due to pregnancy, but after careful consideration of the matter the National Security has rejected your application, for South Africa has enough laws protecting working pregnant women, unless your pregnancy is dangerous. Are you declining this?"

"I do agree," she responded.

"A few weeks later the force discovered that your husband, Colonel Themba, had suspicious activities with the underworld business and a conclusion was drawn from there. You're leaving the force not because of any pregnancy-related problems but because of your husband's activities. That's why your demand for your resignation has been rejected. Any correction?"

"I do agree with you," Lieutenant.

"A statement of loyalty was signed by you when joining the force to remain loyal to your government no matter what. Are you aware of it?"

"Yes, I am," Lieutenant.

"We understand you Sipho considering also the nature of your job with the risks attached to it, but the government should be a respecter of nobody and also your government remembers it has spent a lot of money for your training to become a qualified secret agent."

Colonel Ramaphosa left his seat and sat on the desk.

"Colonel Themba was a teammate and was one of the best of our division but what went through his mind? Why such a surrounding? A very dangerous one."

The Colonel showed some photos in which Sipho saw her husband talking to one of her father's executives. Actually what the government needed was enough evidence to incarcerate them. Sited in her shame she found the strength to ask them. "What do you want me to do?"

"Good question," said Lieutenant Keegan. "You're the right person we need. First of all, you sign another contract with the government with a salary increase; you sign another statement of loyalty, you don't divorce your husband and you make sure that you enter their world and that will be more convenient considering your state."

"To enter their world?"

"Yes, Sipho. You must start working for this man and show consideration."

Colonel Ramaphosa exposed another photo with a man she knew very well, Mr Nhlakanipho her father. She immediately started.

"We also know that this person is your biological father, Sipho, but we have no evidence against him," said the Colonel. "But rather a community leader for his Not-for-profit organization is of great benefit to the government and he's also receiving a lot of donations internationally."

"Why are you doing this to me?"

"We know this is a very tough assignment secret agent," said the Colonel, "But you're a loyal agent of our government, you have proven it in the past and declining this will mean protection of the culprits and an act of treason against your government."

"You're one of our best agents Sipho, integrating their world is the knowledge that you know and should be applied with care, and diligence and you will be greatly rewarded for a service of this magnitude."

"Betraying my own family," she said in distress.

"We wish you all the best," said Colonel Ramaphosa.

And they all left the office, except secret agent Dumisane who left his seat to take place beside her.

"Take it easy, Sipho. The national security of this country is in your hands right now."

"You mean I have the key through betraying my own family."

"You and I are here to uncover secret information and we have to penetrate their world clandestinely and I either don't like it or stop being emotional and turn cold, please turn cold to be able to face them."

Sighing and knowing that this is a way of no return; she wiped her face of all the tears and stood up.

"Are you with me, Sipho?"

"So I don't divorce him now and I have to accept my father's offer as one of his executives."

"Easy!" said her colleague excited.

"Perhaps I won't divorce him anymore, that father of my children."

After saying that; and after caressing secret agent Dumisane's face, she took her bag and left. Dumisane without saying anything. left her to go and face the dilemma that she had to surmount.

Yes, she was hand-picked by her superiors not because she was the best but as part of the family, they all hated and wanted to see her incarcerated forever. The deal was patched together and had to be executed without fault, and she was the main actor. Any mistake from her could end up with fatal results. She was going to pierce their hearts with a sharp instrument and some were going to hate her forever. This way of casting the lot was inconceivable but nothing was impossible with God, she thought. She needed wisdom and peace to bring justice to prevail against her father and her husband, men she loved with all her heart and for the first time, she was going to work for her father, Mr Nhlakanipho, the mastermind of the whole empire, unstoppable with his petty ideas.

And again tears coursed down her cheeks, leaving traces of great tribulations to be overcome.

Chapter 8

The North West province was hot but attractive; the sunshine filled the town of Rustenburg and being distant from Johannesburg helped him to forget about all the worries that haunted him. At the same time facing a dilemma concerning the paternity of the two children he had with Nthabiseng, Colonel Themba tranquilly waited for the coming of the medical doctor who did the paternity test.

In his smart navy-blue suit, matching his suitcase, the colonel's heart exploded when he saw the doctor stepping into his office with the results. He loved his daughter and son and he could never imagine them not being his until his wife reminded him. His house didn't have a homely atmosphere anymore and he knew he was the cause of it.

Without wasting time the medical doctor opened the file to tell him, "According to the results, Colonel, the boy matches your DNA but not the girl."

"What!" He said.

The doctor sighed and then handed over to him the file with the result. And calmly taking the file he effectively realized it was sadly so.

"You're welcome to a second opinion, but this is what we have found."

"Thank you, doctor."

He loved her with all his heart and strength for turning into someone else's daughter. Discouraged he left the hospital thinking about his wife Siphokazi like never before. She was the only one he could trust but she was about to divorce him and marry another man, and thinking that way caused a lot of hurt. He suddenly felt so alone and realized his money couldn't redeem the pain he felt.

He declined to call her thinking it was going to cause more worries and desperation. He was pathetic but not yet ready to give up for he still loved her, and signing the divorce documents was no question. Nthabiseng was dead and buried, meaning he had to move on without her and make sure that still, the business was a priority to him. And his wife calling him a heartbreaker was founded for he deserved her punishment, but still had no plan A to by-pass and win her again.

The colonel made sure to switch off his cell phone, avoiding any contact with close friends and family members. The pitiful wage paid to him by Nthabiseng had to be swallowed and digested for the organization never tolerated emotional instability that could cause damages.

While peacefully cooking in the kitchen, Siphokazi heard her cell phone ringing in the lounge. She rushed to the phone but the ringing suddenly stopped. When verifying she realized that someone was at the gate trying to enter the premises, and again her cell phone restarted ringing. She answered. It was her mother, Helena, trying to enter the premises.

"Ma'am! I'm opening."

It was a surprise visit that she welcomed anyway; seeing her mother after two full weeks delighted her, besides she was already thinking about how to let them know of her decision to cancel divorcing her husband and accept her father's proposal as one of the directors of the group holding companies.

It wasn't long when her mother entered the house followed by her mother-in-law.

"Ma'am, you're both welcome."

"Sipho my daughter; how are you? How is the baby doing?"

"I'm alright, the baby also, what a good surprise."

After hugging each other and with her mother-in-law busy caressing her belly to feel the baby, she took them to the kitchen where she was cooking.

"I didn't include you when I started cooking, but don't worry, I have plenty."

"Where is my son?"

"I haven't seen him for two days and when trying to call, his phone is on voice mail."

"Why? He didn't call me for the entire week."

She had a table in the kitchen so they comfortably sat down at the table looking happy, but concerned for they came to carry out a mission.

"We won't take long my daughter for your father is not feeling alright."

"What's wrong with dad, Mum?"

"Your father is getting old and I've been advising him to consider taking more rest."

"We have many resting places in South Africa, out of South Africa; advise him to take a vacation in Mauritius or Seychelles.
"

"Your father loves his business and thinks he's still in his fifties to be running all over the city, talk to him."

"I will ma'am, but you only came to tell me about dad?"

"We brought you a message from your father."

"Is it for his proposal?"

"He doesn't want you to divorce your husband."

"And he also said that before he dies he wants you to accept his proposal," said her mother-in-law.

Siphokazi refrained to mention anything of what the Holy Bible says about honouring our parents. It was going to be a lie.

"Ma'am, you tell dad that I won't divorce my husband anymore but for the proposal, I'm not ready yet."

That was an agreeable big surprise to the parents and it was accompanied by a scream that alerted the kids that were playing in the TV room.

"Do you mean so my daughter?" Said her mother very excited.

"Yes, I'm serious."

"You've made my day, your father will be very happy."

Half an hour later, the whole family, excluding Colonel Themba, was busy eating the delicious food cooked by their daughter and mother, and for a very long time, she never saw her mother that happy. She was a strong woman who had supported such a man for so many years; things that she couldn't do. But it was never going to be like before anymore, the lot was cast and the damage had to be consumed for the

113

government wanted her to execute their orders as the government was resolved to cease any illegal activities within its borders and the risk was immeasurable.

Three days later and while in the North West Province Colonel Themba decided to switch on his cell phone to check the messages and missed calls. He realized with great interest how many times his wife tried to talk to him. She tried five times and he asked himself why. He was lonely and a long way from home and always bewitched by her charm; she was the woman he married without thinking twice and still loved her with all his heart. But one of his weaknesses was his inability to resist women pestering him for a ride. So curiously he decided to call her back to hear from her.

It rang twice before responding but it was his son on the other side.

"Daddy, how are you?"

"Ntombisi! I'm alright my son, and you?"

"Fine."

"Where is your mother?"

"She is here."

"Hallo!" It was Sipho already responding.

"Hallo Sipho! How are you? I saw your missed calls so I decided to call you."

"Your mother and my mother wanted to talk to you, where are you?"

"In the North-West, I'm coming back today."

After a moment of silence, she said, "Ok, I have to take the kids to the park."

"Alright, alright, see you then, I'm on my way back."

And she hung up but left Colonel Themba perplexed; there was something fishy, he wondered. He had no clue of what was going on but his mother and mother-in-law's presence in his premises meant a way to reconcile them. Actually, almost everything was getting on his nerves and the quantity of money he had could not even solve his problems; it could only help him to bring the painful truth to his awareness. But his time in the province was up, what he wanted to do now was to go back to his family and tell his wife that he still loved her and that he was not ready to sign any divorce papers.

But first, he was going to apologize because he was convinced that he was part of the crisis, she had concrete evidence of his cheatings and improper conduct towards the South African government. But exiting from the family business was no question for the covenant was fatal and only God could restore his situation to normal.

Another thing was bothering him, he wasn't the father of the little girl he always considered as his but the boy was. The question was how to make Siphokazi accept him as hers? Truly his life was a big surprise to her and distrustful; everything was on the brink of collapsing and she wasn't any more to be fooled around.

Taking courage he wondered how and when all of these were going to end, for to date the victory wasn't on his side concerning his family, but he was gaining more ascendancy towards the family empire for he was a genius of the underworld and his father-in-law bestowed him with much of his.

Secret agent Dumisane with Siphokazi's picture in his hand didn't know that his ex-fiancée that he deceived eleven months ago had just entered the apartment. It was an apartment they co-owned for there was certainty they were going to get married; a story he never told Siphokazi that he believed marrying one day.

"Dumi, why?"

He looked at her, keeping his mouth shut.

"You'll never marry this woman, she doesn't belong to you. Why are you hurting yourself like this?"

He smiled and left the apartment to avoid unnecessary quarrels. But once outside and in the street, the quietness questioned him to be careful, thinking about the kind of job he had; but suddenly he received a phone call telling him that he was requested to quickly intervene in a dangerous poaching situation in the Kruger National Park. The anonymous voice told him to remain still until he was picked up in the next quarter-hour.

Recognizing the voice, secret agent Dumisane quickly went to his apartment where his ex-fiancée, while singing, was busy cleaning. It was a beautiful three-bedroom flat in the middle of Johannesburg and every day he was wondering how to never have anything to do with his ex anymore because she was taking advantage of the situation.

What he needed was not far away from him and he only had ten minutes left, so he quickly went into his bedroom, took some clothes from his wardrobe, toothbrush and lotion and left the room to enter the kitchen where he opened the fridge to take his bottle of juice that he had started drinking that morning.

His ex was curious and demanded, "Are you going forever for we are about to pay this heavy electricity bill?

Just pay it and I will reimburse you the difference.

You're the man here.

Don't worry I won't be long when I'm after a poacher and show me some kindness; I need it from a beautiful lady like you.

You need Jesus to keep you alive in that wilderness, which will profit you more.

The secret agent smiled and left his premises; but once outside the flat in the corridor he leaned for a while against the door thinking about what was going on with him. The truth is that he turned paranoid towards Phumzile, his ex-fiancée, she had nothing of an abusive woman persecuting her man for no reason. The problem he had was just he couldn't get over the sudden death of the one he had always wanted to marry and now he was busy seeking for the Suzy that he couldn't find and even secret agent Siphokazi couldn't understand what he wanted to do with a woman who was about to be divorced with three kids.

He had to leave his deceitfulness and focus on what was waiting for him in Skukuza.

Driving three hundred and sixty kilometres made Colonel Themba realize that he lost so much of his dignity. He had a lot going on in his mind but he had to remain serene to overcome the bad wind stronger than him. And while driving, he touched his Bible that has always been in the back seat of his car but refused to consult it, and because of that hesitation, he realized how powerless he became to overcome the gold of this world. But there was something that he needed to do; to see his pregnant wife and his children that he truly missed every day.

But it wasn't going to be a reunion for she was hurrying up to divorce him and start a new life, perhaps with another man. What did I roll up on? He wondered. And once in front of his gate, he cried aloud "finally" and pressed the button of the remote, the gate released the space that allowed him to park his car in the garage. And while parking the car he already had the visit of his two sons stationed at the back of the garage and those made him so happy; he could finally with the love of a father hug and kiss them.

He entered the house with both of his sons and found his wife watching TV in the TV room but she was different, truly pregnant with his child and that he belonged with her. He let go of his children's hand, stepped into her direction and fell to his knees and said "I love you Sipho, please don't divorce me."

It was a miracle to see her standing up to help him up on his feet. He couldn't believe it was coming from the woman who was about to divorce him forever.

"I'm no longer going to divorce you," she just said while helping him up.

"Are you telling the truth?" Said the colonel, confused.

"Don't ask me that again," she said calmly. "I'm not going to divorce you, Themba."

The colonel expressed a cry of happiness, at the same time hugged her to show how much he missed her, appreciating her gesture. Stepping back but holding both of her hands, he started looking at her with that smile he had the first day he met her.

"You look beautiful and very pregnant; your face expresses the peace that I need."

She just laughed.

"Yes, I am carrying your baby daughter."

"I love you Sipho, my wife."

"I also love you, Themba, my husband."

"I'm going to throw a party."

"You're welcome."

The following day in front of Lieutenant Keegan, secret agent Dumisane was about to receive some directives regarding his mission in the Kruger national park, one of the biggest national parks in Africa, covering an area of 19,485 square kilometres in the provinces of Limpopo and Mpumalanga in north-eastern South Africa. He was all alone without Siphokazi backing him up, it was going to be a very risky adventure to enjoy.

"We have received some phone calls from the South African National Park about some strange activities happening in the Kruger National Park. There's a suspicious oriental couple that twice a year visit the Park for two to three weeks and each time there are some poaching activities carried out. They need our intervention to investigate the couple."

Secret agent Dumisane was quietly listening to what his superior was telling him and wanted to know what his task in this affair was going to be, but surely they wanted him to build up a relationship with the oriental couple to know more about if their presence in the park was merely for tourism or to destroy an animal species.

"The headquarters are in Skukuza and you will meet a certain Wolmarans, one of the directors of the National Park who will give you further information including how to work in collaborations with the rangers. Everything has been set up and you're leaving for Skukuza tonight at 07h00 with South African Airways. Good luck secret agent."

"Is no one coming with me?"

"Do you need help?"

"Yes sir, a lady who will play the role of my wife, two rings that will prove that we are married and on honeymoon."

"That's a great strategy, you'll meet her once in Skukuza together with the rings, I mean a lady who is part of the government secret agency and who has played this role before but be careful, she doesn't care who is around her but any misplaced hand on her can cost you your license, so be careful with what you wish."

"Thanks a lot, Lieutenant."

"You're dismissed."

Yes, this time it was not going to be Siphokazi; yes she was constantly in his mind dragging his thoughts towards her.

What a fantastic morning it was for Colonel Themba and Siphokazi. It was a long time since they experienced a wonderful night together as a couple. Siphokazi even knowing the real motives of not divorcing her husband was happy to be back with a smile in the family she loved with all her heart. After all, he was the father of her children and will remain faithful to him no matter what, and thinking that way gave her the peace of mind she needed. She was determined to face the worst and her worst was the day her husband will realize that justice should prevail but still will love him with all her heart.

Meticulously she had to operate and put an end to this empire of cheaters and Colonel Themba watching the brightness of her opened eyes thoughts about their early days. The smile she communicated was of endless life and after days of reflections, he became conscious that nothing could substitute the woman of his life.

"Themba!" She called.

"Yes, my love."

"Don't be alarmed to tell me everything, I'm your wife and nothing will change it."

"Are you still working for the government?"

"After much thought, I decided to resign, it is better like that."

"All of that because of me, Sipho, forgive me."

"So when are you throwing the party since I have an announcement to make."

"Which one?"

"It's a secret, it will be revealed at the party and that party must happen here."

"Let's set it for this Saturday afternoon."

"Make sure that you're the one informing the cartel, I won't call anyone, and you're doing this for me."

"Of course."

"Something else I would like to know."

"I'm yours."

"What about the children you had with Nthabiseng?"

Colonel Themba's face suddenly turned to sadness.

"I need to know the truth."

"One of them is not mine; I discovered it while in the North-West Province."

"Who's not yours?"

"The girl," he said with concern.

"You have a girl on the way now."

"I thank God for that."

"And where are those children?"

"With their grandmother."

"Support them. It is your responsibility."

"I am Sipho, thank you for your support, but the girl…"

"The girl what?" She cut him off. "She knows you as her father."

"Yes, I will provide for her too."

And he disappeared in the bathroom and while left alone she looked around, apprehended his presence, the presence of a husband lost in the deepness of the greed of this world. But the way to getting to the bottom of this was narrowed and deceiving but also very dangerous for she was about to eat every day with the enemies of the state, eating with those who kill for the convenience to prove that he is the man, and every day she was walking and sleeping in a reflective mood on how to cause as little damage as possible.

The South African Airways flight had just taken off flying towards Skukuza where the administrative headquarters were. When checking his wristwatch, it indicated 07h20 in the evening and within thirty minutes he was going to land in Skukuza, in Mpumalanga. Mpumalanga province is a very interesting one in terms of landscapes and its people. The diversity of its attractions has made the province the most visited one after the Western Cape. Even if his mission was dangerous, he was excited to explore for his very first time the gigantic national park.

He had no clue what kind of people he was going to meet there; who was Mr Wolmarans? Of course, one of the directors but was he credible enough because the next minute was dangerous with his kind of job? Who was the woman to play the role of his beloved wife? He was getting fed up with his kind of job. He was always ending up as the traitor to knock down and because of his loyalty, he was very much in demand by the government, especially concerning crimes happening within the country.

He decided to stop thinking and sleep during the flight to feel stronger once he arrived for the meeting which was maybe going to be held at once after landing at Skukuza airport.

He woke up after about twenty-nine minutes when he felt the wheels of the aeroplane touching the tarmac of the Skukuza airport and a few minutes later he was outside of the aircraft walking to the airport building. He hired a taxi straight to the South African National Park administrative headquarters. It was quarter to eight and the weather was warm but manageable. Once he arrived at the headquarters a few minutes later, he entered the building after being allowed through by the security guard. The reception area was vacant with a young white lady in her thirties seated in one of the chairs of the reception area reading a magazine.

She was elegant and wearing glasses that made her meet the criteria of a lady that respected the principles of a decent life.

"Excuse me please," he said while getting nearer.

"You are secret agent Dumisane?" She suddenly said.

The secret agent surprised said, "Yes, I am," he said smiling at her.

"I am your wife, I hope you're not racist."

The secret agent laughed.

"Of course, I'm not."

"My name is Lizzy Wolmarans, don't worry about my surname, one of the directors that you'll meet in the next hour is my biological father, he used to be a secret agent too during the seventies and eighties and he is strategically based here for the security of our national treasure."

And after saying that she stood up and hugged him like a wife should hug her husband.

"Thank you for guarding my steps, responding to her kind gesture. I'm Dumisane," then he said, "And your husband."

"Beloved husband. And we have three weeks to make sure that no laws against our natural conservation are broken."

"Of course my beloved wife."

Her cell phone suddenly rang.

"It is my father," she said. "Yes Dad, I'm here with secret agent Dumisane."

Dumisane for a while looked around and admired the establishment; it was a beautiful building with great South African art décor.

"My father is already inside," she said walking towards the main doorway.

A vending machine selling cold drinks was ten meters away from where they were next to the lifts and Dumisane checked in his trousers pockets where he found a 20 Rand note. He was thirsty and tired, ready to get a nice sleep before starting his espionage. But when he started walking towards the vending machine Mr Wolmarans made his way into the reception area followed by two other individuals wearing ranger's uniforms.

"Good evening, secret agent Dumisane."

"Good evening, sir."

He came across with an average height man with a chest like a Gorilla and with a quick speech that he had no difficulty understanding.

"I'm sure my daughter has introduced herself, she is just like her father who doesn't waste time, she is also one of the finest in this industry, and mostly used to go after poachers or any suspicious park invader."

"She already introduced herself as my wife."

"Great darling," he said to his daughter. "My first contact with this young man assures me that you'll work productively."

"Thanks, Dad."

"But be careful, she's my only daughter among four boys."

The secret agent laughed, he was a funny man who used to terrorize suspicious tourists.

"Follow me to my office, I'm aware it is late but we need to talk now."

His office was on the second floor of the administrative building, and the two rangers were left behind in the reception area. While in his office he went straight towards the small fridge located on the right-hand side of the door where he took out some cold drinks and put them on the table of his reception lounge. Truly it was the office of a big company director.

"You may sit down, secret agents. It is very hectic when every time a particular tourist arrives in this country something very wrong happens. Most of the time he comes alone but in this instance, he came with his partner. They are a middle-aged couple from Thailand and discreet, especially the man. We have cross-examined him every time he entered South Africa."

"But there's no smoke without fire," said the secret agent.

"Well said secret agent because his presence here since he started coming to our country coincides with some poaching activities."

"You mean every time."

"Yes, and with your help, we need to uncover what is hidden that we don't know about the couple. What do you think will be the first thing to do?"

"Listening to their conversations while in their game lodge room can help us to intercept their daily plans."

"Very good idea, they've been here for two days already, and your room just opposite to theirs is yours however you need to find a way to install your micro-phone."

"What about the rangers you brought, Dad?"

126

"They are good friends of the oriental man and after booking for a tour of the park they usually take him to different locations in the park. That's why you also need to speak to them."

"Do they bring a lot of money in, in terms of tourism?"

"They are the kind the tourists we need for our economy, and two years ago when they came they frequently they used the Phalaborwa entrance gate using the National 1, and while here the poaching of two male elephants was confirmed, and that same evening the couple was already out of the province."

"A very interesting coincidence."

"I have to retire secret agent, darling I'm not dealing with beginners in this field, you know what to do. The rangers with the secret agent will take you to the park and in your game lodge; a sumptuous one that you will never forget."

"Thanks a lot, Mr Wolmarans."

"Be careful with my daughter, she's never been yours."

"Dad!"

Chapter 9

It was the first time that she was in the John Foster police station, in the Johannesburg CBD without secret agent Dumisane by her side. She felt lonely and in real danger for this time. She was forced to use all her skills alone to the benefit of her government; which was expecting a breakthrough into stopping the drub smuggling caused by her husband and father.

Lieutenant Keegan was waiting for her to sign the new contract that was going to bind her with the government until the accomplishment of the mission. She was advised to comprehensively read the contract to avoid any confusion that could jeopardize her relationship with her employer. It was a tough contract but with great benefits in case of tragedy or a breakthrough.

Finally, she decided to sign the contract and told Lieutenant Keegan who was enjoying drinking his black strong coffee.

"Ready to sign?"

"Yes sir."

"Here's the pen."

Signing the contract discharged her, firstly because she was obsessive about her job and secondly it was time to turn the page of her family history. She was ashamed and ready for anything, and thirdly she was going to spend more time at the side of the family she loved no matter what. She was missing her father and her beloved mother by no means ceased loving. She wanted to hug him like she never did before.

"Is secret agent Dumisane alright sir?"

"He is on duty in the Kruger National Park, some poaching activities are taking place there and we are about to make some arrests. We needed one of our spies there; he's the right person for such a challenging piece of work."

Wishing to have not been followed by her jealous husband; after signing her new contract, secret agent Siphokazi made a copy of the new agreement and left John Foster police station. It was good and painful at the same time since the bad feeling of betraying her family was already haunting her, although she knew she was doing that for a good cause; hell shouldn't prevail. She thought about her pastors far from where she was, but she didn't want them to know about her Machiavellian plan for what she was about to do was going to hurt everyone, but this was the only way to scatter them, and they won't be remembered.

Holding his wife's right hand, secret agents Dumisane and Lizzy were looking exceptional as a mixed couple among the other folks that were there. They could attract the awareness of almost everyone in the game lodge restaurant. Soft music came from invisible speakers was playing to make the atmosphere welcoming and it suited them. Wearing fancy clothes and facing unknown people to them, secret agent Lizzy rapidly identified the oriental tourists sitting facing another oriental man wearing glasses and a hat.

Installing a microphone in the oriental couple's room was going to help them to hear some of their secret conversations, which Mr Wolmarans will capture with his team. With his wife, he only had two weeks to capitalize on the situation and make a very important arrest that will propel him to one of the best secret agents of the nation. Turning his back on the oriental tourist while Lizzy faced the tourist; Lizzy could calmly monitor their moves, noticing at the same time that the conversation was very serious.

Enjoying eating their salads, Lizzy saw another oriental but this time she was a tall woman, who according to her, didn't bear a resemblance to the photo of the lady who was considered as the oriental's wife.

"What's going on?" Asked Lizzy. "Why are you looking at the photo?"

"She's not the lady in the picture."

"His wife? Just be vigilant for they are all the same."

"Yes, it's her."

"Are you sure? Because if it is her, it will be the right moment to go into their room and install the microphone. They won't return now."

"What are you waiting for?"

Composed, secret agent Dumisane left the table and the restaurant to try what he was used to, prying his nose in other people's businesses. It was risky but worthy for scores of rhinos were losing their lives and then what was going to be left for the next generation to explore? Hastily he went up the stairs certain that secret agent Lizzy was going to keep on checking on their moves.

With both WhatsApps on, the secret agent couple was ready to abort at the sign of any change of mind from the Oriental couple. In case the couple changed their mind and decide to go back to their room, she would have already informed him. Like a flash, the secret agent managed to enter the suspect's room using the master key provided to him by one of the best crime units on the continent, and once inside the room he made sure to lock it again to avoid any unprofessionalism and with serenity he started looking for the best place to install the microphone for the reputation of the game lodge was at stake, even the management of the game lodge didn't know their role in the park and just considered the special agents as normal tourists.

Watching around to detect the best place to install the most sensitive microphone, he received a WhatsApp note from Lizzy informing him to hurry up for the couple was left alone and seemed bored. After reading the message he realized it wasn't dangerous so quickly he installed the smallest microphone, sticking it under the bed. Just after finishing, he was sent another note from Lizzy updating him to not leave the room for the woman suddenly stood up and quickly took the stairs, surely going to her room.

The best place to hide was under the bed. He was halfway under when the door was unlocked by the Oriental lady. Luckily she was singing in Thai so Dumisane heard her coming. She went to the bathroom where she spent a couple of minutes and then left the room.

Dumisane realised that his next move was going to be substantial for the success of his mission. He quickly left his hiding spot hoping not to see the door opening again. It wasn't long before he received another WhatsApp message from Lizzy advising him to leave the room without delay. That's what he did, checking in the mirror that he still looked presentable before leaving the room.

The Oriental couple were no longer there when he arrived back at the restaurant. His wife wasn't there either. He checked his WhatsApp she dropped another written note saying she was outside sitting around the swimming pool. This lady, he thought, we are surrounded by wild animals and a huge crocodile hidden in the deepness of the swimming pool wouldn't surprise me.

Lizzy, well trained, stood up calling his name when she saw the secret agent appearing in the swimming pool area. He was surprised to see a number of people enjoying the fresh air and the different noises coming from the wilderness. It was completely dissimilar to Johannesburg, and the people were celebrating the way of life of the wilderness. The Oriental couple was nowhere to be seen. In a kind gesture, she gestured her husband to sit down and they both started enjoying the fresh air far away from the fast life of the endless Johannesburg highways.

"Is it done?"

"Well done, Madam."

"I will talk to my father to get ready."

It looked as if it was happening in a dream but it was all real. It's been a long time since Colonel Themba had seen his wife as happy as she was, and he was decided to offer her hours of enjoyment to cheer her up. She looked beautiful during her pregnancy and with warmth and affection, he was enjoying taking her to the different tables to greet the guests that she met for the first time the day. She discovered how big the family empire was.

Everybody was radiant, especially her parents and husband. Deciding to no longer divorce her husband made her father the happiest father in the world for he loved his daughter, and he was positive that she married the man he wanted for her well being. He expanded his business territory for his children's interest, and he was willing to be that man that leaves an inheritance to the children of his children; he believed in that.

He was convinced that his existence was no longer meaningless to his daughter for the rejection he experienced from her hurt like a knife piercing his heart. He was proud of the couple and knew that after him his empire will continue to exist; besides he hated to see her working for the government, his enemy.

Colonel Themba and her were in an animated conversation with a long time friend of her father who was one of the directors of his hotel. After the conversation and already one hour into the party, she said to her husband, "I would like to address everyone now."

"Are you sure?"

"Yes, Colonel," she said.

Colonel Themba took the microphone to let everybody ready to hear what his wife had to say.

"Dear guests and family, my wife Siphokazi would like to address all of you; I don't know what she has in mind, darling here's the microphone."

She took the microphone shying a little bit. "I don't have a lot to say but I would like to thank you for accepting this invitation, you're all energetic and spirited and may God bless you all. I mostly would like to speak to my family that I love so much and especially to you dad, I'm accepting your proposition of becoming one of your directors, section Not-for-profit organization, nothing else."

Everyone began applauding while her parents started crying, they were walking towards her with their arms widely opened, and both hugged her. Then her father took the microphone and said "My daughter, Sipho, thank you, you look so much like your mother, a determined woman with much faith and patience. You are welcome."

And the party continued until late at night with the best South African music that could be played.

Having a lot to cope with the ministry of defence, Colonel Themba had just received the instructions to bring his wife to the company headquarters in Roodepoort. Malume (Pty) Ltd was a complex organization involved in diverse industries but its main one was the underworld, secondly, the hospitality industry with its many hotels throughout the country and then followed by its chain of Not-for-profit organizations; and Siphokazi knew that all other industries were financed by the massive sale of drugs.

While on Ontdekkers, the main road to Roodepoort, west of Johannesburg, Colonel Themba drove while holding his wife's hand. He was delighted and honoured to have married such a wonderful woman.

"You did very well to have turned your back on this government."

"Why?" She asked.

"Because you belong with our empire," he said at the same time entering the premises.

Siphokazi was astonished to discover such a beautiful administrative building belonging to the family business.

"Have we arrived?" She said delightedly.

"Do you remember the video that Malume ran at the hotel, showing you your office?"

"Yes," she responded.

"It is here."

"Wow!" She exclaimed.

"Note that you're your father's main heir."

"I don't want to talk about this."

"Your Malume is a genius and he wants you to replace him one day. Come on, this is the jackpot."

Siphokazi made sure not to get cross for she was about to get furious, instead, she just looked at him with the look he was expecting from her. All here was about money and greed, and she wondered what the existence of the Not-for-profit organization was hiding; surely the covering of their evil doings.

After parking the car the couple went into the fourth-floor of the administrative building by taking the lift to where her office was, but while in the lift her husband touched her belly.

"I'm so happy that I'm going to have my first ever baby girl."

"You are," she said caressing his face with her right hand. "I am too, Themba."

And he tenderly gave her a kiss on her forehead that she accepted delightedly. While going out of the lift some tears trickled down her face, at the same time doing her best to dissimulate the emotion, but without avail, because just after the lift the opposite door was her office. And when he saw her wiping her tears he said to her, "I understand Sipho."

The Colonel opened the door and the office was exactly as shown in the video. It was sumptuous and classic, and once inside he turned around to look at the expression on her face, but what he saw were more tears running down her cheeks.

"Thank you, Colonel," she said.

"You don't have to worry because your father's office is just at the bottom of the corridor, and your husband's office is beside yours."

"You're kidding."

"Not at all, just next door, you're a director now. I love you Sipho, I was waiting for this moment for a long time," he said to her.

"I love you too," she responded.

And they suddenly both realized that someone was at the door; it was Mr Nhlakanipho with her mother watching and listening to what the couple was saying to each other.

"Dad, ma'am," she called walking towards them.

"Are you satisfied?" Said her mother after hugging.

"I am ma'am, thank you, dad."

There was another person behind her parents who was nicely dressed and smiling at her.

"I would like you to meet your assistant," said her father. "She has been in this industry for more than a decade, and she will explain everything to you regarding our not-for-profit organization."

"My name is Tasha," she said introducing herself.

"Nice to meet you, Tasha," Siphokazi greeted her with a handshake. "My name is Siphokazi; you can call me Sipho if it's too long for you."

"With pleasure."

"There is," said her father, "You're welcome, this belongs to you my daughter, I'm so proud of you." Both her parents left followed by Tasha, her new personal assistant.

Left alone with her husband, she walked around the desk and sat on the chair; afterwards, she started caressing the desk with both hands, and after finishing she looked at him and said, "For many years you hid this from me."

"Because you were not ready."

"I'm ready now," she said holding his hand.

Proud of a well equipped national park, the spy couple was standing beside the Bantam Ultra-Light Aeroplane waiting for the pilot to arrive. An aerial view of the last poaching event not far from the Malelane entrance gate was going to help them to detain an overview of where the incident happened and how it's happened for it wasn't far from the southern gates of Malelane.

A few minutes later the pilot arrived followed by a ranger carrying an automatic gun.

"My name is Bongani and I have received some instructions from Mr Wolmarans to take you south where the last poaching occurred."

"I'm secret agent Dumisane and my wife is secret agent Lizzy."

"Very interesting," he said looking at both of them.

Pilot Bongani was in his forties with the calibre of a rugby player. He invited them to take place on the plane and they went south towards the Malelane entrance gate.

Poachers don't use aeroplanes but daylight walking closer to their target to cause damage and loss to the country.

The Bantam Ultra-Light Aeroplane was flying at normal altitude to get a clear view of the area, and what a beautiful view it was with all kinds of animals on show. This operation was not a cross-border one as it came to pass in Mozambique in the past with many poachers arrested and imprisoned by the South African and Mozambican authorities.

"Here's where the last poaching happened," said Bongani.

It was an area with many elephants around beside an area of water that could be seen from where they were.

"Can you see those Rhinos?"

Two Rhinos were running away from the noise caused by the aeroplane.

"Yes," said Lizzy.

"The poachers want to kill them all," said Bongani, "And if it wasn't for our rangers with the help of our government no Rhinos were going to be seen again. They are doing a great job and the Mozambican government also has been very helpful to apprehend many of them, but the last year distressed us."

"You mean, this is an area with a big concentration of Rhinos and elephants?" Said Dumisane.

"Yes, it is and also a much-visited area said the ranger. And the rainy season is convenient for some poachers."

From above the aeroplane, many tour buses could be seen going around the national park.

"Who do they use to do the nasty job?" Asked Lizzy.

"Anyone who has the courage and experience or even themselves responded to the ranger, and arresting one of them doesn't mean you have the big boss."

"Of course," responded Dumisane.

The aeroplane tour gave both of the secret agents a clue of where the poaching activity came about; in the wild and secretly and catching a poacher was more than silver to save from harm the environment for future generations to explore and enjoy. But why not use the southern entrance gate for it was closer to where the opportunity was, thought secret agent Dumisane at the same time taking some pictures.

It was not going to be easy, some poachers were professionals, cunning and also very patient. Money without patience makes one's ways very slippery, but he knew he wasn't around for a waste of time and money, but to assure that the Oriental man was not linked to any poaching activity, but if he was involved his return to his country was going to take very long for the destroyers of natural resources weren't welcome in South Africa.

The board of directors of Malume (Pty) Limited was complete except for Colonel Themba who was absent and unnoticed by the rest. No one mentioned his name even his father-in-law who was busy talking about the great return on his investment. Some goods were sold to Malaysia and no cargo was missed on the way, but Sipho had no clue of the kind of goods it was, but everyone applauded when he said the return was as expected.

The only thing she was interested in, was the kind of goods sold to Malaysia. Exporting was good news to the economy of South Africa, but what was taken out of the country was the big question. She was not in a hurry to ask such a question for she was not around the table with apprentices, so talking less or nothing about what was in that cargo was going to make her unsuspicious. She was very dangerous for anyone seated around the table and they didn't know, and anyone noticing anything out of the ordinary about her presence could, without informing Malume, silence her to protect his interest.

"We are honoured to have you with us around Siphokazi," said her father.

"Thank you, Dad."

"The session is adjourned," said Malume.

Very little was said during the meeting, just to inform everyone about what happened in Malaysia. And once said everyone, except Sipho, stood without asking any question. Sipho was surprised so she followed the crowd walking towards the canteen that had a table full of food and drinks. She understood why most of the directors and personal assistants were overweight.

Her father came closer to her with his best smile and asked her, "Why are you surprised?"

"All this food, Dad. Why? This is a waste of money."

"The company is making good money and we have more than enough to allow this to take place once a week."

"Once a week?"

"How is your assistant? Tasha knows a lot about our not-for-profit organizations."

"I have already started understanding the industry and I'm proud of you dad, I was very happy to have a word with one of the directors of the Cancer Association of South Africa."

"You're doing well but I want you to do something for me. Talk to your big brother."

"Malume you know Bongani, I haven't spoken to him for more than five years and I don't have his number."

"I have his number but he doesn't want to speak to his father. I don't want to die without his forgiveness."

"Why are you talking like this?"

"I've made many mistakes in my life to end up with all of this, but still, they can't fill up the emptiness I have in my being. I wasn't always there to take care of you, and he hates my business."

"I will try, Dad, although I'm not promising anything and don't forget to text me Bongani's number."

"I will and your mother is a formidable lady, a strong woman able to handle a stubborn man like me," he said smiling, "I have to go, and take care."

She was pleased to hear her father talking this way about her mother. He was a happy man with the woman of his youth, but she was the opposite of what he was. Tasha approached her holding her glass of red wine.

"Are you alright?" she asked kindly.

"I'm alright. let me have something to eat."

"I also wanted to inform you that our plane tomorrow morning for Port Elizabeth will take off at 09h00."

"Which flight?"

"Our main storehouse is in Port Elizabeth and only three directors have access to the main storehouse and you're one of them."

"Is it the way you treat your directors in this company?"Sipho laughed.

"A weekly cross-examination of the main company's warehouses is made by the authorized director and your father wants you to be the one handling the task this week, but mostly to gain a good understanding of the business products."

"Products?"

"The not-for-profit organization receives diverse donations mostly internationally and the managing director directly linked to the different warehouses of the organization will certify to you once there that what was expected has surely arrived and has been seen and counted, and of course, verified by you."

Busy drinking her glass of water, secret agent Siphokazi took heed of what her assistant was busy making clear to her, and this was very interesting because any prohibited goods could well be kept safe in some of the company's storehouses., Daring to ask her many questions was not going to be of assistance as she was certain that not only products about the not-for-profit organization were kept there. Surely drugs and cocaine were kept there for distribution. Besides her duty was getting very interesting for her father trusted already on her and was about to entrust her with his best part of the business.

Chapter 10

Sipho arrived in Port Elizabeth, in the Eastern Cape Province, 770 km east of Cape Town. She and her assistant were seated in the back seat of the car that was already driving on Donkin Street. It was an attractive street with many luxurious townhouses that lifted in her the desire to reside in. She was happy to visit for the first time the Sunshine Coast of South Africa with its beautiful beaches and wildlife attractions, just to count some of its attractions.

But she was there on business experiencing an opulent lifestyle; which she was ready to abandon anytime for the sake of her well being and her family.

"Have you been to Port Elizabeth before?" she asked Tasha.

"Every month I'm here," she responded.

"Who was my predecessor, Tasha?"

"Your father, Malume."

"Malume!" She said surprised. "Do you mean this position has never been filled by any other person apart from my father?"

The driver had already taken another street along which many companies existed.

"Not all Malume directors know these warehouses in Port Elizabeth, only his family members and me."

"You're not part of my family Tasha and you've been coming here every month."

"I've been the family personal assistant for more than ten years and all profit organizations are in the hands of Malume's family."

"All of them?"

"Yes, Malume always says to me this is my inheritance to my family, nothing else."

"What about the hotels?"

The driver was already entering a big warehouse, and from far she saw two men standing like waiting for them.

"He is the prime shareholder, but the not-for-profit organization entirely belongs to him."

Secret agent Siphokazi realized that Tasha still had a lot to tell her; she was very well informed about the family commerce and had a big mouth that she needed to expose everything. But she seemed sharp-eyed and there for a very good reason, also very connected to her father and the least mistake could expose her intention. After all, they knew she once was part of the South African secret agent industry.

"Who are those people?"Sipho asked.

"They are both experts in managing warehouses of this magnitude, so they always make sure and let us know if this warehouse is still worthy to be considered as one."

"Are they working here?"

"Yes, they are and well paid."

After the driver parked the car, they were greeted by the two managers who invited them inside the warehouse where all donations to the not-for-profit organization were received for control and dispatch. And after that, they went up the stairs along a corridor for about ten meters long until they reached a well fitted out board room.

"You may take a seat."

"We are very happy to notice that we have a new director," said one of the managers called Van Wyk.

"Thank you," said Tasha, "I would like to present you to Siphokazi Themba, Malume's daughter, and she's our new director."

"So glad to meet you, Siphokazi Themba."

"Glad to meet you too," she said kindly.

"So without wasting time this is the complete report about the activities conducted in the warehouse for the last week. As usual, our sponsors have honoured their commitments and if ready we can move and check them together and take account of what has been furnished."

Walking around the warehouse was what she and the tour took about thirty minutes. She was very satisfied with the cleanness, the layout and the way they were organized; this was truly a family heritage to cherish. The company used more than ten warehouses, making her assignment very difficult for she wanted to discover where the dangerous goods were kept. She needed miracle information to break through and organize the perfect set-up.

It was time for them to go to the hotel and when they were about to leave the boardroom for the final face to face with her managers, the door was opened by Colonel Themba dressed like a tourist visiting the city. Sipho was surprised since he left him in Johannesburg.

"You're here!" She said at the same time leaving her chair to give him a warm hug.

"I decided to follow you, not only you're pregnant but that baby is mine."

"So!" She said at the same time giving him an affectionate smile.

The management present looked at each other smiling.

"No longer am I able to leave you for a long time."

And they hugged each other, joyful to belong to one another.

"Now we are on vacation and this city has the most beautiful beaches in Africa. Is your meeting over gentlemen, Tasha? Because I m taking her from you."

"We're done," said Tasha.

Secret agent Siphokazi realized once again that her assistant was well known in the company.

"Crazy boy," she said.

It was five days already in the Jungle without any positive outcome. The Oriental couple were truly behaving like tourists on vacation in South Africa. There was no breakthrough yet with the microphone installed in their room but according to Home Affairs their stay was three weeks and anything could go off.

Was the immediate threat to the wild nature really in the Kruger National park? The most desirable outcome was for any poaching activity to dare happen because he was there for that and to stop it. But the curious thing was the constant visit to the Southern gate area where most of the Rhinos and Elephants lived. The Oriental couple were in love with the area and went there four times in a row and that was a good sign for the last successful poaching that occurred happened there, disappointing the whole nation.

While eating some peanuts his cell phone rang and it was Mr Wolmarans.

"Secret agent Dumisane, I want you to keep a pencil and paper handy because the Oriental is about to meet one of the suspects that disappeared many years ago to Mozambique. He used to be one of our prime suspects at the beginning of the nineties."

"I have no clue about the guy."

"His name is Alfredo, a Latino who seemed to regret having been born in South America."

"Why?"

"He spends most of his time in Africa and I believe he is the mastermind at the back of the poaching happening in the rest of Africa, and now he seems to have decided to revisit the scenes of his crime."

"He won't escape this time."

"And what's conspicuous is that they are about to revisit the same area tomorrow afternoon around 10h00 a.m. I want you and Lizzy to be moving around about that time, connect with them as tourists try to get some pictures with them, and if they refuse then they will look very suspicious; I don't believe he is a converted man."

"Consider it done, sir."

Lizzy Wolmarans was dressed like a lady ready to impress, and both had to be impressive to create the best impression they could. They made sure to swim together, play tennis together and even touch each order's lips to give the impression that they were beyond doubt a happily married couple. Secret agent Dumisane enjoyed her company for she was beautiful and highly professional and unpredictable with her next move, and tourists enjoyed meeting them.

The bar was open and smelled of the South African fresh wine from the Cape. A traditional dance show, Indlamu, according to the guests' speaker was about to begin, and it was the first time that the secret agent couple was going to experience the dance while in the Kruger National park game reserve. Indlamu was a South African dance associated with Zulu culture. The Ndebele language is very similar to the Zulu language in Kwazulu Natal. The men dancing were wearing regalia including ceremonial belts, shields and spears with their traditional headpieces.

The dance started to great applause and with everyone enjoying the unique moment., While looking around, the secret agents' realised they had not seen any sign of the Oriental couple. They were there for them and they wanted them around all the time to know what they were after. Courageously and after a glance to her husband, Lizzy programmed to do what she was about to do left the place, treading carefully across the path in the middle of the grass that she was observing considerately for they were in the middle of wild merciless animals.

Understanding what she did, Dumisane left her completing her move for she was about to discover if the Oriental couple was still in the Province or gone already. She arrived in the reception area and noticed that the keys to the room were absent. Immediately she turned back to her husband.

"The couple is there because the keys are not at reception."

"I would like you to fall in love with him," said Dumisane.

"Why get that much closer?"

Out of the blue, the Oriental man appeared without his wife beside him and he began moving his body at the rhythm of the Indlamu dance. It was spectacular because he seemed much attached to the way of dancing. He had to enjoy the opportunity for nothing was gratis and if this was part of the game reserve menu then he was happy that it was finally happening. However, the Oriental man seemed to know everyone, especially the employees of the game reserve.

While dancing he looked in their direction and gave them a warm greeting. Truly the atmosphere was great with those filming and taking pictures.

"Tomorrow while together in the park, give him your best smile."

"I don't see his wife," noticed Lizzy.

"Very good news if she's gone."

"You still didn't answer my question?"

"We need to get as close as possible to him."

"And why not you become his friend?"

"A lonely man is well repaid with the presence of a beautiful woman like you."

She laughed and during the whole dance the Oriental man was alone and without his partner.

From a distance of about one kilometre and in the oppressive heat in the Kruger national park, secret agents

Dumisane and Lizzy, driven by two well-armed rangers, were with their binoculars following Alfredo and the Oriental man. They were going south en route for the Malelane entrance gate where most of the concentration of Rhinos and Elephants were and the area was about three kilometres away from where they were.

This was a unique mission for Dumisane being in the wild and without the presence of his beloved secret agent Siphokazi busy betraying her family. The current goal was to remain in their surroundings looking like tourists with the ultimate opportunity to cross or overtake them, and then have a conversation with them, take some pictures in the wild and see their reactions. A poacher seeks the right moment to activate his plan and an early hour of the day is perfect for such an action, for most of the tourists are tired sleeping or taking their breakfasts.

Clint called Dumisane, "don't you know a way to cross them, and we have a good surprise for them."

Ranger Clint's perceptive of the secret agent's plan immediately accelerated to go around them, and he did it perfectly. It was very important for they didn't want to give them the impression that they were following them, and that worked perfectly despite the serious incident that could happen with an errant buffalo running away from a contingent of starving lions.

When he was a few meters away from them, ranger Clint reduced speed to create the meeting. He stopped just in from of them, smiling at the Oriental tourists and the suspect Alfredo who looked surprised by the meeting.

"I know them, I know them."

The Oriental man said it excited and loudly, allowing the secret agent couple to hear and without more ado, Lizzy expressed her best smile to the Oriental man who noticed with gladness. His wife seemed absent and that could facilitate intimacy.

Both drivers had stopped their cars at the same time being careful to avoid a fatal surprise with a leopard; and right away the couple as they were a few meters away from them, with much courtesy and with their cameras hanging around their necks approached them, with such wonderful contentment on their faces.

"This area is the best one for elephants," said Lizzy.

She was followed by her husband who suddenly turned around and took a picture of the giant tree that was about ten meters away from them, really behaving like tourists. But they both said nothing just smiled at the couple who was very kind to them.

Mr Kim remembered the lady who during the traditional dance gave him one of her best smiles, and she was busy doing the same just two meters away from him.

"Darling come and let's take a souvenir picture with Mr..."

She said it at the same time stretching her arm to greet him, and Alfredo rather surprised by such kindness remained calm and his eyes also meet hers, but the plan was to bruise Mr Kim and his allies.

"I'm Kim," he said delighted, "and my friend is..."

Alfredo, introducing himself as a naughty boy, cut Mr Kim off.

Without wasting time secret agent Dumisane gave his professional camera to the ranger to take some pictures of them in the wilderness with the two suspicious poachers.

"Thank you for the pictures," said secret agent Lizzy with a wink at Mr Kim.

The Oriental man welcomed it with a broad smile, happy to double-cross someone's wife.

"Will see you next time," said secret agent Dumisane.

Three hours later the secret agents' couple arrived at the South African National park administrative headquarters where Mr Wolmarans was waiting for them. They were tired and indeed hoping for a quick breakthrough that could send them to rest and wait for another less risky assignment. This one had to happen in the middle of the jungle where anything was possible with wild animals.

Mr Wolmarans was already waiting for them when they went to the second floor and entered his office, They found two glasses of water waiting for them to cool down. When they entered, he was busy checking on the pictures received from the agents as they were in the Kruger national park with the two suspicious poachers.

"You can sit down," he said without looking at them.

"Good afternoon, dad."

"Lizzy," he called standing up from his chair to hug her.

"Thanks, dad for the hug," she said.

"Good afternoon team, you are doing a good job with these photos showing Alfredo who escaped almost twenty years ago from Mozambique. A professional poacher with the best evil plan to exterminate our nature, and we want him in our custody in the next few hours."

"Does he think you forgot about him?" Demanded Dumisane.

"I'm very surprised to see him in South Africa again."

"Maybe he has a twin brother," said Lizzy drinking her glass of water.

Mr Wolmarans again attentively looked at the pictures.

"Let me show you his pictures from twenty years ago."

The two agents after checking those pictures noticed the big resemblance.

"So what's your next move?" Asked Mr Wolmarans.

"Close contact between Lizzy and Mr Kim."

"What do you mean by close contact? She's your wife."

"Dad, we want to get into his files, his notes."

"It's a good idea but be very careful and you'll need to act quickly before they notice anything fishy with both of you."

"You're right," said secret agent Dumisane, "But what about Alfredo?"

"Check tonight if they are still together, and if so then they are about to hit South Africa again."

"Thank you, sir."

"How is mum, dad?"

"More attractive than ever my daughter."

"Send my greetings to her."

"I never told her what you're busy doing right now, please don't call her and start telling her everything, she will hate me."

While in Port Elizabeth, Colonel Themba and his wife were busy spending some unforgettable moments at the King's beach. Themba turned her business trip into a vacation that he wanted his wife to never forget. After all, she needed the presence of a husband caring for the future of their marriage and children, and the beach was a blue flag one able to offer safety and beauty to its visitors. She was delighted and felt so welcome to be far away from the prejudices caused by her affiliation with the government of South Africa.

After spending one day of exploration of the Addo Elephant Park, South Africa's third-largest national park and Algoa Bay watching whales and dolphins, the couple decided to go and spend three days at the King's beach. The exploration was just unforgettable, and she was already grateful, feeling like forever running away from her government and never being found again, but she knew she was unable to decide that way. That made her bleed in her heart for she wanted more than what she had in her hands right now.

Without question, she was certain in her spirit and mind that Colonel Themba was the man of her life, the only husband she will ever marry and be submissive to. The cruelty of the world shall never bring to an end the task God gave her towards her husband. And while eating she had sufficient time to observe the man of her life who perhaps won't be spending many years by her side anymore, in favour of the state she was going to betray him as he has never been before. She was looking forward to seeing him able to handle the shock of the betrayal and truly realize his wrongdoing, and especially the latest was the best of the reasons to see him behind bars.

She wished him to become conscious that he was lost without her, for she regarded herself as the perfect choice of God for his life. And now that they were constantly together and eating the food cooked by her hands, he looked radiant and whole. He followed her to Port Elizabeth because of her qualities that many men would like to appropriate for their happiness. But it was a great idea to take her on vacation for he knew that she enjoyed these kinds of surprises, and they were also opportunities for her to make him get the picture of what she truly represented in his life.

She was that flower with thorns that he deceived for the love of the treasures of this world. He was the man that she had forgiven for the sake of love, the man she has never ceased to love and be willing to love. Right now eternity was not on the side of their union for he had to pay for his sins to the South African government, and even the justice of God was closer to him like never before and she believed being that instrument to make an end to what dishonoured her and every justice.

And while looking at her he saw some tears of love falling down her cheeks, and wiping them out was not enough for more went downcast with a tender look that he believed he understood. Yes, she was crying because she acquitted him a long time ago but could not stop what was about to happen that they were both going to hate, and it was going to be the end of everything between them because justice would have won forever. But still, she was going to love him and care for his children; he will see her coming to visit him while in prison even after refusing to see her, for her betrayal and nothing would change it.

She wanted him to apprehend one day through the tribulations ahead that women are not the same. That she has never been like Nthabiseng, but just an example of a helper that he neglected for many years, and that he has found again and for eternity, for he won't be lost again.

Chapter 11

The longing to hold her in his hands was booming. The Oriental man very wisely looked around and realized that Lizzy was all alone without her husband in the restaurant of the game reserve. She was turning her back on him so this was an opportunity not to miss to surprise her with his best Oriental smile, and an offer for a drink. His partner was not around so adding to the Kruger National Park's menu a Western African woman was a great triumph.

Approaching with great hope for what he had already experienced with her; the Oriental man came and sat next to her making sure that he didn't scare her off; they were in the middle of the jungle after all. But she was at the restaurant before dawn expecting his visit, and by that time he was also out of his room since he wanted to encounter her and know more about her.

The Oriental man by her big surprise was a fluent speaker of English because he said, "A woman who knows her ways is mostly desired by men."

"Good afternoon Mr Kim," she said turning around and showing delight. "But I don't trust men," she reposted.

"Good afternoon Lizzy, I didn't forget your name. But why don't you trust men? Do you think I'm dangerous?"

"Are you? Because I kind of like dangerous men."

He laughed and said, "May I offer you a drink?"

"Not now, I was just thinking about my family in law," she lied.

"What's wrong with your family in law?"Kim asked, sitting beside her.

"They don't like me."

"Because he married a white woman? That's ridiculous."

"It has been like this for many years, but let's forget about my sad story," she said with a tender look that he couldn't resist.

"What do you want to know about me?"

"Your origins. What you like in life."

"I'm a proud Taiwanese as you like saying in South Africa, a proud South African."

"Wow! I like it, Pyongyang, a very curious destination for a woman like me."

"Why?"

"I know very little about Chinese culture."

"I'm not Chinese," he said correcting her, "But a Taiwanese, proud one. By the way, where is your husband?"

"He went to the city of Nelspruit until tomorrow evening."

"Ah! Mampumalanga," he said wrongly.

"No, Mpumalanga."

"Mam..., oh! I will never say it well. I've been trying to say it like someone from this Province but I'm still failing. But what do you think about going to my room? With all the respect due, this place is a bit noisy."

"What do you have in your room?"

159

"Some good South African wines," he said, in his best way of being charming.

That's what she wanted and so far he was pushing things according to her plan, she could read his corrupt mind.

"Why not, after all, this entire place is getting busy and noisy. And where is your wife?" She asked.

They were already walking when he responded.

"She went to Johannesburg for a week, her big sister lives in Pretoria where she runs her business."

While in the room, Lizzy noticed that the room was similar to theirs and that she just needed a moment alone to rummage through his belongings. A man like him, if he was a poacher should have some contacts to help him with such a delicate mission. She just needed a point of contact to the poaching industry that could be added up to him having a relationship with a well-known poacher like Alfredo. She sensed that she was busy having a cup of tea with a dangerous man who didn't care about her. What he wanted was to just use her and then forget about her.

"This is your cup of tea, green tea if you've already heard about it."

"I've heard it's good for your health."

Mr Kim went to the small fridge and out of it took one bottle of Champagne and came to sit next to her. She understood the move and let it go for she needed to be trustful until she obtained what she wanted.

"You don't waste time, Mr Kim."

"I just like your company. You're a very attractive and kind woman."

"Thank you but I don't make love to a man on our first date," she said softly.

"I'm sorry, I didn't mean to disrespect you," he said at the same time as changing seats to face her, but very pleased about the foothold he had on her for she was at his mercy according to him.

And while Lizzy was in the Taiwanese man's room, secret agent Dumisane was in Skukuza at the headquarters with Mr Wolmarans listening to the conversation. They were both surprised that the Oriental man was speaking such good English with his Mandarin accent and was Taiwanese and not from Thailand.

"She is doing very well," said Mr Wolmarans.

"Yes, she is. Do you have any clue as to where Alfredo is?"

"Alfredo is still our main suspect and one of your colleagues confirmed he stays in one of the game reserves not far from Malelane."

"Surely they are up to something."

"Of course, two lions working together help each other to eat the best meals out there in the wild. Listen there's no way she will get anything from him today; the first contact is a success and let's see tomorrow."

"Do you want me to call her and interrupt?"

"Yes, an emergency."

While talking with the Oriental man Lizzy received a phone call from her husband.

"Oh! It's my husband," she said. "Yes, Dumi."

And after talking for a while she said, "Mr Kim."

"Call me Kim, just Kim," he interrupted her with a gentle smile.

"Great," she said, "I will see you tomorrow before 10H00, is it alright?"

"Of course, I will be waiting for you."

To leave him with great thought to stay overnight with, she came forward and kissed him on his left cheek.

"Bye," she said.

The following morning, Mr Kim had every reason to be the happiest man on earth. When he heard someone knocking at the door he knew it was her, for the business was still unfinished. He was persuaded that the woman after him was just uncontrollable towards men from the Far East. For him, this woman will not resist trying to get his complete attention and make him hers.

He opened the door for her with his best Oriental smile that went straight into her eyes; assuring that her Machiavellian mission was about to break through. She could see that this man had great expectations and was determined to behave like a fake gentleman. But she was used to that for since childhood her life revolved around talking about such people full of evil thoughts.

"Lizzy," he called, "you look excellent."

"Thank you."

"Come in as our breakfast is ready."

"And the champagne?"

"I was thinking about it, let me quickly go to the reception and get one for you."

"You're welcome, Kim."

"Awesome."

That was quick for such an opening was what she wanted, she had no time to waste. Very quickly she went and opened the drawers and finally found a notebook that she took and started paging through. But after a few blank pages, she dropped it to get another one that seemed already in use, and after paging through the second notebook for a while, she finally fell on a list of many African names that she photographed for a check-up; and just after she took the picture, she heard some people speaking from the corridor and that was risky so she let the notebook fell on the floor and with her right foot pushed it under the bed, closed the drawers and laid on the bed. And just after playing that game, the door was opened by Mr Kim who was very happy to have found what he knew was going to please her.

Lizzy Wolmarans instantly realized that she was facing a clandestine man ready to hit some Rhinos and enrich his life. And such a man was dangerous and casual; every situation had to turn in his favour and he would do anything to get from her what he wanted. But he wasn't cheeky, he seemed to treat women with respect and was ready to spend his money to get what he wanted.

"Are you ready for the champagne?" He said.

She immediately left the bed, walking towards the dining table, so he followed her there, where the breakfast was laid out.

"Thank you, Mr Kim, sorry Kim."

"It's alright, I have for you good champagne quality, you will enjoy it."

"Wow! Sorry before I start eating I would like to send this message to my father."

Lizzy in a calculated move sent the photographed list of names to her father who was listening to everything they were saying from the game reserve's room. There were about twenty names, and all were African names. And after sending she refocused her attention to Mr Kim and the delicious breakfast that she started eating.

Mr Wolmarans while busy listening to what was happening with his daughter heard a beep from his cell phone announcing a sent message. He checked the screen he realized that it was a message from his daughter. He saw what was sent to him; a list of many African names that surely his daughter wanted him to assess. Immediately he called the South African police department of Skukuza for verification. He was busy talking to Lieutenant Leah who was the number two at the police station previously involved in the arrest of poachers.

"Give me a few minutes and I will come back to you."

"Thanks a lot, Lieutenant Leah."

And a few minutes later Lieutenant Leah came with very exciting news.

"Mr Wolmarans," said Leah.

"Yes, Lieutenant."

"Very interesting information because some of these names on the list are in our custody."

"Lieutenant, there's no time to waste you better organize the police force to arrest the perpetrators of poaching our Rhinos and Elephants; besides my daughter is with one of the poachers right now."

"Where about?"

"Mbalula Game reserve, the famous one."

"We know that one. We are going to inform the security service of the game reserve to arrest them before we get there."

"Awesome Lieutenant."

Thinking about the security of his daughter and without telling her mother about what was going on, Mr Wolmarans had to let his daughter know that she immediately had to leave Mr Kim. Paying attention to their conversation he heard Lizzy saying "your food is so delicious"; she was still alive so he decided to send her a WhatsApp note and leave the dangerous man without delay.

While enjoying their breakfast, secret agent Lizzy expected some feedback from the team listening to her date with the suspect. She was also concerned about the small notebook that she kicked under the bed that had at her point of view crucial info that could help them arrest the suspects. Why did an Oriental man have many African names written in his notebook? She knew she was doing a fantastic job and she was expecting the best feedback ever received in her career.

Suddenly she received a message on her cell phone.

"Let me check, maybe it is my husband."

It wasn't her husband but her father with a message she was expecting. The message said, "leave at once for the names on the list are poachers and the police are on the way to arrest him".

"Sorry, Kim, I was about to say Mr Kim; give me ten minutes, I'm coming back."

"Don't take too long."

165

Five minutes later after finishing eating his breakfast Mr Kim left the table very excited for he knew that the next step was to hold her in his arms. He went to the bed to make it look welcoming and laid on it, however, something pushed him to look under the bed and he realized that his notebook was under the bed and that the drawer was slightly opened. He immediately left the bed confused and nervous, noticing that Lizzy was something fishy, someone sent after him to spy on them.

Without wasting time and under the influence of a dangerous substance; the Oriental man decided to call his colleague Alfredo who responded within two seconds.

"Alfredo," he responded.

"We have been set up."

"What? Don't say more, maybe we are being listened to, get out of there, they are after us."

Mr Kim realized he had very little time to escape for his mystery was uncovered and the woman who was with him was not returning after ten minutes as she had said. He was no longer the tourist visiting the country but the fugitive so much wanted; too bad.

Secret agent Dumisane standing beside Mr Wolmarans heard the conversation between Mr Kim and Alfredo.

"Give the order to secret agent Lizzy to arrest the Oriental man," said secret agent Dumisane to Mr Wolmarans who was protective of his daughter.

"Maybe he carries a gun."

"With all the experience she has, she knows how to protect herself."

166

He had to call to quickly act on the arrest of the Oriental man if not he was going to be held responsible for his escape. So he dialled her number and she responded instantly.

"Yes, dad."

"Arrest him; get two rangers with you before he leaves the hotel because he knows who you are."

"Really, ok dad."

"Stay with me here Dumisane, in case he escapes you will go after him from here."

Lizzy with her pistol in her hand, slipped it down the back of her trousers to avoid any panic. Mbalula game lodge was one of the best and any scandal could harm their turnover so she had to work with care, but the killer of wildlife had to be apprehended at all costs, no matter the location.

At the same time watching out for her back; secret agent Lizzy Wolmarans opened the door of her room and noticed that Mr Kim's door room was half-opened with no one inside. The poacher was gone but where? She immediately mentioned it to Dumisane.

"Go to the reception and ask."

"That's what I was thinking."

Getting to reception she found the manager of the lodge who seemed impressed by her beauty and was keen to help her.

"I'm looking for Mr Kim. Have you seen him?"

"He just left, he never said where. Can I offer you a drink?"

"We must arrest him, he's a poacher."

"What! He is one of our best customers."

"Inform the security of the lodge, we must look for him."

"He just left for Skukuza in a helicopter."

"Stop that helicopter."

"As said, Madame."

After calling many times with the help of two rangers the manager could not intercept the helicopter and that was unusual.

"Mr Kim is in a helicopter and we cannot intercept him," said secret agent Lizzy.

"Any idea of where he's going?"

"To Skukuza."

"But where possible can he land? Maybe they've stopped somewhere."

"I've already been given orders to close the South African frontier with Mozambique."

"Thank you, sir," said Dumisane to Mr Wolmarans.

"Thank you, dad."

One of the helicopters of the South African National Parks was available with the pilot already in the helicopter. With two rangers accompanying him, secret agent Dumisane started flying around the gigantesque national park trying to locate, in an area of 19,485 square kilometres, an abandoned tour helicopter of the Mbalula game lodge. According to the game lodge managing director the tour helicopter could not be intercepted, meaning they landed somewhere and took the pilot with them as a hostage.

The mission was risky but of value, for they were about to make some interesting arrests, and all the time Dumisane thought about Phalaborwa entrance gate and the Giriyondo border post; so going further north-east was not a bad idea.

And travelling from Phalaborwa via Letaba rest camp to the Giriyondo border post for 95 km was one of the most discreet ways that could be used to escape the South African security force.

"We need to close the Giriyondo border post to Mozambique," said secret agent Dumisane to Mr Wolmarans surprised to hear such development from the secret agent.

"Good idea, let me call Lieutenant Leah."

Flying above the national park wasn't an easy experience, especially those areas with many trees, making the view of the area difficult. But from far and using his binoculars, the secret agent saw what he undeniably wanted to see; an abandoned helicopter without anyone around it and they were not far from Phalaborwa in the Limpopo province.

"I'm sure they've taken the pilot hostage," said Dumisane to the rest of the team, "and they are driving towards the Giriyondo border post to Mozambique. Carry on piloting towards Phalaborwa. But first, let's get closer to the abandoned helicopter."

"This is a very dangerous area with many snakes around," said one of the rangers.

"We want them alive; we want to question them than to find them in the belly of a giant snake; which won't help us at all."

Because of the vegetation, the landing had to be executed by a specialized pilot, and getting closer to see who was inside the helicopter was the ultimate so the experienced pilot positioned the helicopter with a clear view. Through the binoculars, the secret agent was using and as he thought nobody was in the helicopter.

"Let's head to the Giriyondo border post to Phalaborwa, I'm sure they are busy driving that direction to escape."

Dumisane had to be brave for his country's sake with a fervent hope that all the poachers had to be neutralized. His cell phone started ringing and it was Mr Wolmarans.

"We have found an abandoned helicopter belonging to the game lodge and we have lounged an attack towards the Giriyondo border post."

"The SAPF is already stationed to all the borders going into Mozambique."

"Please would you inform the game lodge management about their helicopter before any elephants sit on it?"

"They are already informed."

"And Lizzy, where is she? She did a great job."

"She is still at the lodge watching out for any suspects."

"Thank you, sir."

"All the best secret agent Dumisane, get them alive."

"I will sir."

Secret agent Dumisane was carrying with him an R5 assault rifle and a 9mm Z88/Beretta pistol on his waist. He was ready for any ugly surprise.

"We need to identify the road and pursue them from there."

"Yes sir," said the pilot.

And the road was not far because a few minutes later they were above it, flying, following the road., The GPS indicated fifty kilometres left to reach the land border post, and for the secret agent, the day was sunny and different from other days. He was sweaty, nervous and ready to hit the offenders of our wildlife.

With his binoculars pointed towards the road the secret agent watched.

"Did you see anything?" said one of the rangers who had a chin of a boxer and was well physically built.

"Do you see what I see?" said Dumisane, handing over the binoculars to him.

"I see a 4X4," he said a few seconds later.

"They are on the run, but let's be careful for they can be dangerous. I'm sure they are carrying guns with them."

"Let me go around them and force the car to stop."

"That can be more dangerous; we can end up becoming an easy target to them. But I'm sure they know the police are after them. Just carry on flying above them and just a little bit behind them, I will call for the driver to stop the car."

"I'll be very surprised to see them halting," said the ranger with a chin of a boxer.

Dumisane called Mr Wolmarans, a woman's voice answered and it was Lizzy.

"Dumisane, it's me, Lizzy, how are you doing?"

"Lizzy my wife, we're just behind a blue 4X4 going towards the Giriyondo border post and we believe it is them trying to escape."

"We're at the border post, they are surrounded then."

"We're twenty kilometres away from the border post; I will try to stop them."

Suddenly a gunshot was fired in their direction and immediately secret agent Dumisane dropped the phone to pay

171

more attention to what happened around him; fortunately, nobody was hurt.

"Give me the microphone."

"You have it just on your nose," said the experienced pilot.

"You're being surrounded by the South Africa police force, pull over the car."

And another shot was fired, this time it broke the left window of the helicopter's door and hit mercilessly the second ranger who cried out in pain holding his left shoulder.

"We are being attacked," he said to Lizzy when he took back control of his cell phone.

"We are sending two helicopters in your direction."

"Please do so but they shouldn't kill anyone, we need them alive."

"Promise."

The ranger suffering from the bullet was bleeding, but with his experienced colleague, he managed to position him with a cloth covering the wounded area to avoid excessive bleeding.

The driver of the 4X4 was driving at 100 km per hour panicking the tourists that were using the same road, and secret agent Dumisane with his binoculars was holding fast to identify the driver of the 4X4. He hated the decisive moment but he was about to reduce the number of poachers exterminators of the African fauna.

They were now fifteen kilometres away from the Giriyondo border post and he was impatient to see the appearance of the promised two helicopters of the South African police force. He didn't want another casualty from either side. Where was the South African police force?

"They are behind us," suddenly said the ranger with the chin of a boxer.

"Behind us?" Repeated the secret agent.

Rapidly both McDonnell-Douglas 369E helicopters overtook them with such a dizzy speed. It was impressive and at the same time intimidating because the 4X4 suddenly stopped, without polling over with no one getting out of the car. Secret agents prayed that they won't commit suicide for there was no escape available for them; the border post was impermeable and dangerous.

The secret agent decided to inform the police force to let them drive up to the border post and see what other ways were available for them to enter Mozambique.

"Let them drive to the border post, they cannot escape."

"Good idea," responded one of the police agents.

But stopping the 4X4 without pulling it over meant to seek a different way that could make their lives difficult especially if they decided to make their way into the savanna. And that what they did for they surely realized that a trap was waiting for them at the border post.

"Ranger, shoot the wheels," said the secret agent.

Without wasting time he managed to flat both left wheels of the 4X4 but they continued stubbornly refusing to surrender, then the police force ordered them to surrender or they will shoot to kill. But they refused to stop and proceeded east despite the flat wheels.

"Don't get closer, they can shoot," said the secret agent.

One of the McDonnell-Douglas 369E helicopters impressively and at a significant speed got so close to the 4X4 panicking them, and one of the policemen noticing the opened driver's window threw two tear gas canisters into the car; causing more panic that forced them to halt the car and escape from the terrible damage of suffocating and to never wake up.

Understanding the brave move of the South African police force, the secret agent with his AK 47 ready to shoot ordered the pilot to lower the altitude of the helicopter. There was nothing else substantial the poachers could do to escape the police bravery unless they wanted to commit suicide and never be arrested.

Jumping out of the helicopter was not a problem because he was trained for such an event and the move was followed by more than ten other, national police members. But trying to run was not going to solve the problem because the police started shooting in the air when suddenly secret agent Dumisane saw Alfredo turning around holding a pistol ready to discharge merciless bullets. But the secret agent was faster than him.

In a calculated move he shot the right shoulder of Alfredo who fell rolling over like a soccer ball.

"Don't shoot," he said to the police, we need him alive.

But it wasn't over because the Oriental man took the pilot of the game lodge helicopter hostage, threatening to kill him if they don't let him go.

"Let me go or I shoot him."

"It's over Kim, please surrender."

"I don't want to go to jail."

"Or you get eaten by wild animals because we're surrounded by them here," said secret agent Dumisane.

Another helicopter had just landed with secret agent Lizzy on the scene.

"It is this woman, she betrayed me," said Mr Kim screaming with rage.

"Free the man," said secret agent Lizzy.

"I hate you," said Mr Kim stretching his right arm to shoot.

The police force was quiet but ready for the quickest move to be executed. To the surprise of everybody, Lizzy with boldness started walking towards the Oriental man. Secret agent Dumisane kept his self-control and allowed what she was about to do. She walked until she got four meters away from Mr Kim and said to him, "Why are you killing our Rhinos?"

Mr Kim with the gun on the head of his hostage said nothing but watched everywhere.

"Just put your gun down and face a fair trial."

"Why did you betray me?"

"You are killing other species, Kim."

And he began weeping, dropped his gun down and let his hostage go.

"You did very well."

The police force came and arrested him together with Alfredo who was already handcuffed in one of the helicopters.

"You're a fascinating wife," said secret agent Dumisane to his colleague Lizzy Wolmarans who turned around to hug him.

"I didn't want him to die. We cannot replace the life of a human being with anything else."

With her head leaned on his chest, she was resting in the arms of a brave man that she will perhaps never see again.

175

Chapter 12

Many good memories were filling her mind while she was busy watching the family photos. Their most recent photos while in Port Elizabeth were the symbol of the love that has been refreshed forever and only death could separate their union. She held those photos against her chest at the same time watching the news that has just started on national television.

Suddenly the face of someone she knew very well appeared on television for a few seconds. The person was secret agent Dumisane involved in ending poaching activity in the Mpumalanga province; the man who was much in love with her. She was happy for him; she expressed a smile that her husband who just entered the house saw on her face; a smile expressing the joy she could feel within her.

Colonel Themba took time to observe her. With both hands, she was pressing those pictures against her chest watching television, and at the same time singing a peaceful song that she seemed to love and enjoy. While deep at the moment he felt being far away from the real world full of a trip up, and remaining forever by her side listening to songs of peace and enjoying her softness. She looked happy to him and that made his day because he wanted her cheerful and to have the baby girl they both craved to have.

For so long he missed her kindness, and the vacation in Port Elizabeth restored a hundred times what has been stolen from them. Just after the poaching news and without panicking her face turned towards him; smiling at the man she has never stopped being devoted to.

"Your colleague has done a great job, they've arrested one of the most wanted poachers."

"We were the best team spying around darling."

"Spying is not for you, but managing big amounts of money looks just like you."

"That's what Malume (Pty) Ltd is all about?"She said standing up. "The good money and I'm so happy to be your wife."

"I'm happy that you understand, Sipho."

Six months later in Edenvale, Johannesburg and at the assembly of Ps Thabiso and Tshepang

While singing a song of worship, Ps Tshepang saw Colonel Themba and his wife Siphokazi, followed by their children coming into the church. Siphokazi, radiant, was pushing a pushchair with a baby girl inside, and the greeters of the church took the couple and their children to the family room.

Forty-five minutes later after praise and worships, Ps Tshepang started preaching about the power of forgiveness in a relationship.

"I salute you people of God for He is love and His love is in us all, and to forgive us as part of his plan. Let us also forgive one another for a bright future. Husbands forgive your wives and wives forgive your husbands so that God also can forgive us our trespassers for none is perfect."

"Hearing that, Colonel Themba held tied his wife's hand and said, "Thank you for forgiving me, Sipho."

"And you, will you forgive me?" She said.

"I have already forgiven you, Sipho."

"The power of forgiveness produces breakthroughs in our lives," continued Ps Tshepang. "God is able in Jesus' name to give you the desires of your heart, but only if you can forgive. It is a decision that you have to make for God to hear your prayers. Do you want restoration children of God, forgive?"

And one hour later after the service, the pastoral couple were talking with Colonel Themba and Sipho and were very happy to see reconciliation reigning in the couple.

"It is very good that you came back to the Lord after so many months without seeing you," said Ps Thabiso, "And a baby girl, that what you wanted right?"

"Yes, Ps," said the colonel and from his pocket, he pulled an envelope full of cash that he awarded to the pastoral couple saying, "This is an offering to you man of God for what you're doing for the community with so much passion, please accept it and do whatever you wish to do with it."

"This will help the assembly," said Ps Thabiso, "God bless you, Colonel and carry on serving this nation with integrity."

"Thank you, Ps, see you next Sunday."

"May God be with you."

While leaving the premises of the assembly, Ps Thabiso wondered if the problem was solved; if the colonel was no longer part of the underworld for what he had in his hand was a lot of money and on top of the cash amount a cheque showing an amount of 50,000 Rand was also given, and with his wife, beside him, they prayed over the donation.

"Put this money somewhere until the Lord speaks to us," he said to Ps Tshepang.

"I will Ps," said his wife.

The following day whilst in the premises of Malume (Pty) Ltd, secret agent Siphokazi was calling her personal assistant Tasha via the intercom but she wasn't responding. When she checked her mail she didn't even act in response to a short message concerning the delay with the clothes that were expected to arrive in the Limpopo province on Tuesday. Sipho decided to go to her office personally and see what was going on as the only time she had seen her today was when she entered her office early on.

There was no trace of her presence; even her big handbag that she carried with her when she arrived was not there. She walked around her desk to check if her laptop was on and it was. Then she decided to have a look and see what she was busy with, and the screen exposed a building that looked like a warehouse with the address written underneath.

Her first instinct was to instantaneously write the address on a piece of paper before Tasha came back and that's what she did before she all of a sudden saw her coming into the office. Sipho met her at the entrance of her office so she couldn't notice anything and the screen of her laptop was already dark.

"Where were you? I was looking for you."

"I forgot my cell phone in my car. I saw your e-mail about the clothes destined for Limpopo but everything has been sorted out, the delay won't affect the warehouse for they have some extra clothes they can use."

"Good news then I was concerned about it, I don't want Malume to come after me. "

"Yes, he is very sensitive when his not-for-profit organization is threatened."

"See you, Tasha, and thank you for the feedback."

"Secret agent Siphokazi went back into her office with what could perhaps help her to unlock the mystery of the family business. Her father without telling her anything made sure to distance her from the underworld business that was generating multimillions of Rands. The not-for-profit organization was just there to cover up, and also because of the strong marketing of the organization, some donors could give up to ten million Rand a year.

She needed some time off to go to Isando, in the East of Johannesburg to pay a visit to the building that seemed like a warehouse that could hide what she undeniably wanted to discover. Her watch was indicating 10h40 so she had to excuse herself to her assistant and conduct some investigation that she needed to do first on her own.

Johannesburg was hot and a little bit windy, and driving east was clear so she drove on R21 going towards Tambo airport at 110 km/h. Ahead of her on her left side, there was an off-ramp called Barbara Street, so she took it abiding by the direction provided by the GPS. By the red lights, she turned right on Barbara Street while the GPS was already showing her the next turn left, so that was what she did hoping to find the place and satisfy her curiosity.

By the next red lights, she turned right again and 500 meters ahead was her destination. Delighted, she reduced the speed and started driving slowly until she arrived in front of the building. It was a warehouse with a big panel at the front of it written "caring for the nation". That was it and that was not enough to know who the owner of the warehouse was and what was hidden inside.

Looking straight into the warehouse she noticed that it was well protected with electric fences all around it, supported by three well-armed security guards. She immediately left when one of the guards approached her. She didn't want to be noticed by anyone for she was convinced that the installation could well belong to the cartel and Tasha was one of the suspects not telling her everything. She suspected that Tasha was assigned to her because she knew a lot and might end up one day revealing more secrets to her. But she was not going to wait until that day. She needed to find a way to enter the mysterious warehouse, see what was in there and take some pictures.

It was already more than seven months on the case and her pregnancy had been an element of delay, but she knew she was on the right track. The scene of the crime was often revisited by the perpetrator and she thought about a keen spy who could move around the premises and get some pictures for her. She wanted to know who goes in and out of the premises that seemed very well protected, and such protection was hiding some treasures dear to the family that she was unaware of, but was the warehouse for the family?

Without wasting time she looked for secret agent Dumisane's cell phone number that she finally found, hoping that he still used the same number. She dialled the number and the good news was it started ringing for almost ten seconds before someone responded.

"Hello!"

She immediately recognized his voice.

"Wow!" She exclaimed, "That's my partner," she said.

"Siphokazi!" he called, surprised.

"Yes, baba."

"I've tried to reach out but was unsuccessful."

"I've changed my number Dumisane, how are you and many congratulations on arresting the poachers?"

"Thanks a lot but that happened a long time ago, what can I do for you now?"

"I need some help; I'm here at Isando not far from the city airport facing a very strange warehouse that I discovered in my own assistant's laptop."

"Ok."

"I believe there is something suspicious about this warehouse and I need a spy to get some pictures of those going in and out of the premises."

"It could be a hiding place for illegal goods, and how is the baby?"

"My baby girl is fine."

"Congratulation Sipho."

"Thank you. So I'm sending you the address of the premises and I need feedback from him within three days, please insist this to him."

182

"I can arrange that for you, consider it done."

"Thank you but don't ever call me on this number, but once you have the pictures please send them through this number."

"I also would like to see you Sipho."

"But not now, very soon."

"Keep well Sipho."

"Bye."

Forty-eight hours later while serving her husband his food Sipho's cell phone announced a message. She first looked at her phone and pushed it in the back pocket of the jeans she was wearing. She wanted to make sure Colonel Themba was happy with his food and eating and then check what could well be a message from secret agent Dumisane.

But she waited until Themba finished eating his food.

"Are you not eating?"

"I've already eaten, Colonel."

"Very nice food, thank you, my wife."

"You're welcome."

"I'm going to rest a little bit in the room before watching the late news."

"See you just now."

While in the kitchen secret agent Siphokazi took the courage to check her WhatsApp message. It was Dumisane's number with four messages sent to her. That was a quick reaction from the force with the expectation of getting something out of it. But what she saw was at the same time very informative and sad because two photos were showing her husband with another woman beside him wearing sunglasses entering the premises, and she felt horribly jealous, but she had to keep her calm.

The other photos surprisingly showed one of the executives of Malume's empires with Sipho'sassistant, Tasha, sitting on the passenger seat, and that was not to be ignored for she always considered Tasha as a prime suspect knowing a lot about Malume's business deals. But keeping those pictures on her cell phone was dangerous so she decided to keep them in her flash disk that she hid in her purse.

After saving the pictures, she quickly thanked her colleague with a WhatsApp to which he responded instantly. So what she had dreaded was real. She was still far away from knowing everything about the business, and Tasha was one of the pivotal parts of the organization's activities. Maybe Sipho wasn't trusted because of her past involvement with the government secret services, and Tasha had been assigned to watch on her activities, or at the right moment to start telling her more about the company's hidden secrets. It wasn't the first time she thought that way about Tasha, or perhaps they didn't want her, by order of Malume, to be part of the underworld section of the empire.

While in her office with her assistant facing her, secret agent Siphokazi received an unknown phone call; to which she finally responded after hesitation, and it was the voice of a man that she almost recognized.

"Hello!" She answered without saying her name.

"I can still recognize your voice after so many years."

"Bongani! Is it you? Oh my God!" She exclaimed happily.

"Why are you so excited?"

"Dad and mum are also looking for you, how did you get my number?"

"Don't talk to me about dad. How is mum?"

"Very worried about you. Where are you? We need to meet."

"I'm in Pretoria."

Where? I can come now.

I can only be available after hours, about seven pm. Come to my hotel and I will text you the address."

"I'm so happy Bongani, see you tonight. Do you know Bongani?" Sipho turned to ask Tasha.

"Yes, the elder of the family."

"Please don't tell my parents, they also want to see him but I need to talk to him first."

"Trust me Siphokazi, ok your letter is completed, do you want me to send it now?"

"You can send it and don't forget to forward me a copy as well."

"Thank you, Sipho."

Left alone secret agent understood that her assistant was the prototype of a secretive observer hiding behind her glasses acquainted with the game she was playing, but she was not going to wait until she starts telling her everything about Malume's business because then she will be already corrupted. What she needed to accelerate her investigation was the use of a specialized team that could infiltrate the warehouse unnoticed, and locate the owner of any illegal goods. But that had to be decisive, for any illegal goods discovered on that particular day will cause the arrest of her husband and the rest

185

of the executives. She could do with calling secret agent Dumisane to make such an arrangement since she was deceived and tired to see this taking longer.

After explaining to her husband about her big brother's call and their appointment in Pretoria, they both decided to visit him. The idea to go together appealed to her husband. But she knew it wasn't a good idea because he was also unhappy with his brother-in-law who was part of the cartel. Suddenly his phone rang and he briefly talked with the caller who was a man

After the call, he said, "I can't make it with you anymore. The minister of defence has called for an urgent meeting, drive safe."

"I will tell you all about our conversation."

After a soft kiss on her right cheek, he left the premises. She was happy about the circumstance, for after her talk with her brother she intended to go to Malume's headquarters and check on her assistant, Tasha. She required more evidence that could support the photos taken at the Isando warehouse, and she would be in seventh heaven if she could find her laptop at her office.

Getting to the capital city of the country was going to take her about fifteen minutes, so after giving some instructions to her nanny, she departed from her home to Tshwane. She was very happy to see Bongani after several years of absence without even talking to him. She had a loyal brother who was just like her but she decided not to tell him what she was up to. She wanted him to reconcile with his parents despite the family identity.

The road to Tshwane using National 1 was free, and twenty-six minutes later she was in the Arcadia suburb driving towards the hotel close to the Saudi Arabian embassy. Her brother was already waiting for her in the restaurant of the hotel tranquilly drinking wine, and once in the hall of the hotel, she couldn't mistake him despite the many years that went past without seeing him. Even with his back to her, she recognized him.

A tap on his left shoulder made him turn around and guess who was there, her little sister who was no longer a teenager but a grown woman.

"Siphokazi, look at yourself, little sister."

And they hugged each other so happy to meet up again after many years.

"Let's go upstairs to my room."

"You haven't changed, still have that cute face," she said.

"Look at yourself, you've flourished."

After ordering some drinks, they took the lift up to the fourth floor and entered the room.

"You're welcome; this is my modest room and you may have a seat."

"Thank you, Bongani. I haven't seen you for several years."

"For a very good reason, I love dad and mum but I can't be part of their dirty games."

"I know but they are getting old and you need to see them, they want to see you, my brother."

"Dad is a greedy psychopath ready to sacrifice anything for his money, look at what he did to mum."

"Please."

187

"What about you? Even your husband is absorbed by dad's craziness. They are all going to fall."

"Please don't go back to Cape Town without meeting them, they are our parents."

"Are you still in the force? What are you waiting for to arrest them? I mean all of them."

"Don't speak like that; I also want you to see my children."

"I'm here on business for ten days; I will see them before going back."

"Thank you, thank you."

Forty minutes later, she left the hotel for Roodepoort, towards Malume headquarters. Protecting herself with a firearm, secret agent Siphokazi was resolved to put an end to what has for several years dishonoured the family. She was facing was a craggy mountain to be flattened to nothing. She was craving to see them all under arrest and start a new life with her husband while in jail. In her opinion, only the hard way could change Themba's mind and turn his back on the underworld.

Dressed like an executive, she parked her car in the underground parking and took the lift. And with her keys, she opened her office door, locked herself inside and immediately went into Tasha's office. Regrettably, her laptop was with her so without wasting time she began checking every document on her desk, drawers and what was in her dustbin. What she needed was a solid foundation that could support the well-taken photos she had of the mysterious warehouse.

Searching for a while gave her nothing, and then she decided to go back to her office for Tasha was too smart to allow any infiltration. But on the right-hand side of her desk when entering her office stood against the wall, very expensive old fashioned drawers locked with padlocks; so what was in there, she wondered? That was going to be another problem to get through. She had no idea about where possibly the keys were.

She started searching for the keys, opening her desk drawers without getting anything and finally, she went back into Tasha's office and rummaged through what was there but found nothing. This was very disappointing and tiring. But her secret agent's instincts sent her to check what could maybe be hidden behind the big mirror installed against the wall on the left-hand side of her desk. Quickly she went to check what was behind the mirror and surprisingly saw a bunch of similar keys on a hook on the wall.

Delighted, she took the bunch of keys and immediately walked to the drawers. It seemed like there was a key for each drawer, and she started opening them ready to face any bad surprise. And after opening all drawers she saw that each of them had a folder with a name written in bold, and when paging them they all represented the names of all the warehouses owned by the company including their physical addresses. Very interesting but there was no folder with the Isando address.

Discouraged she put them back one by one, she noticed that the middle drawer had another folder deep in it that she didn't spot. Right away she took it but no name was written on it. She paged through it until she finally found on the fifth page what she wanted to see, the file belonged to the Isando warehouse. She first put all the files back and locked the drawers except the middle one and then considered taking some time to examine the file.

Secret agent Siphokazi sat on her desk and began analysing the mysterious file page by page, and was focused on unveiling what the Isando warehouse was all about. Everything she was reading was ultra-secret and exposed the very nature of the Isando warehouse. Some pages had photos exposing the very inside of the warehouse that was luxurious. There was a hall where the company parties were held every last Friday of the month that no one had told her about it. But on closer inspection, it was a ten-year-old folder forgotten by the management but very instrumental to her for most of the secret meetings was held there without her knowing. Very quickly she took some pictures of the folder and put everything else back as they were before, happy to have found something.

Secret agent Dumisane heard his cell phone ringing and rapidly left his kitchen for his room to answer the phone call.

"Hello!"

"I need to talk to you."

"It's you," he recognised her voice and avoided calling her name.

"We need to meet, it is urgent."

"I'll be glad to meet you after so many months, but where because last time your husband followed you."

"This is a risk that we have to take, and I will advise you to meet at the 50th floor of Carlton Centre in Johannesburg CBD around half past twelve today."

"See you there."

190

Three days later, she left her office to meet her father who possibly could be in his office. But she decided first to ask her assistant, Tasha, who was next door.

"Tasha, would you check if my father is around?"

"Ok, madam."

And a few seconds later via intercom, she came back to Siphokazi.

"Yes, madam. Malume is available in his office."

"Thank you, Tasha."

She found Malume rather relaxed and smoking his cigar with both feet on his desk watching a local soccer game on television.

"Sipho," he called when she entered his office, "My beloved daughter. Come and sit down beside daddy."

"Morning dad, how are you?"

"I'm alright, come this weekend and see your mother."

"Yes, dad I was about to tell you that I'm coming this weekend but not alone."

"Not alone?"

"Yes with Bongani, I met him three days ago in Tshwane."

"You met him!" He exclaimed at the same time taking his feet off his desk.

"Yes, and he also wants to see you."

"He should also come and work with his family; all I have to belong to you, my children."

"So let me tell mum not to worry, she will see us this Sunday afternoon."

"I want to be reconciled with all my children before I die."

"Why not dad, but please don't be aggressive with him."

191

"I just want him to be part of what belongs to him."

"But don't envy him if he doesn't want to. But he actually wants to see his parents, dad."

"We shall warmly wait for you, my little girl."

"Thank you and see you, Dad."

"What! You are going already?"

"Just to catch up with my work."

She came near to him and kissed his left cheek.

"See you, Malume."

Off she went leaving him in his office.

Chapter 13

The Carlton centre tower was planted in the middle of the Johannesburg CBD with restaurants on the 50th floor of the building. The tower was used heavily for tourism with the 50th floor offering a fantastic view of the city of Johannesburg.

What a great choice it was to meet her at the peak of the highest tower of the city of gold. Secret agent Dumisane already waiting for her on the 50th floor knew deep in his heart he was still in love with her. He was patiently expecting her to appear from the lift that he could catch sight of her through the regularly opening doors as many tourists visited to get a great view of the city.

Soon he saw her materializing from the lift, the doors closing behind her. With a gesture of the hand, he let her know that he wasn't seated far from the lift. He got to his feet to warmly welcome her; happy to smile at the lady he loved and with who he wanted to spend the rest of his life.

"Dumisane!" She called happy to see him again after many months.

"Sipho, really I missed you, colleague, look at yourself, you look amazing."

"You're going too far now, congratulations again on the arrest of those poachers, what a great achievement, I'm very happy for you."

They hugged each other for at least three seconds and then sat down.

"I don't have much time, Dumi."

"Then go straight to the point, but let me order you a drink, quickly."

"I'm alright, listen to me I believe that the warehouse at Isando has the answer that we are looking for. Besides, I've never been taken there and my assistant, Tasha is the executive secretary of my father's company and she never told me anything about the warehouse."

"Let arrest her."

"What?"

"We do have pictures of her in front of the gate with the executives of the organization including your husband."

Secret agent Sipho sighed and then held her head with both hands.

"You're doing very well Sipho and I know it is not easy but your father made a big mistake in letting that woman assist you with your duties."

"I also have these pictures from a ten-year-old folder I discovered about the warehouse confirming that this is the main warehouse of Malume (Pty) Ltd."

"We should arrest her as quickly as possible and take her to our installations to pressurize her to give us the secret on how to have access to the warehouse, we want tangible evidence for this is not enough, and I promise you she will panic and will tell us all, which will be strong evidence.

"I know but how are you going to arrest her?"

"Give us her physical address and we arrest her after work in front of her home."

"Crazy boy," she told him. "Don't arrest her from her home, family members or the neighbours might inform the organization; just use a police car to arrest her on her way home with no one from the company noticing, and force her to lie to the office saying she's sick."

"Good idea, keep your serenity my dear and it will be fine; justice must be done."

She sighed again and finally said, "I have to go and I will text you her physical address tonight, please don't physically hurt her."

"Promise, Sipho."

"Bye!"

"Don't you like the view?"

"Not today, bye."

And with compassion he let her depart to face her tribulations that he couldn't solve, only her. Nobody could wish to take her place and experience her deception. She was a betrayed woman always in a hurry to leave him alone, let down by those she was affectionate towards for the most part and ready to surrender to their enemies; which was the state. Left alone on the 50th floor of the highest tower in the Republic of South Africa, secret agent Dumisane took some time to view the economic capital of the country and at the same time, plan a future with the woman he loved no matter what.

Mr Nhlakanipho and his wife were taking a walk inside the garden of their Roodepoort mansion. It was Sunday and they were impatient to meet their long-gone son Bongani who was upset with his father's business. They knew it was not going to be easy to re-establish their relationship as it was before, but an effort had to be made to forget and move on. He still would like him to be part of the business and take a major decision for he had the personality, but knowing his son's values, this was not going to be easy.

"I don't want you to start bothering him to become an executive of the company."

"I know he's not coming for that, but he's my son."

"Wait until the right moment, promise me."

"Ok, I won't bother him with that, but maybe he changed his mind."

"He will tell us himself; I first want my son back to us and make peace with his parents."

"It's a good idea, Helena."

A few minutes later Siphokazi emerged from the garden followed by their long time gone son. Both parents had their back to them when his mother felt the presence of someone behind her turned around to see both of her children, and there she started crying with joy. She ran towards them to hug them. It was a treasured moment, especially for the son who also began weeping, blissful to find once more maternal love. Nine years without seeing his parents were a lot and they truly missed each other. Their hope was to meet again under different circumstances, nevertheless, it wasn't to be.

After hugging each other they went straight into the living room where the cocktail cabinet was opened with some snacks already served on the table.

"Bongani my son," said his mother, "so many years why? Not even one phone call to your mother."

"We're not perfect my son," said Malume with his right arm around his wife's shoulders.

"I'm sorry Dad, Mum for the pain I have caused you. It is great to see you all over again."

"Let me take some pictures of this moment," said Siphokazi busy taking some already.

"So what are you up to now?" Said his father.

"No," interrupted Helena, "we will talk about your career later, first of all, how are your wife and children?"

"They are doing very well; let me show you some pictures of them and see how they've grown up."

He took his smartphone from his pocket and went into the gallery, stood up and went sit in between both parents to show them the pictures. And with much delight, they watched together with his sister busy taking some unforgettable pictures. What an incredible afternoon it was to see everyone happy talking about other things than business and power.

After taking those pictures she listened to the stories behind the pictures that Bongani was enjoying showing to them, busy laughing at the same time. So far everything was taking place as she wanted, talking only about the family but she knew the time to talk about the business was getting closer for their father was not going to let him go without knowing what his son was up to in Gauteng province.

"What's this?" Asked the mother because the picture showed him in front of a hotel holding a file.

"The company where I'm working, I'm one of the managers," he said.

"That's my son, we are a family of managers. Your sister Siphokazi is one of the executives of our not-for-profit organization.

"Dad," called Siphokazi, "can't we talk about something else?"

"It's alright Sipho," reposted Bongani, "dad likes talking business and congratulations, my little sister."

"I'm very happy my son that you're one of the managers of this hotel," said her mother.

A delightful spread of food was already put on the table and Helena invited everyone to come and sit around the table to start eating. She was very happy with both men's behaviour that tempers did not escalate despite their divergences in opinions. They were both grown up with self-control and all those years without seeing and missing each other gave them a good lesson for sons and fathers should meet.

Monday afternoon at 16h47

Tasha, after a great day, was ready to leave her office for home., Siphokazi in a deceiving way offered her a meal at her favourite restaurant at lunchtime. Siphokazi's move was strategic for she was looking to know if Tasha looked suspicious of anything, but everything seemed alright.

She unusually allowed her to leave the office first to let her colleague, Dumisane, know and arrest her on her way home.

The whole thing was set up to generate great fear in her to confess everything. She knew about her father's underworld business, but it was painful to Siphokazi.

Due to the high volume of traffic at that particular hour of the day, going to Florida Park, even still within Roodepoort was going to take her more than thirty minutes.

"Goodbye and see you tomorrow," Tasha said to her boss who was still sitting in her office.

"Goodbye Tasha and have a nice evening."

"Same to you and thank you again for taking me out for lunch."

"You're welcome Tasha," she said that hoping to see her part of those people who will testify against Malume Pty Ltd one day.

Driving at that particular hour of the day was not easy for people were in hurry, nervous, tired and also lacking patience. Losing Tasha for many days without her coming to the office would be a grievous blow to the company because she knew too much to be separated from the executives of the organization.

The secret agent was curious to see all the executives' reactions once discovering that Tasha cannot be found for jobs.

While driving, Tasha saw on her right a teacher leading a parade of pupils, marching along the street singing. She remembered how she used to do that many years ago while in high school, it was both a good time and a learning experience. But today she was an executive secretary full of secrets to divulge to those in search of them and she didn't know she made a dreadful mistake working for the most powerful underworld business in South Africa. It was time to end it with her help.

A twenty-month stretch in prison was nothing to what she was going to hear from those after she double-crossed them; the truth was that she got herself into a frightful muddle that was going to cause excess fear. But the truth was that she loved taking care of Malume's business, she enjoyed managing the fortune that went with it and was prepared to never betray him.

Secret agent Dumisane had been informed about the executive secretary leaving her office and was calmly driving behind her ready to stop her before she got in front of the gates of her townhouse. He didn't want the neighbours to notice her arrest and inform some family members or her colleagues. The best story to tell was that there was a very unfortunate situation that happened in the family and she won't be around for a week so. That way there is no way to figure out that she is busy confessing everything she knows about the business.

She was going to be the perfect witness to destroy the cartel for they were not ready to relinquish their evil power from the community. Dumisane was excited about the confession that was about to materialize and humiliate everyone at the cartel, and the public was going to be stunned by the tragic end of a merciless powerful cartel.

The time had arrived to ambush her. Secret agent Botha was driving and Dumisane gave the order to switch on the police siren at a red traffic light., He instantly got out of the car and walked towards Tasha. The light turned green and hearing the sudden frightening sirens sound behind her, Tasha panicked. With a quick look in her right rear-view mirror, she recognized the police so there was no point in trying to escape for they were going to make sure to pursue and catch her. Besides they looked like security agents for they had firearms around their waists, and she thought maybe they just needed some information from her.

Causing a traffic jam, the two secret agents made sure to quickly deal with the matter at hand.

"Would you step out of your car?" Said secret agent Botha.

"Why? What have I done?" She asked anxiously.

"You need to come with us; we have some questions to ask you, we are the police," he said showing his badge.

"Can I call someone about this?"

"You will do that at the police station, don't worry about your car someone will drive it for you."

Secret agent Botha gently took her cell phone from her hand for no one should know about her arrest, especially Malume (Pty) Ltd. Yes, she was taken aback and for a cause she was still unaware of but she was close to being told about. Rapidly they left the scene, and surprisingly a few minutes later when she looked behind someone she had never met before was busy driving her car following theirs.

"Can just the police arrest someone like this without a warrant for arrest?"

"Don't worry about your safety; everything will be fine if you cooperate with us. By the way, my name is Dumisane and this is Botha. We're from the South African intelligence. We're secret agents.

"What do you want from me?"

"Be patient, you will find out."

She had a strong suspicion the intelligence was after Malume (Pty) Ltd, and it was not going to be easy for her to give up information, but why target her? she wondered. She was scared and aware that she was dealing with the government that expected her to tell them what they wanted to discover from the business. Already in their building and tired after a long day at the office with her cell phone confiscated, Tasha realized that there was nothing that lasts forever under the sun. She was in front of unknown people who could at any time kill her. She was in their hands and there was nothing she could do about it.

The office where she was smelled nice and was clean but she was without a telephone to use to call a family member or her boss Siphokazi. Her watch indicated already 18h20 so what time were they going to release her? She was confused and ready to please them to let her go home.

Suddenly Botha entered the office, smoking at the same time.

"Do you want a coffee?"

"No thank you."

"Don't worry, it is free."

Botha was a blond middle-aged man trusted by his government for this kind of difficult task.

"What do you want from me? I haven't done anything wrong."

Secret agent Dumisane also entered and heard what she said.

"We don't want to harm you lady but know that you won't get home today until you tell us everything."

"What are you talking about? Everything like what?" And she started crying.

"Crying won't help you but cooperating with the intelligence will," said secret agent Botha.

"Botha and one of our ladies will kindly go to your apartment and get what you would like them to bring for you. Do you live with anybody?"

"No," she said angrily.

"Good news, provide the address and they will take care of everything."

"And if I refuse."

"You will remain in custody until you tell us everything and also become the only government's witness."

Botha came holding a piece of paper with a pen that he put on the table for her to write the address and everything she needed. It was like a dream to her but those moving around her were real and determined to start their interrogation.

"So are you holding me hostage, my government?"

"Your government needs some good confessions from you, Tasha," said secret agent Botha.

"You also know my name."

"We are well informed," responded Botha.

"I'm tired and hungry," she said trying to get their sympathy. "I am not involved in illegal activities in this country, just a secretary."

"We can give you food to eat," said secret agent Dumisane. You are not just any kind of secretary, but an executive one and working for a powerful cartel that makes millions of Rand every month."

"I want some water and some food; you are going to drive me crazy."

"Are you on medication?" Asked secret agent Botha.

"I'm taking some cholesterol medication."

"Write everything you need on the piece of paper and we will bring what you desire."

"I don't want men to touch my things."

"We promise, only ladies will touch your garments and any other stuff you want."

Convinced, but with her hand trembling Tasha took the pen and started writing all she wanted to have, however deep in her being her conscience was already telling her of a possible investigation into the activities of Malume (Pty) Ltd. The time was grave and merciless, and calling her advocate was the only option to get out from this place and say nothing, but how to call him because they took her by surprise to ensure she didn't call anyone.

"What you're doing is illegal; I have the right to call my lawyer."

Unexpectedly secret agent Dumisane put many pictures of her on the table together with her executives.

"Do you know these people with you?" Demanded Dumisane.

Surprised she said, "Yes."

"You know very well what they do."

"I don't understand Mr Dumisane. I'm just a secretary."

"A rich secretary," said Botha between his teeth.

"Don't protect them," said Dumisane, "for they are all involved including you in the selling of illegal goods like drugs, selling gold without a license, money laundering and multiple assassinations."

When checking those photos she saw herself with Siphokazi walking outside Malume's premises.

"What do you want from me?"

Secret agent Botha came with pictures of her with many executives in from of the Isando warehouse, and she panicked more when she saw the front side of the warehouse in all those photos.

"Do you know this warehouse?" Interrogated Botha.

"I am just a secretary."

"A secretary who knows what we need to know to arrest all these deceivers."

"I'm hungry and thirsty, please."

"We don't want to stress you out, but don't take us there," said secret agent Dumisane.

"Ok we are bringing your food and water," said Botha.

"If she refuses to cooperate with us she doesn't deserve food from us, you can give her water."

"I haven't said I'm not going to cooperate with you."

"What about this warehouse? Botha, bring to her the food and water she needs."

At that same time in her husband's home office, secret agent Siphokazi was busy paging through an old chequebook showing colossal amounts of money spent by her husband who had been so in love with the deceased Nthabiseng. There was more in the last drawer where she found beautiful self-taken photos of him with a woman other than Nthabiseng while walking in what seemed to look like a natural park.

It was painful and disappointing because the pictures were the most recent of them all. She felt like committing a crime that she would never regret, for the level of betrayal she endured from her husband was devastating, and that woman was beautiful and exposing her best smile to the camera, and he seemed to enjoy her company. Nevertheless, after glancing at those photos for a while she put them back where they belonged.

It was time for him to experience the betrayal that will change his life forever, and he shall know that it was her, Sipho his beloved wife and that she did it for a good reason, to stop him from dying one day like a dog in the street of the city of Johannesburg. But it was a beautiful office and her picture was on his desk so he could look at her all the time. He was still in love with her, still, he needed her in his life, and still, he was hoping for a better tomorrow.

Her husband suddenly entered his office and was surprised to see her inside sitting at the desk.

She smiled at him as if for the last time and said, "It is nice to know you're back."

"You look so beautiful," he said manipulated by his wife's beauty.

And he hugged her with compassion and she felt it, happy to know that he still loved her.

The secret agent duo made sure to not question her while eating to let her enjoy her food. They needed her strong and cooperative. Watching the room from outside through the glass, she was eating with a concerned look for she was sometimes looking around in case something could surprise her.

They also had a long and tiring day, especially planning how to arrest her without causing any chaos. So far secret agent Siphokazi had worked perfectly, and the whole division was happy with her professionalism, except still, Dumisane felt sorry for the reason that she was deceived by the family she loved so dearly, especially her husband, the father of her children whom she enjoyed cherishing; he was the man really in charge with all the company operations.

And after all those vain thoughts secret agent Dumisane went back into the office alone when all of a sudden he saw her exposing a firearm. This was a big mistake from the force for she wasn't checked thoroughly.

"You let me go or I shoot you," she spoke with a trembling voice.

"Botha, did you put any evil substance in her food?"

Botha heard it and carefully walked towards the interrogation room to see what was transpiring.

"Show me the way out."

"You need to calm down, Tasha. This place is full of policemen and they will kill you before you reach the lift."

"I hate you," she said crying.

"We are going to help you to get out of this situation, but you have to cooperate with us."

"How?" she shouted.

"Give me your gun, Tasha. It is going to be alright.

And she suddenly dropped the gun and wept. She was about to pull out the trigger and make the biggest mistake of her life. And calmly Botha entered the room and took the gun from the floor.

"You did well," said secret agent Dumisane.

"Do you have a license for this gun?"

Sat and pensive she realized that the moment wasn't at her advantage; she had to negotiate for the government wasn't playing around.

"Yes, I do have," she responded wiping her tears.

Suddenly the door was opened and Lieutenant Keegan entered wearing his uniform When Tasha saw him it was like the whole world turned against her.

"Is she cooperative?" Coldly asked Lieutenant Keegan with an eye posed on her.

"She better be because if she isn't then this night is going to be the longest one of her life," said secret agent Botha scratching his hairy chest.

"I never said that I wasn't going to cooperate."

"The secret agent came with a recorder and put it on the table in front of her."

"Talk," he said.

Many pictures of her with the executives of Malume (Pty) Ltd were laid in front of her on the table, including the recent pictures she took with Siphokazi her boss.

"All these executives already have a warrant for their arrest except you," said Dumisane, "unless you tell us everything you know about the business. They all have thirty years in jail for polluting our country by smuggling goods."

"Smuggling?"

"So you don't know about any illegal activity conducted by all the executives you know?"

"But," she said.

"We're about to assault the warehouse and we believe that illegal goods are stored there with your help," said Botha busy drinking his cup of coffee.

"And if you don't tell us the truth now, and we go there and discover that you hide information from us, then we are going to treat you as an accomplice, and treat you equally as a smuggler," said Dumisane, "and you will stay in our custody from today until you serve thirty years in jail, and believe us many never made it."

Tasha resumed crying, wiping her tears with her hands with no one offering her a serviette.

"I've been very loyal to this company. Twenty years is a lot and they have always respected my contribution with very good remuneration, but I've learned to turn a blind eye to those illegal activities. And also many things happen without me knowing or being there but because of my high education level, they've involved me in all sorts of activities including smuggling drugs."

"Only drugs?" Demanded secret agent Dumisane.

"Gold and even diamonds."

"Without licenses?" Demanded secret agent Botha.

"I was making them and Colonel Themba was the one taking them I don't know where to legalize them for export and so on."

"Good, very good," said Lieutenant Keegan. "At least you are aware that illegal activities occur in the organization."

"What about the warehouse?" Asked Dumisane.

"Which warehouse because the company has many warehouses?"

"You know which warehouse we're talking about, look at those pictures," said Dumisane.

Before responding Tasha covered her face with both hands and then slipped them down up to the chin and said, "It is over."

"What is over Tasha?" Said Botha approaching.

"I have betrayed the company."

"There's nothing eternal under the sun Tasha," said secret agent Dumisane. "The government for many years has been in your case, and it's the end now, and if you refuse to tell us you drown along with them."

"This warehouse is the main one and you will find what you want to know there."

"Thank you," Tasha, said Lieutenant Keegan attentively listening.

"Can I leave now?"

"You can't until you testify against the organization in a court of law, and we are going to keep you in a safe place until we're done with this case."

"Please don't keep me here, and I can't testify this is too much."

"We need a strong witness and you're it," said secret agent Botha. "You will get your reward for helping the state to put them all in a box."

"You cannot go back to your decision, Tasha," said secret agent Dumisane. "There is one last thing we will need from you, it is the right time to arrest all of them and at the same moment, and we know that you organize meetings and parties in that warehouse; we want to know which day and at what time."

After saying that, Lieutenant Keegan called both secret agents to talk to them outside the interrogation room.

"We need all possible information for we don't know what this woman is capable of; we don't want her to commit suicide without telling us everything she knows."

The duo went back to her to get the rest of the needed data.

"Did you think about what we asked earlier?"

"Mr Dumisane I'm tired."

"Today is Monday and the week is long, when is the next party for God's sake?"

"This coming Thursday we're having a big meeting but Malume won't be there, I've already booked a flight for him to Cape-Town."

"Malume the founder?" Demanded Botha.

"Yes sir."

"What time?" Demanded Botha.

"From eleven O'clock until four p.m. "

After saying that again Tasha covered her face with both hands, she was going through the worst nightmare of her life. There were no more big parties thrown with her involved and enjoying. The realization of her fondest dreams was

211

jeopardized, and her life, in a blink of an eye, was synching down to the obscurity.

"I'm tired and I want to sleep."

"Yeah! It is late now," said secret agent Dumisane to Tasha. "We won't keep you in our custody, but at a very safe place without cell phone access. You did well and you are our witness now. Your work laptop is also in our hands to avoid any access to the internet, and know also that you're already in danger and they can kill you for you know too much, we don't wish for anyone to locate you. Your SIM card has been already removed from your phone until the day you will be taken to court to testify against them. Understood?"

"I can't even speak to my family members?"

"We cannot allow that, Tasha," said secret agent Botha.

Lieutenant Keegan reappeared in the interrogation room and called both secret agents.

"Take her now to where she will stay, make sure there is no opportunity to commit suicide, she is the only witness who can help us to jail some of this wicked generation."

And he immediately left.

Chapter 14

Siphokazi arrived in her office around 9am and found a message from Dumisane in her inbox. The message confirmed what the plan of the intelligence was all about, the complete disappearance of the executive secretary until the date of the trial. Since Malume had arrived he was trying to get hold of Tasha to come to his office.

Sadness overwhelmed her for a while until she decided to join her father in his office with the best lie that could exist.

Mr Nhlakanipho saw the door of his office being opened upon her beloved daughter who looked beautiful in her outfit.

"Sipho my daughter! How are you? Where is Tasha? What's wrong with her?"

"Dad, I don't know, her cell phone is off since yesterday after leaving the premises."

"She can't do this to us now."

"What is it dad that I can do for you?"

"Don't worry my assistant can always help with that and if you need anything as well talk to my assistant. But you need to be there," he suddenly said.

"I beg your pardon dad?"

"This Thursday. Ok, don't mind."

"Bye, dad."

After leaving her father's office, secret agent Siphokazi thought about what her father said about Thursday. She was certain that the coming Thursday was going to be the right day to make a warehouse collective arrest followed by a thorough check, so she just simply had to enter into contact with her colleague Dumisane who was keeping the witness with him. She speedily went back to her office and sent him an SMS that he received and responded within five minutes, confirming that the assault was set up for Thursday morning before twelve and that she was welcome to join them if willing.

In the vain hope of seeing her marriage surviving; Siphokazi calmly sat on her chair in front of a family photo showing her husband sitting in the middle of them carrying their little girl with the two boys on either side. She was pensive as the upcoming event was close, and she didn't want more than ever her husband to be hurt. The assault was forever going to revolutionize the history of her long relationship with him that her father destroyed. And besides, he was unable to let her know about the great executive meeting and party that will be held in the mysterious warehouse.

Of course, she knew that her mother didn't want her involved with the illegal activities that were occurring in the company, but the truth of the matter was her marriage was no longer glowing in the darkness as once it used to be, even unnoticed in daylight and only God could shelter her with her children since after the trial their father was no longer going to be the protector of the family, but just a memory that will haunt her forever.

Her fixed-line rang and it was her father.

"Sipho are you busy now?"

"No dad but trying to get online with Tasha."

"Take me to the airport."

"Are you travelling or receiving a visitor?"

"Going to Cape Town my daughter."

"Alone?"

"Your mother will join me in two hours, I need some rest.

"Now?"

"Yes in five minutes."

"I'm coming, dad."

Her father was the number one accused for harbouring illegal goods in the Republic of South Africa and driving around with him without protection but just her fire-arm uneased her. But still, she loved him very dearly because he was after all her father who was just doing what he thought could protect his family.

"I am old now my daughter and I need a successor, Bongani refused to take over and I only have you to continue the legacy and there is more to know about the business."

"You still have many years to live dad, you're just seventy-two."

"Yes, but I have children and the capable ones are you and your brother Bongani. Think about it and let me know."

"I will dad."

Driving on the R21 going to Oliver Tambo International Airport was agreeable, however, a long way from Roodepoort, and taking the highway way was safe to her for the reason that her father had many enemies in the same kind of business ready to get him cold.

"Why don't you have some bodyguards to protect you wherever you go?"

"They are behind us following us."

"What!"

"Yes, my daughter, they know I'm with you, they know all about my movements."

She checked her rear-view mirror and saw a car that was always following theirs, keeping a normal distance away.

"I see now," she said.

"So dad is well protected, including your mother and you must also get some of them because you're my daughter. My enemies can be your enemies too."

"I'm fine, Dad."

"Are you saying that because you are part of God's Kingdom or since fear is not part of your agenda?"

"Because I don't want to live the kind of life you live dad," she interrupted him.

"You're like my deceased big brother, Ntombisi, a maniac of lawfulness, but he died poor like your big brother is going to if he continues working for other entrepreneurs."

"But he has a good salary."

"What's a salary? The salary of a greedy man will never make you rich my daughter; he will make sure that you are sucked until you can't be anymore."

"Should we all go after the treasures of this world dad?"

"Not everyone but us yes, we're part of that bloodline, and no one can change it and it will continue in perpetuity. You're the one who told me last time that God's gifts are irrevocable."

"Of course, paps then make me the number one of your not-for-profit organizations, just after you."

"Is it what you want? Consider it done. You make me think about your mother when she was about your age, knowing what she wanted. In the next twenty minutes while on the plane I will make sure to drop you an e-mail kindly signed by dad."

"Thank you, Dad, I love you."

And as they were about to arrive at the airport secret agent Siphokazi saw the bodyguards' car overtaking theirs.

"Follow them. You don't need to park anywhere, follow them to the drop off zone area upstairs and they will take you home, I'm travelling with one of them and two are waiting for me at Cape-Town International Airport."

"Ok, dad. You spend a lot of money on your bodyguards."

"For your security, it worth's it."

The Gautrain was also arriving at the airport to drop the passengers coming from Sandton, Midrand and Tshwane, and it was beautiful to notice the infrastructure development in the country, and in particular in the Gauteng province where they were living.

The drop off zone of the domestic side of the airport upstairs had many cars parked so she followed everything the driver of the bodyguards did and parked behind them.

"Stay well my daughter, and he kissed her on her forehead. Check your e-mail in the next twenty minutes."

"Bye dad and thank you for trusting me."

Ready to cover her head with a hood, secret agent Siphokazi was busy listening to the last questions asked to Tasha by secret agent Botha. She was behind a one-way mirror so Tasha was unaware she was there. The unit, with the help of the South African police, was ready to take by surprise everyone involved in that meeting and party within the mysterious warehouse. The intelligence was very motivated to see this coming to an end, and Siphokazi was holding fast to be part of the set-up and see her husband beginning the transformation process as for her it was the only way to see him dying with dignity.

Secret agent Dumisane noticed that she was lost in thoughts and it wasn't good for what they were about to do.

"You don't have to come with us Sipho; stay behind if you can't focus."

"No one should shoot him, warn everyone."

"Of course no bloodshed especially to the man you love."

"Oh my God! Very few men understand why women cry sometimes, but at least if he gets shot and dies I'll be there to hold him in my arms, Dumi."

"Come on Sipho, I understand your fear."

But she was happy knowing her father was escaping the danger that was around the corner ready to bring desolation into Malume (Pty) Ltd.

Colonel Themba walked down the sumptuous corridors of Malume (Pty) Ltd and opened his wife's office door but no one was inside, it was completely deserted. Not even Tasha was there and it was almost a week where she had been absent from work. This was unusual for her who usually made sure to make everyone aware of any unforeseen situations. He settled on calling his wife whom he hadn't spoken to since eight o'clock that morning.

"Hallo, Themba! Are you alright?"

"I am, where are you your office is empty?"

"I am in the mall with Tasha; she left for the restroom."

"Great news, finally. what happened to her?"

"A long story, I will tell you all about it once back at the office with her."

"Yes but I won't be there for the next three hours for an urgent meeting is waiting for me, will see you once done."

"Then enjoy the meeting and don't forget to bring me some fresh flowers."

"Ooh! I love you Sipho, you're the garden that refreshes my mind."

And she suddenly started crying.

"Why are you crying Sipho?"

"I just loved what you said, thank you."

"See you in three hours."

"Bye."

Left alone and without anyone to console her, she watched the growing excitement of the agents from a distance. Their excitement at arresting those she loved so much. Secret agent Siphokazi with her back against the wall and with both hands touching the wall felt sorry for the father of her children. The children who, before having a nice sleep every night, had their father tell them a nice story to make them sleep. But here everyone was ready to silence the biggest dinosaur of them all, her father, and nobody else than her knew that he wasn't around but in Cape Town to rest his mind and body.

Nevertheless, she decided to tell secret agent Dumisane who was just coming towards her to embark.

"I wanted to tell you something," she said.

"Look at yourself Sipho; I won't advise you to come along."

"Listen to this."

"Ok."

"My father isn't around but in Cape-Town. He left two days ago, but everyone else is here."

"Great Sipho but listen you can stay."

"No, I'm coming."

"Are you sure?"

"Yes, Dumi."

"Then let's go."

They both left the corridor to rejoin the rest of their secret agent unit which was mixed with the South African police force. They were all ready to react with brutality and professionalism.

Colonel Themba's hand was behind held by a lady as he drove towards the warehouse in Isando. Every executive of the organization was accompanied by his mistress who usually played the role of a spy for the boss to receive remuneration in exchange for information, and Colonel Themba, through her, managed to forget about the late Nthabiseng's professional attention.

Miss Morefi was elegant with a sharp mind that warned Colonel Themba of the danger that his wife, Siphokazi, could represent. Her determined character made her even spy on Colonel Themba's house while on holiday in the Eastern Cape but found nothing, and the colonel was even surprised about the courage she had and gave her a bonus for such commitment. She had a sneaky unfair advantage and that element brought confidence to the colonel who needed such a corrupt mind that wouldn't think twice about the job that must be done.

They all arrived within minutes of each other at the warehouse whose gate was opened to allow quick access into the compound. The echelon of security was as usual with four heavily armed security guards, for fifteen company executives all ready to commence the meeting, and then after, the party. However, they didn't know that booking a party on that day was a gamble, for the intelligence was not far from the mysterious warehouse.

After parking the cars they all went into the boardroom. Colonel Themba, holding Ms Morefi hand, was going to be the one to lead the meeting in the absence of Malume who travelled to Cape Town. Once inside four other well-armed guards were going to surrender the warehouse to assure hundred per cent security to the executives of Malume (Pty) Ltd.

The sumptuous warehouse had two boardrooms, two-party halls and a swimming pool, but the other spaces were to keep the most valuable goods of the organization ready for distribution.

The secret agents, including Siphokazi were advancing towards the warehouse in a car. Agent Botha was driving, following the South African Police force that was about to reach the warehouse. She could feel her heart beating against her chest for the moment was intense, and the way she knew her

221

husband he would not let the raid happen without defending himself.

They stopped the cars at the gates. Officers carrying Kalashnikovs jumped out of the police car. One of the guards tried to get inside the warehouse, but he was brought to a halt with a hand move indicating not to try to move. So neutralizing them was imperative to avoid any bloodshed for they were going to try to protect their bosses.

"Don't try to move."

Immediately they were surrounded, disarmed and locked in one of the police's vans, however, what was happening outside was already seen inside for there was a team watching every move coming to pass at the main gate.

Without wasting time the police followed by the secret agents, their heads covered with hoods, penetrated the warehouse, but a surprise was waiting for them because the alarm went off causing a general panic. Right away the police called through a loudspeaker to announce their presence and that everyone should admit defeat.

"We are the police and want everyone out of the warehouse with their hands up. We don't want to cause any physical harm."

All the secret agents were in position behind the police force waiting for the right moment to make their move inside the warehouse. They needed to discover what was hidden there that could give them enough proof to cause their immediate imprisonment. One of the four security guards watching from inside managed to escape through the back of the warehouse. Neither the police nor the secret agents, were aware of the existence of the four security guards. But quickly the intelligence made sure to encircle the warehouse to avoid any possible escape.

After unsuccessfully calling for everyone to come out of the warehouse with their hands up, the three secret agents consulted each other for a possible invasion into the warehouse because wasting time could give the cartel the advantage to escape by a means so far unidentified by the agents or the police. Secret agent Dumisane drew near the sergeant with the loud-speaker.

"I believe we need to go inside, they are hiding and we don't know this place."

"I believe it is a good idea, let's do it."

The main entrance was closed and had to be forced, so the police, still followed by the well-armed secret agents, started marching towards the warehouse main gate.

Colonel Themba and the rest of the executives panicked; the moment was grave and not at all at their advantage.

"Why are the police here?" Demanded Colonel Themba leaving his chair.

"There is a traitor among us," said one of the executives already holding his gun.

"You don't have to fight them," said Colonel Themba smoothing down his colonel's uniform, "put your gun where it belongs."

And again they all heard the police speaking through the loud-speaker saying they want everyone with their hands up to avoid casualties.

"We have been betrayed," said one of the executives.

"We need to decide on what to do," said the colonel, "either we surrender or we react aggressively."

"We can't react aggressively, they are going to shoot us. We need to ask them what they want."

"What do they want?" Said one of the executives.

"All our goods are stored here," said the colonel, "they are here to arrest us because they know we're hiding something they want to catch sight of."

"So what do we do Colonel Themba?"

After asking the question the executive pulled his gun out.

"What are you doing?" Demanded another executive.

"Shoot me."

"You cannot do that."

The police heard a powerful explosion coming from within the warehouse, not far from where they were followed by some screams, including women. That frightened secret agent Siphokazi for she knew her husband was with the rest of the executives; so what went wrong?

Walking along the corridor ready to shoot at the first sign of a threat, the police followed by the three secret agents went straight towards a door made of marble. They pushed it open and encountered the biggest shocking truth, for all the executives were holding their guns pointed towards the door and ready to shoot.

The three secret agents with hoods covering their faces tagged along with the police inside the big boardroom, while Siphokazi was alarmed to catch sight of the place with well-dressed women, all laying on the floor trembling like never before together with the body of one of the executives lifeless on the floor in his blood.

"We are not here to harm anyone," said the sergeant with his gun targeting the executives, "And what happened to him?"

"He killed himself because of your infringement," said one of the executives.

"He killed himself because of his guilt," corrected the sergeant.

Siphokazi could read the dread on the executives' faces and she felt remorseful for her husband who was among those holding their guns. Fortunately, he wasn't the one who killed himself.

"What do you want from us?" Demanded the colonel.

"Put your guns down first," said the sergeant between his broken teeth.

"What do you want from us?" Repeated another executive.

"We are the police and here to investigate, put your guns down. I hate repeating myself. I am sergeant Mthethwa of the South African police force."

"Drop your guns," said Colonel Themba to the rest of the executives.

From where she was, secret agent Siphokazi thanked God for the wise decision taken by her husband who she knows as a risk-taker, and able to do anything to save his life. Calmly, they dropped their guns to surrender. Without wasting time the police expropriated all the guns and initiated a thorough search for any illegal good.

Stressed by what was taking place, secret agent Siphokazi followed by Dumisane left the boardroom.

"Are you alright Sipho?"

"It will be okay," she responded worriedly.

"We shouldn't stay here on our own."

"But some of the police force members are outside, and this scene is killing me, I'm moved to see him this way."

"Don't be apologetic for what you did so courageously, you're doing so well, my sister."

"This will be breaking news," she said.

"You did this for a good cause."

Suddenly sergeant Mthethwa left the board room with some police officers. He instructed them to follow him and start searching for the illegal goods.

"They don't want to speak," he said, "But we cannot wait for them, let start searching until we find something to stop their evil ways. And then we can get out of this evil place."

"Ok let's go," said secret agent Dumisane.

Followed by some well-armed members of the South African police force, secret agents Siphokazi and Dumisane followed the spirited, determined sergeant Mthethwa. Secret agent Botha was left with the rest of the police force in the boardroom, keeping an eye on the executives of Malume (Pty) Ltd who were overwhelmed by the circumstances and with their cell phones confiscated by those keeping them hostage.

The strategy had, so far, gone well with only one tragedy caused by the executives themselves with one committing suicide. Going down the stairs with the rest of the intelligence, sergeant Mthethwa and the two secret agents opened a door that took them straight to a big party hall that Sipho had not seen before, and all of that belonged to her father. She was amazed, but at the same time saddened by what was coming about. A big party was going to be held after the big meeting, which explained why the hall was not empty. The catering staff inside started screaming when they saw the police force appearing armed as if they were going to battle.

"Calm down," said secret agent Dumisane, "We won't harm anyone of you if you cooperate, and if you refuse you're all under arrest. Where is the storeroom?"

Everyone kept silent.

"Arrest all of them," said the sergeant.

"No please," said one of the ladies, "we know nothing about this place; we have been hired to do this. We are just a catering company."

"Keep an eye on them," ordered the sergeant to some members of the police force.

After looking around, secret agent Siphokazi saw on the far left of the hall a door locked with a big padlock that created a centre of attention. Without delay she pointed out the door to the rest of the intelligence, so the three leaders walked towards the door at the same time anticipating what might be beyond it.

Of course, the door had a big padlock that needed to be broken, but what to use?

"Let me break it," said secret agent Dumisane holding his gun.

He shot three times but was fruitless.

"We need something stronger," said the sergeant with a sweaty face.

"Like what?" Demanded Siphokazi.

"Bring your AK 47," said the sergeant to one of the elite that was close to them.

The man ordered them to distance themselves from the door, however and shot. The effort paid off for the strong padlock without making any noise fell on the sumptuous fitted carpet. They opened the door but beyond it, darkness was reigning, causing fear and it was accompanied by a funny smell.

"I suppose some science occult practises happened here," said sergeant Mthethwa to the two secret agents whose faces were still covered.

"We need to look for a switch," said Dumisane.

"Look for some switches where you are," commanded the sergeant to the rest of the police force.

Refusing to be ruled by fear the two other leaders watched Sipho taking her cell phone out to put the light on. They all followed the move to see beyond but what they saw were stairs going down like going straight to hell and to by no means come back.

"Any switch on the side," said sergeant Mthethwa perhaps already busy thinking about his wife and children.

"Nothing," said Dumisane after checking. "What do we do? An area like this one could be full of wild rats eating each other."

"Actually what we need to do is to go downstairs with some guys and leave some of them at this point with the rest of the crew."

"Ok, let's go," said Siphokazi sweating inside her hood.

Followed by the two secret agents, the sergeant took four of his men, all carrying AK47s, and started to descend the stairs that were long, worrying and dark like a city without electricity. Practically it was like going too far with one's expectations, and consciously knowing that the Lord is everywhere including down there. But with their cell phones torches, they could all see just what was close to them despite the extreme darkest, perhaps hiding the most precious treasures of the organization.

But time was running out especially when unaware of their opponent's ability to counter-attack the intelligence with a high standard manoeuvre that may neutralize them. Even one of the executives committed suicide to indicate that the warehouse was maybe the most strategic point of the organization.

They suddenly came to a door made of iron and set off the alarm that the executives heard, worrying them to death for the alarm meant getting closer to where their hearts were; their treasures.

"That's it," said secret agent Dumisane.

"Why? This is just a panic alarm," said Sipho.

"Are you sure? We need to go beyond this gate," said Sergeant Mthethwa with his eyes wide open checking on the guys that were a few centimetres away from him.

"Maybe this path is taking us straight to a lion cage."

"Come on Siphokazi," said Dumisane, "let me check for a switch, maybe there is one."

"Please do," said the sergeant sweating and shining in the dark.

With the help of their cell phones torches, the trio followed by the well-armed policemen tried to see through the iron doors' spaces if the stairs were still going down, and the good news was they weren't for the area seemed flat. Immediately secret agent Dumisane passed his right hand on the side of the door in search of a switch to put on the light to make the darkness disappear, but it was unproductive.

"We don't have the whole day," said sergeant Mthethwa; "We must break the lock, let's move back to allow the guys to shoot."

And again they all moved back to allow the four elites to shoot and break the powerful padlock, and once the shooting began it created again another threat to all those who were in the warehouse including all the executives who were with secret agent Botha hard-working watching on them.

The strong impact of the AK's 47 bullets broke in pieces what seemed to be the strongest padlock used by the company, and that allowed them to enter the flat area, but there was still no switch to put on the light. Surely the switch was somewhere but purposely made difficult to find.

Colonel Themba was sweating, his eyes fixed on secret agent Botha who was with well-armed members of the South African Police force. The boardroom was silent with the sad view of the executive who killed himself. He was laid on the floor with a vest covering his upper body, and the ladies could not stop weeping.

"At least allow these ladies to leave the premises," said the colonel with a trembling voice for he was very nervous.

"We will, only if those checking on the warehouse come back with some news," said secret agent Botha.

"Why are you after us?" Demanded the colonel.

"Remember we are the police, and what is suspicious is a focus for us."

"Are you a secret agent?"

"Why do you want to know? Is it important to you?"

"But why some of you are covering their faces, it means they are undercover right? Maybe we know you."

Secret agent Botha tightened his mouth and then said, "Shut up, I don't have to answer you."

Out of the blue, the colonel aimed a firearm at the police while amid the other executives who panicked to see such bravery, but it was downright stupidity for the police aimed their AK's 47 at him causing total insecurity.

"You don't have to do that, Colonel," said one of the executives.

"This is committing suicide, Colonel," said Botha very calmly where he was, for he knew he could not escape.

"You let me go or I shoot myself as one of us already did."

Secret agent Botha kindly smiled at him and said, "Killing yourself, Colonel, won't help your wife and kids."

"I don't give a damn."

While talking to persuade the South African police force, secret agent Botha had enough time to shoot one bullet that broke the bone of Colonel Themba's right shoulder. Screaming in pain he went straight down on the floor trying to stop the blood that was coming out. While the colonel was swearing at them with all his strength, some of the ladies went to his rescue to see what they could do to help him.

"Next time we will shoot to kill," said secret agent Botha content to have reached the right target.

What a difficult task it was for they were in an area without a switch around to set up lighting, and with wild rats surely running all directions, the force hoped for the next discovery to be the breakthrough, and the thought of betraying her family was constantly visiting Siphokazi.

"Do you see anything?" Demanded secret agent Siphokazi.

"What we need is more lights," said Dumisane. "One of us should go back up there and get something that can help us to see more for I judge we are at the right place."

"Ok, I'm taking one of the guys upstairs," said Siphokazi.

"Great Sipho!"

Going back upstairs was quick but worrying for those held hostage by the police were terrorized by what was happening.

"I need help, do you have candles or torches," said secret agent Siphokazi to the frightened warehouse labour force.

And one of them lifted her hand.

"Where are they?" She asked.

"In the kitchen," she said.

"Where is the kitchen lady? We don't have time to waste."

"Let me take you there," she said trembling.

Secret agent Sipho took with her three members of the police force and followed the maid.

"You don't have to be afraid like this," she said to keep her under control.

The kitchen was similar to a restaurant one with almost everything inside, and what she was looking for was not difficult to find. She managed to obtain three torches with batteries inside of them, which she immediately took down after testing their functionality, and they were in good condition.

Chapter 15

Left behind with the three well-armed policemen, secret agent Dumisane and sergeant Mthethwa saw someone from the stairs coming down with what seemed to be some torches. And they knew it was secret agent Siphokazi coming back with some good news for they were two minutes away from discovering what the warehouse was hiding. But he had no good news to tell her for after she left secret agent Botha phoned to let him know about the incident that took place with the colonel, however, he was only going to let her know once the operation was finished. He didn't want to cause any discouragement right now.

"Finally, we have what can help us to see well," she said.

"You did well young lady," said the sergeant.

She kept one for herself and gave the rest to her colleagues, and the systematic search went on. The space was big with wooden cases spread all over the place on pallets. The trio, followed by the four well-armed policemen went after them determined to stop the illegal activity.

"I believe this place is full of poisonous wild rats," said the sergeant.

"I prefer them to venomous snakes," said Dumisane.

"Would you stop?" ordered Siphokazi while busy violating her father's trust.

They all went straight towards the nearest case to try and open it to see what was inside, and after opening them the surprise was discouraging because it was full of cutlery.

"What is it?" Said the sergeant with disdain.

"I'm not surprised to see this here guys," said secret agent Siphokazi, "this place is not far from the restaurant."

"But why make it scary to get here?" Demanded Dumisane.

"Because they are hiding something," whispered the sergeant.

"Then let's walk further down," said Siphokazi.

With courage and determination, with the help of torches, the mysterious warehouse began exposing what appeared to be very interesting to the trio. Many metal cases were superimposed with many statues nearby, hence what was inside those statues? They were beautiful to behold and have in one's house.

"Let not rush opening them, they could be explosive."

"You're right sergeant," said Dumisane.

"What do we do then?" Whispered Siphokazi.

A simple gesture of both hands by the sergeant brought the three well-armed policemen to come close to the statues, verifying if any dangerous device of detonation was present. After checking them for a while they indicated with the thumb that there was no sign of a dangerous device that could detonate. So without dragging their feet they broke some statues that were there to discover, without surprise, that they were all full of drugs.

"There we go," said secret agent Dumisane.

"Fantastic," said the sergeant with a strong voice proportional to his stature.

Secret agent Siphokazi remained calm and saddened. Everything from now on was going to change starting with her life, for no husband for a very long time was going to hold her in his arms, as well as a father to play with her beautiful children. They all had to get used to loneliness after betraying her family and especially her children who were going to complain about the sudden disappearance of their father.

"I found precious stones in this statue," said the sergeant.

"Precious stones," she asked surprised.

"They look like diamonds, maybe fake diamonds."

She struggled to open one of the cases but then one of the policemen joined her and broke the padlock with the butt of his firearm; and what she unearthed was more interesting because the case was full of the South African local currency; the Rand.

"Oh my God!" She exclaimed.

"What is it?" Demanded secret agent Dumisane.

"These cases are full of money; I believe fake money," she said.

"Ok, well-done team," said sergeant Mthethwa. "Let's arrest all of them since we have enough proof against them. Let's call more force members to encircle this warehouse and thoroughly check this place of darkness, I'm sure what we have already seen is nothing but more than enough to lock them for many years."

"I agree with you," said secret agent Siphokazi.

Following the three well-armed policemen, the trio, full of excitement maybe except Siphokazi, went out of the darkness, to the direction of the board room where secret agent Botha was with the rest of the executives. But before arriving there secret agent Dumisane took care to let his colleague know about what transpired with her husband.

"But I have something to tell you, Siphokazi."

"What is wrong?" She asked panicking.

"Colonel Themba tried to flee and he got shot in the right shoulder."

She stopped walking and covered her mouth with her hands.

"But he is alive, sorry my dear."

"I'm finished."

"I already told you to be strong."

"Please take them without me, I don't want to see them, I'm going outside."

Feeling despondent, secret agent Siphokazi with her hood hiding her tears of a lonely woman witnessed those millionaires being taken away from what they cherished more than their spouses and children. Colonel Themba among them and with a bandage around his right shoulder didn't know that his beloved wife was amid the merciless assailants ending the existence of one of the most profitable businesses in the Republic of South Africa.

Driving into his luxurious mansion in Cape-Town, Malume parked his car in the garage followed by his three bodyguards who parked their car outside but in the compound. He enjoyed driving in the Cape, allowing himself some freedom he didn't have in Johannesburg. Most of the time coming to Cape-Town was to relax with the company of his beloved wife Helena; who he loved so much. She was the love of his life and could never be matched with any other woman. Consulting her after a hard day was always the best decision to take to bring peace in his being; she was the helper that the Holy Scripture was talking about.

Today was the day she had to join him in the Cape, and he knew she was waiting for him with the best reception ever experienced in his life because she was committed to welcoming him with her best smile. They met fifty years ago in Cape-Town while he was working as a bus driver, and remembering those moments about their youth was extraordinary and irreplaceable. She was beautiful like a flower that has just flourished, and he always made sure to be the driver taking her to her restaurant job at the waterfront, hence whenever she entered the bus he made sure to express his best smile whilst helping her to climb onto the bus, and she noticed with much enchantment that this gentleman was in love and ready to say it loud.

Yes, it wasn't long after that they started dating when he dared to invite her to the movies, and she accepted with the same smile she has to this day. On that particular date, he dared hold her hands with affection, at the same time commenting on how beautiful her fingers were.

However, she wasn't there when he entered the lounge and the kitchen. Where was she for he missed her company? He decided not to call her and went upstairs where the bedrooms were, and he finally found her sitting on the bed weeping with both hands covering her mouth.

"Helena!" He called. "What is wrong?"

"Ooh, you are here!"

"Why are you crying? Come on I've travelled safe, I'm here."

"Helena stood up and came to hug him."

"I didn't want you to find me in this state, but you need to watch the news, please sit down."

Helena put the TV on and went straight to the news channel that was still showing the breaking news about the arrest of all Malume (Pty) Ltd executives.

"What is this?"

Immediately he fell on the floor and lost consciousness.

"Malume!" She screamed at the same time.

The bodyguards that were outside heard the screams and immediately came upstairs to Malume and Helena.

"Please let me take him to the hospital, quick."

Walking through the corridors of the Johannesburg general hospital where her husband colonel Themba was hospitalized, secret agent Siphokazi thanked God he was still alive. He had been transferred to casualty under high surveillance with the police watching him twenty-four hours a day. When she entered the casualty, there were many beds on both sides and while walking in the middle, she finally identified one of the policemen standing beside the bed where her husband was lying.

Getting closer was even more difficult for she was the mastermind behind the casualty, and when he saw her he smiled at her.

"Finally, Siphokazi," he said with a dry mouth.

"I am his wife," she said addressing the policeman with some tears going down her face. "How are you? I heard what happened."

"I am so sorry, Sipho. I should have understood that when Tasha suddenly disappeared. Besides, you warned me many times."

"Just know that we love you, I don't know what to say Themba."

"I couldn't call you because they confiscated all the cell phones."

"Don't worry it will be fine."

"I won't be around for a very long time but know that I love you; I'm truly sorry to have hurt you with the children this way," Siphokazi witnessed some tears coming out of his eyes.

She hugged him with all her strength and left.

"Sipho," he called.

She turned around with endless tears going down her face.

"Don't forget to come to court with my children."

"I will, Themba."

With her children in front of her TV set secret agent, Siphokazi couldn't grow weary of watching the same breaking news about the arrest of Malume's executives. What a sad day it was without a way to turn back the hands of time. The dice were cast and the sentence had to be pronounced against what she dreamed her marriage had to look like, but the fierce opposite was real and heartbreaking.

Suddenly her phone rang and when checking it was her mother calling her.

"Hello mum!" she answered.

"Are you watching the news, my daughter? What happened? I'm here in Cape-Town at the hospital with your father who has collapsed after watching the news, come I can't handle this alone."

"Ooh my God! I'm going to the airport right now."

"Please come."

"I'm on my way, please remain strong."

"What's wrong mum?" Her son Ntombisi asked as he saw her sad face.

"Grandpa is sick my son; I have to go to Cape Town, stay well with the nanny."

Her nanny was there with her daughter in her arms.

"I must travel to Cape Town now and I hope to be back tomorrow night, please stay well with the kids."

"Don't worry madam, everything will be fine."

"Thank you."

"Drive safe madam."

"Thank you."

South African Airways were about to take off to Cape Town for what seemed to be another very difficult chapter to live through in her life. What was coming upon her was the result of her faithfulness towards her government and especially towards God. After the security procedures, they were already flying towards the country's tourist capital, for the province was one of the most beautiful, welcoming most of the tourists visiting the Republic of South Africa.

But she was not this time heading there to enjoy the landscapes or scenery, but to take care of her father devastated by the terrible news of the arrest of his executives, and she understood she had to face the dilemma with courage and bravery, for this was part of the damage that was caused by her action to stop forever the evils done by her family members. Yes, it was a complex decision that made her cry every day of her life until the day the arrest came to life, however she had always been ready to face the consequences.

Her government expected so much from her and to fail to bring good results would have cost her the reputation built. Deep inside of her existed a hidden great joy of accomplishing what she aimed for; she wanted her husband to die the way a man of integrity should die and not in the street with a bullet in his stomach for the reason that he was found violating the law.

Two hours later outside Cape-Town International Airport, secret agent Siphokazi with her P38 pistol hidden in her vest, ready for the unexpected, took a taxi straight to the hospital where Malume was. She was acquainted with how dangerous a heart attack at that old age was for her beloved father that she ashamedly betrayed. She was diffident at the beginning for it was just too much to carry the weight at the same time with the pregnancy that she undeniably wanted to protect.

The city of Cape-Town was hot and windy on that day, and the taxi driver, knowing where he was going, understood after checking his rear-view mirror that the woman he was transporting was stressed out and out of ideas. To encourage her he finally said, "Everything will be fine madam."

"Thank you," responded secret agent Siphokazi using a kind smile. "Essentially, I'm going to check on my father who is ill."

"They become fragile at that old age," he said sympathizing.

"Yes, he is old but full of life and I don't want to think about the worst. Are we still far?"

"Five minutes. We won't be long.

"Thank you, what is your name?"

"Ashraf."

"Thank you, Ashraf, for your kind talk; I will double your fare," she said to encourage him.

"Thank you, madam, that's why I like carrying Jozi customers."

She smiled nicely at the driver while paying him double, went out of the taxi, and went into the highly equipped hospital of the Cape; With a heavy heart, she approached the receptionist who welcomed her with a good smile of encouragement.

"What can I do for you madam?"

"I'm here to see my father Mr Nhlakanipho."

"Ok let me check, yes Malume, he's your father? We have known him for many years for his check-up at this hospital."

"Yes, he is my father."

"It is nice meeting you. He is on the first-floor room number eight."

"Thank you very much."

"You're welcome."

Going inside the room was painful. Her mother, Helena, was sitting by his side with a face full of tears, while Malume breathing with the help of a mechanical ventilator had his eyes on his wife as if he was busy telling her goodbye. She was still beautiful in his eyes like the first time they met and that also provoked more cries Surprisingly her big brother, Bongani, had just arrived and was standing behind her.

"Dad," she called, "What happened?"

"Sipho my daughter, thank you for coming as quickly as possible. Thank you, my son."

"How is dad, Mum?"

"He's very tired, your father is dying," and she added making sure that Malume didn't hear.

"Was it a heart attack?" Bongani asked.

"Yes, it was; I'm sure he wants to talk to you, come closer."

And when Siphokazi got nearer, he whispered, "Why did Tasha betray me, my daughter?"

"I don't know, Dad," she responded weeping.

"She killed me. Bongani you must take care of your mother."

"I will, Dad."

And suddenly, he breathed his last.

"Malume!" Helena called, "Your father is dead."

"Dad!" But it was too late.

Crying like never previously, the agony of losing a dear husband and father was an ordeal that she could not avoid turning away from. It was the end of destiny that many wouldn't wish to be subjected to; and in each other's arms and encouraging their mother that despite all she went through, being the wife of the great Mafiosi and remained faithful to him until his death.

The following day and still in Cape-Town busy with the arrangements of the burial, the family was waiting for the papers to take the body back to Johannesburg. One of his wishes was to be buried in Thembisa Township, in Ekurhuleni east of Johannesburg where he buried his parents and grew up until the age of thirty-two. Besides, it was the custom of the family to be buried in the Thembisa Township.

It was a silent house full of sadness with just the falling of Malume's empire to praise. But it was time to pay tribute to the first man she ever loved in her life, her father who spent a great deal building a successful group of companies that fed so many families. But now that the outlook of Malume (Pty) Ltd seemed gloomy. Many were going to grind their teeth in fear of desolation, and many had already seen that all the executives of the company were under arrest.

What went wrong, my daughter?

"Mum, my assistant Tasha who was working for Malume when I joined the company a week ago, all of a sudden disappeared. She's still missing as I'm speaking to you.

"I know Tasha very well, meaning she was used by the police."

"Yes mother and I'm sure they will use her as a witness against the family, do you see where we are going now? My husband is arrested and dad is dead, and all of that is because of greed."

"I knew this was going to happen one day with one of us scheming against us, and you see your dad could not take it."

Suddenly Bongani entered the living room with some documents received from the undertaker.

"Everything is all set up to take the body to Johannesburg."

"Thank you Bongani," said their mother.

"We have to be a resilient family for many problems are waiting for us in Johannesburg, think about the trial."

"Are you going to be there my son? I need all of you by my side if not I won't take it."

"This is the consequence, Mum, of your faithfulness towards dad and the whole family, please be strong."

"I loved your father."

"We understand, Mum, and we cannot blame you for that," said Bongani.

Remaining composed, secret agent Siphokazi while taking notice of her mother talking, wondered if she was going to reach the stage of mourning her beloved husband's death. She was not up to her mother's resiliency to handle the character of such a man that was her father for so many years as she did. He was a mighty man, manipulating everyone on his way and only thought about his riches. He was also the one who manipulated the man of her life, Colonel Themba, who was about to spend many years in prison for betraying his government and the nation.

"Themba!" screamed the man as he leapt at the colonel in his cell. It was all the warning Colonel Themba needed as he dodged the boot of the man aimed at his heavily bandaged shoulder. With his good arm, he smacked the man in the back of his head, using his own momentum to speed the man towards the wall. The man's head made a dull thwack as his skull hit bricks.

"You'll pay for that," the man stared unblinking at Themba as blood seeped down from the wound in his head. The man pulled a shiv from his pocket and swung. The homemade blade whooshed through the air as Themba swayed backwards and collided into his bunkbed. Swoosh again as the man again swung for Themba's jugular. Themba raised his good arm to block the blow, the shiv cut into his forearm as he did so.

"Aagh!" Themba cried with pain as he grabbed the man around the throat using his bad arm. The pain from the bullet wound thumped through his body, but Themba ignored the pain. He headbutted the man in one swift motion, his forehead connecting squarely against the man's nose.

Blood gushed down, covering the man's t-shirt as he collapsed on the floor. Themba stood on the man's fingers until he heard the crunch of bone and the man dropped the shiv.

"Get out!" ordered Themba. "And tell whoever sent you they'll suffer the same as you if anyone tries that again."

The man crawled from the cell and ran away, leaving a trail of blood on the concrete floor.

Once in Johannesburg driving on the roads of Thembisa Townships with Malume's body, a very long cortege procession was following the hearse going towards his last dwelling place. The funeral director had accomplished an exceptional job to carry the body until Johannesburg, and he was now busy with the last stage of the funeral. Most of the family members were there to pay tribute to the Malume of the family.

Throwing the last flowers on the coffin already inside the grave, Helena with her children and grandchildren was helped by her firstborn son who was taking her everywhere with secret agent Siphokazi by her side. She never meant to cause the death of her father, only the illegal business, and she couldn't prevent such a tragedy to occur in the family because of her betrayal.

She in no way regretted to have faithfully worked for her government, except to have a long time ago lost a husband and a father. Her marriage ceased existing the day she discovered her husband was amongst the most dangerous men in the city, and that her father was the mastermind behind it. They both were the cause of what was happening to them, one buried and the other jailed, and there was no need to express regret to have worked faithfully for her government, excluding losing the men she loved the most. It was painful and mourning the loss of her father who had such a brilliant mind, was worth it.

So she had to take it easy, and her mother had to do the same to stay alive and move on with her life, for the wages of sin is death, although she would never forgive her from the day she would discover that her beloved daughter was the cause of her becoming a widow today. She still loved her husband with all her heart, and only death could separate them. The early passing away was caused by a daughter she carried nine months in her womb.

When will she get the chance to unwind for going to court was waiting for them, and especially her? Going and meeting her husband in jail was also ahead of her. She was bound to that up to the neck and could do with the strength to trample on

247

them, if not she was going to get depressed. But now she was the remnant of the Malume (Pty) Ltd, the number one executive of the not-for-profit organization she inherited from her father. As he promised her, he confirmed in writing with his signature and the official stamp of the company, which still had to be verified from her e-mail inbox.

Seated in front of her husband at the police station, secret agent Siphokazi was crying whilst explaining the whole situation to Colonel Themba who was attentively listening.

"So Malume died of a heart attack without me present at his funeral? Why like this? I hate Tasha, she betrayed us."

"How has your wound been since the last time I saw you in the hospital?"

"I'm better and please stop crying," he said passing his right hand on his face.

"How do you expect me to stop crying when at the same time my husband is jailed, and my father is buried?"

"I should have listened to you, Sipho; I am still so sorry for all the sorrows I have caused you, the kids; I've been so selfish. Please take care of yourself and my children. Maybe I will spend the rest of my life in jail; perhaps I will die in jail killed by my enemies."

"Don't talk like that, Themba. Have faith."

"Faith!" He sighed after saying that.

With his eyes deep in hers, he caressed her cheeks and grasped it will never be the same again, other than a passing that will haunt him forever and finally slay him.

"When do we appear in court?"

"They will let us know very soon, meanwhile know that we are there for you, your children love you and expect to see them again."

"I'm already thinking about all those who would like to make you their wives."

"I will remain the woman that you know, I still love Themba."

One policeman entered the room and interrupted their conversation.

"The time is up, you can leave now."

"Goodbye Sipho," he said letting her hand go.

"Bye, see you very soon."

The following day in the offices of Malume (Pty) Ltd, secret agent Siphokazi was busy checking her e-mail when she saw her father's nomination letter. The establishment was quiet and a restructure, as quickly as possible had to take place because all the executives and most of the company's activities were suspended. She needed someone like Tasha to assist in such a very difficult time so she had to assemble all the personnel and talk to them. She was thinking of gathering all the general managers of the organization; the internal auditors and accountants to see how to get hold of the balance sheet to find out the organization's financial position.

The treasurer of the organization was among the executives arrested, and one of the most important persons was the C.E.O who was no longer alive, Mr Nhlakanipho. So without delay, she went to her father's office to talk to his assistant who was there.

"Good morning, Siphokazi," greeted the personal assistant.

"Good morning, Lindiwe, how are you?"

"I am fine thank you, and you?"

"I'm coping," she said. "I would like you to drop an e-mail to all the managers including those who are not with us here for I have something to say to all of them. I need everyone ready in thirty minutes."

"Ok, teleconferencing for everyone?"

"No for those with us here, let's meet in the main boardroom."

"Ok, let me do that right away."

Siphokazi left pensively. She was looking at how to calm the situation down as many were already thinking about their uncertain future with the organization. The arrest of all executives, including Tasha, couldn't facilitate her to understand what the organization was all about, especially its sources of revenues. But the truth had to be communicated to avoid another betrayal from her side for the employees could come together and sue the organization for misrepresentation and financial loss; so she had to address it, short and snappy and make sure that the truth is told.

Another thing was she began to strongly miss church, and even at the funeral, she avoided the presence of the members of their assembly and even the pastoral couple Thabiso and Tshepang because of the humiliation she felt.

She truly needed a new beginning and be able to put all she went through behind her and move on with her life. She was fed up and ready to start a new life with no father and husband to disappoint her all over again. Then someone knocked at the door.

"Come in."

"Everyone is there in the boardroom."

"Please come with me."

Well dressed and full of confidence the state secret agent entered the boardroom where all the remaining top managers were waiting for her including those of other branches in Gauteng and other provinces.

"I greet you all," she said sitting down.

Lindiwe came and sat just behind her for there was a place for her behind the C.E.O's seat to take notes or remind her of anything.

"As you know we buried Malume last week and the company is in a very precarious position with all the executives arrested, except me as you can see. I was not with them because I'm dealing with another section of Malume (Pty) Ltd; which is the not for profit organization. Very soon all of them including my husband will appear in the high court since our company is accused of practising illegitimate activities, and I assure you my heart is broken, however speaking to you now is the best option. They are very serious allegations that can cost us a lot if they are proven correct. So let's pray that we don't lose everything. Just continue your jobs as usual until further notice. Thank you very much and please I need to know about the financial position of the company? So I need the chief financial officer with your team to work on it."

And after smiling at them she said, "That's all for the moment I had to tell you so you're dismissed, and thanks for being here."

Left alone in her office, secret agent Siphokazi realized she had too much in her hands to handle, as a result, she had to quit her governmental obligations and focus on her family that needed her support. And what about all these employees who were about to lose their jobs? She also had to look after her mother who was devastated by the sudden death of her husband, consequently leaving her alone for too long wasn't going to be the right thing to do.

Late in the afternoon, driving on the streets of Edenvale, secret agent Siphokazi was speeding to meet the pastoral couple, who were unaware of her visit, but aware of what happened to the family because they were present at the funeral. Sipho was too ashamed to entertain their presence at the funeral and hid in the crowd. She needed spiritual guidance to be strong, and she knew where to go for assistance to alleviate the soreness caused by the abrupt death of her father as well as the arrest of her beloved husband, who she handed over to the police.

When she entered the pastoral office, Pastor Tshepang alone in the office saw the anguish that her daughter in the Lord's face could not hide.

"Come and sit down, sister Siphokazi."

She fell back on the seat, shocked by what she had caused to the family that she had lived with during all her life.

"My deep condolences said the Pastor."

"Thank you Pastor Tshepang. I don't know if I will handle this."

"Do you remember we told you to be very strong? Remember what God said to Joshua. You could not possibly pull off this by your might."

And she began weeping.

"Will God forgive me, Pastor? I have been disloyal to my family and they don't know that."

"But you did that in all conscience and that was part of your job my daughter. Yes, your father died in the process, but what he was doing harmed the country and mostly his family."

"I loved him so much Pastor Tshepang, I never meant to cause him so much trouble up to dying and leaving my mother a widow."

Hugging her with all her strength, Pastor Tshepang realized she needed counselling and follow up to overcome such a tragedy, principally the passing away of her father as she was the cause of his death.

"You need to give your word to me Siphokazi; hold on and trust God as always, you don't open up a door to the devil to engender guilt in you, I believe as your Pastor you did the right thing before God. You had to make a judgment to pursue the destiny that God has put ahead of you."

"Thank you, but I didn't know it was going to be painful."

"Sister Siphokazi, be strong in the Lord."

"I will do my best Pastor."

"Keep on praying and you'll be strong like never before."

"Please pass my greetings to Pastor Thabiso."

"Yes, I will he has a meeting with the leadership of the church, and please come to church as it used to be, we want to see you every Sunday."

"I will Pastor Tshepang."
They hugged and she left.

Chapter 16

The courtroom was full of people and once more another very difficult day secret agent Siphokazi had to overcome to move on with her life alongside her children. The courtroom was noisy with many people curious to see how South African justice was going to handle the perpetrators of very serious offences. What the government needed was enough proof and they had much for the mysterious warehouse contained what could keep the executives incarcerated for many years and shut down the business.

After all, it was a great victory for the country, and secret agent Siphokazi was about to secretly receive one of the greatest rewards awarded to knowledgeable civil servants of the Republic of South Africa. She requested the ceremony to happen secretly without any television coverage or any picture taken except by someone she trusts who will take some for her records.

The day had been hot and already long. The crowd were in a hurry to see what many couldn't believe see happening one day. The cartel was powerful and merciless and had plotted a lot against many important governmental personalities to weaken the state and trample on it. The killing also was a machine used to intimidate their opponents and make sure that any competition is neutralized.

Malume (Pty) Ltd was a menacing machine able to subdue the most influential government strategy as they knew who their number one enemy was, because Colonel Themba played the role of the informer because he was involved in most of the government strategic meetings. If he was absent from the meetings then he had some of his colleagues let him know about the way forward, however, he was present in those strategic meetings most of the time. The intelligence, of course, could not understand why there was a leak and where that leak was coming from, and that was why the need came about to check on the participants and discover where that leak was coming from.

Once Themba was discovered as the leak and also having Mr Nhlakanipho as his father-in-law, quick and embarrassing actions were considered by the intelligence on how to end the evil party that started a long time ago. The intelligence, after noticing that their secret agent Siphokazi was part of Malume's family, thoroughly checked on her conduct and approached her once they were satisfied that she wasn't involved in her father's fraudulent goings-on and that she knew how to help.

Of course, the terrible embarrassment was initiated not in favour of Siphokazi for the intelligence was determined to make use of her and bring an end to what has caused so much damage to many including the government.

Suddenly people started speaking less; something very painful to her soul was about to come to pass with the prisoners appearing in court. She couldn't stop some tears going down her slightly made-up face. After all, she still wanted her husband to notice how beautiful she was, and she also wanted him to know that she still loved him despite the humiliation caused to the whole family. And she was all by herself without brother or sister. Even her mother couldn't make it. Her mother-in-law sat beside her crying interminably.

Dressed like already convicted prisoners, secret agent Siphokazi and her mother-in-law saw what was unavoidable to witness on that day. Ninety per cent of the company executives appeared in court on that day like a bad dream that will never end. The court was also full because their family members were curious to hear from the judge. They knew they couldn't escape many years in prison. And while standing in front of the crowd but with their backs to secret agent Siphokazi, her husband turned around to look at her eyes that were full of tears that he was unable to wipe away.

He caught sight of her attractiveness and was full of remorse that he couldn't resolve, and by the way she was looking at him with her beautiful eyes full of tears, discovering how much she cared about him, and he knew that she still loved him despite the humiliation.

Suddenly a strong voice ordered everyone to stand up for the judge was making his entry in the courtroom.

"All rise."

And after the judge sat, everyone else sat down, except for the prisoners who were ordered not to sit down. The judge was a well-disciplined and experienced civil servant that Siphokazi knew very well that no one could doubt. Siphokazi thought that surely the executives also knew him as the strictest of judges currently working in the Republic of South Africa.

While in her bedroom of the big house, Helena was alone pacing around the room touching every place Malume used to attend to, and she was at the same time talking but to someone who was already beyond the natural realm. Her dedicated maid, faithful to her for many years, was regularly watching her behaviour, making also sure to encourage her.

"Please, mama, don't do that to yourself."

"I will be fine Maupa, I need to do this to finally realize that I'm talking to myself, he is gone."

And calmly Maupa her servant made sure to take her with her in the kitchen, where she was busy cooking.

"Bongani phoned and he is on his way to see you, and he tried to talk to you but you didn't respond. Where is your phone madam?"

"Truly he tried?"

"He is coming."

"Thank you Maupa."

Everyone in the courtroom was waiting for the witness that secret agent Siphokazi knew would appear. She had orchestrated her arrest and knew she was the key to putting all the executives in prison. For many years she had been the personal assistant of Mr Malume, and she just needed to confirm to the court everything she knew about the company and the warehouse that was full of illegal goods.

Besides what was found in the warehouse in their possession was more than enough to prove their guilt. The truth was that it was all over for the executives for no advocates could defend them successfully, it was a closed case finally won by the government.

Tasha, well dressed and ready to enter the courtroom, was standing beside secret agent Botha who was about to take her to the witness stand. Well-armed police escorted them. What she was about to confess was going to alleviate many years that she could have spent in prison and perhaps even die there. She knew what was waiting for her once out of her cell, meeting those executives that had cherished her for many years in the positive reception of her faithful service.

But they were all going to be surprised by such a betrayal, which they hadn't seen coming, and they will also identify with the end of the road for the Malume Empire because Tasha was the daughter of the business, she grew up and completed her masters degree in business administration while working for the company, and it was the corporation that financed her studies.

The courtroom was warm and with a tense atmosphere. It was full of family members waiting for the only witness to appear in court. All the secret agents involved in the arrest of the executives preferred not to play the role of a potential witness. To them, Tasha was enough to prove their wrongdoing and keep them in jail for many years.

Colonel Themba and the rest of the executives had their hearts beating against their chests like never before. Who was the only witness that could prove the existence of illegal activities within Malume (Pty) Ltd? Of course, the police because they saw everything, and that was more than enough to lock them up, but who could come and prove that really what the police saw in the warehouse truly belonged to the empire? Again the colonel turned around and quickly looked at his wife Siphokazi sited beside a crying mother who already felt the end of everything for his son.

Opening statements were read by both the prosecution and the defence. The defence lawyers were the best that money could buy and wore expensive suits. The prosecution called their first witness. who entered from the main door. The executives could not see her until she reached the front of the courtroom where she stood up facing the judge. Botha took her to the witness stand where she sat beside the judge, almost in front of all the executives. All the executives looked at each other, and then looked down so surprised and disappointed by what they couldn't accept as true.

With effort, Tasha looked at all of them with tears running down her face saying, "I'm sorry, I'm sorry."

And when she spoke all the executives looked at her stunned. Themba finally realised who had betrayed them

"Silence!" Said the court speaker.

And all the executives looked down, not knowing what to do, and again colonel Themba turned around to look at his wife who was wiping off tears that were filling up her eyes.

"What is your name, young lady?" Asked the counsel for the prosecution.

"Tasha."

"Speak now, what do you know about these people? Let me say it so that no time is wasted. Are you confirming that all the illegal goods found at the Isando warehouse belong to Malume (Pty) Ltd and that you know all those executives? Respond by yes or no."

Before responding she looked at all of them for she liked them, they had always been nice to her.

"Yes!"

The whole court murmured, nothing could save the executives.

I'm saying this because I've been the personal assistant of Mr Nhlakanipho, the president of the company for more than twenty years. All those goods were delivered with me taking good note of them. I'm sorry," she said to the executives again.

"You betrayed us," said one of the executives, violently.

"Silence in my court," said the judge to the executives.

"I'm sorry," she repeated herself.

The trial continued for two weeks as experts on forgeries, drug shipments, intelligence officers, money laundering, forensic accountants and even the catering staff at the warehouse and more were brought to the stand and interrogated by the prosecution and then by the defence. Each day, Siphokazi went to court and watched her husband become increasingly despondent with every piece of evidence that was presented.

"Ladies and gentlemen of the jury," the prosecutor began his summing up. "You have heard the evidence of many people, including a trusted assistant of Malume (Pty) Ltd. You have heard what was found on the premises of Malume (Pty) Ltd, drugs, fake South African notes, diamonds and gold without a license to possess them. You have heard first-hand accounts from police officers on the scene," said the prosecutor who paused and decided to drink a portion of his glass of water on his desk. "It's up to you to find these men guilty and rid South Africans of these horrible people."

The defence summed up their position, but as they spoke of the "fine upstanding men of honour and decency being framed," Siphokazi could see the stony faces of the jury.

The jury deliberated for less than two hours before coming back out into the courtroom.

"Members of the jury, have you reached a decision on which you all agree?"

"Yes, your honour," said the foreman of the jury. "We find the defendants guilty of all charges."

The courtroom was filled with voices, some happy, some sad. One of the executives started to cry.

"Silence in court," the judge called. He thanked the jury and dismissed them and turned his attention to the hushed courtroom. All family members were present, for they were all anticipating the judge's final decision.

"Because of their involvement in illicit activities forbidden by the South African constitution and considering the severity of the act, the convicted will spend a period of twenty-five years in prison. As for you Tasha; and for your help to our government and your community, your sentence will be of five years in prison. The court is dismissed."

Crying for losing five years of her existence, Tasha with the rest of the convicted left the courtroom unable to say a proper goodbye to their family members, who were busy crying while watching their loved ones being escorted to jail by the police. Secret agent Siphokazi worried and holding her mother-in-law, observed her husband being taken far from the liberty he used to get pleasure from with all his heart.

The following day on the premises of the South African Defence Force, secret agent Siphokazi stood beside secret agents Botha and Dumisane, who were being awarded the South African prize of excellent service to the nation. It was secretly done without coverage for the risk was too high to be uncovered by the enemies of the state. Retaliation was not to be ruled out by those who felt betrayed by those they trusted.

It was a great moment for the three secret agents for the medals and brevets were handed over to them by the commissioner of the police, himself and in the presence of the vice president of the republic.

"You've made it Sipho," said Dumisane.

"Under very difficult conditions," she said with a sad face.

"You're a soldier and a soldier must fight without bias for his nation," said Botha.

"He's right, Sipho."

"I want to forget this chapter of my life but I just can't; I have to live with it."

"That's what you wanted Sipho," said secret agent Dumisane. "What are you going to do now?"

"I'm leaving the force to take care of my father's NGO's, they are all clean."

"I understand but watch and pray. And we can still spend some time together."

"That's kind of you Dumisane, but I would like to spend a while alone until everything comes back to normal, moreover, my children are already asking after their father, and I need to find a way to convince them that he is coming back soon. They are still too young to understand."

"Of course, they are."

"I will drop my resignation on Keegan's desk tomorrow morning."

"Are you sure?"

"Yes, I am Dumi, you've been so kind to me you know. Thank you, Botha."

And she left after hugging them.

"Bye," she said.

"I will call you."

"Do so."

One week later inside the family premises in Roodepoort Helena was feeling better and seemed to have decided to walk in the right direction along with her family. She was better since her firstborn Bongani came from Cape Town. She needed her son's presence more than anything else, and on that particular day, all her five children came to pay her a warm visit that made her so happy. After all, they all wanted to know what was left of their father's inheritance to take care of and Siphokazi was already busy telling them about the remnants of Malume (Pty) Ltd.

"Essentially, nothing from Malume (Pty) Ltd will be left except for his five hotels."

"Why?" Asked Bongani.

"Because there was tax-evasion and we don't know how much it is, and the government the way I know it, will start with the administrative building."

Their mother was listening saying nothing to all of that.

"What about the NGO?" Demanded the youngest of the family who lived in Limpopo province and worked there as manager of one of the public hospitals in the city of Polokwane.

"I don't know but as the head of the department, I will do my best so that the family doesn't lose such a wonderful service to the community, and Mum thank you for being strong for all of us."

"Do we have enough money with that NGO?"

"Yes Mum, however, I'm afraid of what our partners will decide to do with their donations, especially financial. We have full-time employees that cost a lot to the organization and we won't be able to sustain without their financial support."

"Do what you can my daughter and don't worry, don't become like your father who had no rest, really a working machine. Let's hope they won't touch it. And what about our house, I hope they won't come and expropriate our mansion, this is my life, my children."

"We need to be prepared for any eventuality Mum, said her son Bongani. Mum tax evasion is a very serious offence to any government in the world."

"The South African Revenue Service will soon tell us how much Malume owed and let pray that the amount to pay won't escalate beyond the administrative building and the money in the business account."

"I need to be resilient to carry on living with you, my children."

"Thank you, mum," said Siphokazi.

And all her children came to hug her with tears in their eyes, happy to be part of a great family reunion.

"He would be very happy to have seen you all with his grandchildren, he was dreaming about such a family reunion." And again she started crying.

"Please, Mum, stop crying," they all said together.

The premises had many children playing around and far away from all the dilemmas of the family. Helena was so happy to be surrounded by her grandchildren who all the time enjoyed approaching her for a kiss, and most of them came to visit her for the first time.

"I believe she is the one who betrayed all her family."

"She deserves to die with a bullet in her stomach."

"But there is nothing we can do without Colonel Themba'sapproval."

"Why do we need his approval? He is in prison."

"Because she is his wife, you don't just kill someone's wife, man."

"And we are all going to be broke because of what she did to us. She is evil and deserves to die."

"She is no more evil than you."

One of the two executioners was holding an envelope that contained three photos of secret agent Siphokazi's state award ceremony, and they were furiously ready to cause a fatality. It was eight days already since the incarceration of the executives and such truth will infinitely hurt the colonel.

"He needs to see this and tell us what to do, but she deserves to breathe her last."

"When should we see him? Because we also need our money."

"Let's do it after tomorrow."

Holding her three children in her arms, Siphokazi needed strength to visit her husband for the first time in the prison of Soweto. After all, she preferred him in jail than to depart this life in the streets of Johannesburg with a bullet between his eyes, and she was proud of herself for having extinguished what could have turned one day into a terrible nightmare of suddenly losing her beloved husband. But she wouldn't have done such a thing if she wasn't in the force. Her presence in the force was just a very lucky draw by the government; after all her expectations towards God were high and putting Themba in prison to make him reason straight was the only option she had to see both of them one day live a normal life of a couple that behave faithfully to each other.

"It is time now to go to sleep."

"Still, dad is not here tonight, Mum," said Ntombisi her firstborn.

"Dad will come back one day, but not now," she finally said with courage.

"How can he leave us without telling us goodbye?"

"I'm sure he will surely call one of these days."

She instantly thought about encouraging him to call his children by giving him some money. The children were already missing their father, so hearing his voice would make them so happy and give them the expectation of seeing him one day.

Driving south on that day for her was painful but a good opportunity to drive on the streets of the most populous township of the republic of South Africa and even Africa. With the Southgate Mall on her left, she could already see on the signboard the direction of the prison where her stubborn husband was jailed with the rest of the executives. Seeing him in those conditions was going to be agonizing but justice had to be done and she wanted him all for herself. She wanted him to feel sorry for the wicked role he played against his nation and to repent his transgressions and turn his back on what he cherished more than her every day. That time had to arrive for absolute restoration of their marriage and his soul.

A few minutes later, she parked her car in one of the prison's parking bays and walked towards the building that looked like a hopeless dead zone, but there was a hope that these surroundings would help her husband to come to repentance; besides he was better in jail than free sleeping around with other women, and die a painful death one day with four bullets in his stomach.

Colonel Themba was busy reading a military book in his cell saw one of the prison wardens opening his cell door.

"There's a woman who would like to see you, maybe your wife, get out you don't have much time."

"Thank you."

She was seated in front of a glass panel that showed her the other side of the prison where the prisoners were. Suddenly

Colonel Themba appeared curious to know who came to visit him for the first time in prison.

"Themba," she called happy to see him.

Humiliated, he had difficulties to meet her eyes that were already full of tears.

"Why did you come so soon? I just can't face you Sipho."

"You have to; I'm still your wife and you're still my husband."

"What do you want to do with a man who will spend twenty-five years of his life in jail? I haven't been good to you for God's sake, the kids also and I deserve what is happening to me."

"It is hard for all of us, and I brought you some money for you to cope with the situation inside here, and also call your children for they are already asking after their father."

"That's kind of you. Listen Siphokazi, you deserve better than this, I am not worthy to have such a wonderful woman like you, you merit a good man who will cherish and respect you; I haven't been the husband you wished for."

"I have already forgiven you a long time ago."

"That is why I'm saying I'm not worthy of you, please understand."

"I want you to take it easy, Themba."

"How? I have disappointed everyone, my mother who never knew, and mostly my children and you."

"There is hope, and I still love you."

"I love you too much also to keep you away from a man who could treat you better than I did for many years. You suffered a lot Sipho and in the process, you even lost Malume, our Malume," he began crying.

"This is the money I brought, and I will wait until you come out of this place, and don't talk the way you are talking. Worse has come and let deal with it, and tomorrow shall shine."

"Really! Are you going to wait for a man like me? I'm a loser."

The door behind her was opened by the warden who was about to take them out of the visiting room, and she turned around to speak to him.

"I would like to leave him with some money, and how is your shoulder?" She asked turning her attention towards her husband.

"Alright, I will help you with that," responded the warden.

"Much better, Sipho."

"You are still my Colonel Themba and I will always love you. Do you have a Bible with you?"

"Next time if you come bring me one."

"I will come in three days with some food too, but please call the children during the day."

"I will."

"Bye! I love you."

Stepping out of the prison building and driving the streets of the big city of Johannesburg alone, Siphokazi realized that it was a situation to get familiar with. Nevertheless, it was great to have seen him and to have talked to him. Three days was like forever and she needed to be there to encourage him for he needed her presence to survive in that prison, and without forgetting also that everyone had turned his back on him.

She was joyful that he still needed her love, her presence like never before and going back to see him in three days shall be better than the first visit; and still, he was handsome and far from the dangerous underworld he used to be attached to with all his heart.

Chapter 17

Playing in the garden during sunset with the children, former secret agent Siphokazi was patiently waiting for the phone call from her husband to his children. She was holding to that for him to keep hope alive. A place like prison was very stressful for a man of his age and stature but was going to help him to turn his back on what could one day have killed him prematurely.

He had beautiful children to whom he could regularly speak and looked forward to seeing them again once he was free in the future. But still, she had to decide on taking them one day to the prison to visit their father; however it was too early for they wouldn't understand, and end up experiencing a shock that could forever distance them from their father, and that wasn't part of her plan.

After they finished playing and without any phone call from him yet, they all entered the house to get ready for supper.

"Dad promised to call you tonight," she said to them, who were by now watching their children's programs on TV.

"But what is he waiting for?" Demanded Ntombisi.

"He will."

And a few minutes later her cell phone commenced ringing and when she checked, the screen was showing a private call. She answered right away hoping it was him.

"Siphokazi speaking."

"Sipho, it's me."

"Ooh! Let me call the children, come, come, come talk to your father, he's hasting to speak to you."

It was Ntombisi first that spoke so nicely to him, and then the second one and after the little girl. She could hear everything as she put the speaker on. And after speaking to them she took the phone back to continue speaking to him.

"It was nice speaking to them, Sipho."

"You did well Themba, I will see you on Friday."

"I'll be waiting for Sipho."

"Bye and goodnight."

"You must know that seeing another day in prison is a miracle."

"I'm sorry."

"Don't be and see you on Friday."

Remaining pensive she just put both hands on her chest, cheerful for the peace she felt.

Colonel Themba, in his cell alone, had just finished reading his book when he saw the same warden as yesterday unlocking his cell door. He held a long solid truncheon in his right hand, looking like he was about to hit him with it.

You're requested to the visitor's room, some folks would like to speak to you.

Intimidated he immediately stood and wore his sandals.

"If you want a cigarette you're welcome, I've got many of them for a nice guy like you."

"You give me the money and I get it for myself, but follow me first to the visitor's room."

"I like your style."

The prison was calm but with an atmosphere of distress to overcome. As he was walking some were telling him "you are lucky to have a family that loves you, but very soon they will all forget about you until you see them at your burial."

"You need to start thinking about it," said the warden to him.

Colonel Themba just smiled and once in the visitor's room, he went straight to the window that another warden indicated to him, yet a big surprise was waiting for him for he was in the presence of his hitmen.

"What are you doing here?" He said to them.

"Can't you first greet us, boss? We're happy to see you."

"If you're here for your money; I will organize it for you."

"That's good news boss but we have something to show you."

"What!"

One of his hitmen took an envelope from his jacket pocket that he opened to expose three photos.

"Do you know this lady, boss?"

"Yes," he said, "my wife."

"This ceremony, Boss was held two days ago in a secret place without television coverage."

"What do you mean?"

"She received from our government the South African prize of excellent service for the nation."

"What! But she was no longer part of the intelligence, this doesn't make sense."

"We received these from one of us working in the department of defence."

Colonel Themba held his head in his hands and then covered his face, he was in terrible shock.

"She deserves a bullet..."

"Don't!" He stopped what the hitman was saying. "No one should dare touch her, I'm saying no one."

He instantly called one of the wardens close to him to ask him something.

"Would you help me to get those photos?"

The warden showed in a kind gesture and allowed the envelope to get to the colonel and then said to him, "See you inside."

"Thank you."

And then he came back to his hitmen.

"This information must be kept confidential, and thanks a lot for all your services, and don't worry about your money; I will triple the amount because of these photos, good job, but no one should touch her."

"Thank you, boss."

"Someone will call you very soon, goodbye."

Left alone, furious and very confused, the colonel became overwhelmed by a great sadness. He thought he was being smarter than her, but she played it better than him without him realizing it. What game was she playing? he wondered. He thought about the all divorce scenario that he believed was going to occur, and then her sudden change. But she was the only one he wanted to use to secure his fortune. She confirmed declining to divorce him, afterwards that what he wanted to hear from her, and now being the number one betrayer and much deserving to die?

He started to think about the police's well-orchestrated assault on the warehouse at the same time thinking about those who covered their faces, and surely she was among them. "I hate her," he said speaking to himself; but why hand over the whole family? But to gain what? Just for an award? There was something that he didn't understand that he needed to know. Was she promised a lot of money from the government? He had so many questions without answers because he had that much money.

Three hours later it was time to go for supper, and he declined the offer from the warden.

"If you don't eat someone else will at your place."

"I'm not feeling like eating."

"Come on, you have a beautiful wife, don't die now."

The colonel remained calm for he needed serenity to overcome a hostile environment like the prison.

"I will be fine," he said to him.

"For whom are you cooking for mum?" Asked her son.

She calmly turned around to face her son.

"For us, Ntombisi," she responded.

Of course, she was not telling the truth since the food was for her husband, Colonel Themba.

"It smells nice mum."

"Thanks, you'll enjoy it but I will take some to your uncle who is at the hotel not far away from here."

"Can I come with you?"

"Next time because after the hotel I'll be heading to the office."

"Please, mum."

"Next time only."

Disappointed the little man left without saying more, and once alone in the kitchen she sighed finding it strange that her son insisted to come with her on this particular day, maybe he sensed something fishy? She ignored it and carried on with what she was up to.

One hour later Siphokazi parked the car in the parking of the prison, ready to see her husband. She was getting used to such a difficult place to handle, but that was what she finally wanted for a possible restoration of their relationship.

Already in the visitors' room waiting for her husband to come, a powerful alarm went off scaring everyone who was there waiting or already talking to those they visited.

"What's that?" She asked one of the vigilant wardens who was with them.

"I'm sure someone is causing trouble there, just wait until everything get back to normal."

"Thank you."

Suddenly, Colonel Themba appeared and sat without saying anything.

"Nice to see you," she said smiling at him.

But he said nothing.

"Are you alright? Are you not well treated?"

"Why do you care so much?"He asked with aggressiveness.

Siphokazi, surprised by the reaction of her husband, covered her mouth with her right hand. Maybe he's ashamed of his actual status, she wondered.

"But I'm here for you."

Calmly the colonel took an envelope from his pocket, opened it and removed three photos that he presented to his wife who was confused about his sudden change of temper.

"Look at this," he said.

When she got closer she saw herself in those pictures being elevated to a national hero. And she suddenly looked down sighing, not knowing what to say.

"I am sure you were amongst those undercover in the warehouse covering their faces, betraying those who gave you life, your father and mother and the father of your children. Why? Why Sipho?"

"I had no choice," she said with tears filling up her eyes.

"No choice? That's well said."

"I was told by the intelligence it will be considered treason if I refused to help them knowing Malume is my biological father and you are my husband."

"Really! Weeping won't solve the problem because you've been selfish and weak towards our enemies."

"Really! You're not telling the truth."

"Go and get yourself another husband who can give you more children."

"Themba please hear me out."

"I don't want to see you again in my life; I thought you became part of us, our world."

"What about what you've done to me? You and father. You betrayed me, you betrayed everyone, and you only cared about your millions."

"I'm leaving; don't ever come back here again."

"Themba please, calm down I still love you."

"No, you don't, you love your secrets more than me, go and marry the government that entrusted you to kill your father and keep me locked here for twenty-five years. I hate you as well as this place."

The colonel left, leaving her alone; crying for the worst has come into her pathetic life for she was unaware the colonel was still connected to his hitmen. She felt heavy to stand up and leave without accomplishing what she came to do for she was about to tell him again how much she loved him despite the situation.

While driving back and without knowing how to proceed she started thinking about her safety and the safety of her children for how did he receive those photos? Who brought them to him for the ceremony was without television coverage and only the intelligence photographer was allowed to take those pictures? Immediately she pulled over, put on her earphones and called secret agent Dumisane.

"How are you Sipho? Nice to hear from you."

"I'm in trouble, Dumisane."

"What's wrong?"

"I visited my husband today in prison, and he showed me pictures of us receiving the national award."

"What?"

"Maybe they are after me; I'm scared for my life and the children."

"He won't harm his children."

"What about kidnapping them?"

"He won't. I guess only he can order a crime against you; unfortunately, we are also being spied on."

"Who can spy on us, Dumisane?"

"The underworld, they can always come after us, come and let's talk about it."

"Meeting you right now won't be wise Dumi."

"What you should do is to find a way for someone else other than a member of the family to meet your husband. Maybe a pastor, your pastor for example can approach him."

"Let me see them right now."

"Drive safely; don't panic."

The pastoral couple had just parked their car and then noticed the presence of Siphokazi waiting for them at the entrance of their office. She looked concerned and needed help. They knew she was facing the biggest challenge of her life with the sudden death of her father and the incarceration of her husband caused by her.

"It is always kind to see you among us Siphokazi," spoke Pastor Thabiso.

"Thank you, Pastor Thabiso."

After opening the church back door Pastor Tshepang invited her inside, and they went straight into the office.

"Are you alright sister Siphokazi?" Asked pastor Tshepang.

"Things are getting tougher, Pastor Tshepang. During my visit to the prison when talking to my husband he showed me some photos that were supposed to be secret, and…"

She stopped talking to blow her nose.

"Those photos were taken during the ceremony when being awarded the national prize of excellent service by the government."

"Ooh, God!" Said pastor Thabiso. "First of all congratulations."

"Thank you, pastor," she said smiling.

"Yes, continue."

"The ceremony at the department of defence was supposed to be secret, and it was secret without television coverage, without the newspapers, on the contrary, we don't understand what happened because Themba has in possession of some photos of the ceremony with me being awarded. And he doesn't want to see me anymore, and I'm right now feeling at risk."

"Do you think your husband can order someone to kill you?" The question came from pastor Tshepang.

"He's even telling me to get married to another man."

The pastoral couple looked at each other, not knowing how to proceed.

"Your husband is still connected to the world you're not connected to, and you must also understand my daughter that he's right now deceived and confused by his wife, and he won't make your life easy; so you need to back up for a while and give him some times to digest what you did to him. And what did you tell him?"

281

"That I still love him, and that I was under the obligation to penetrate their world, and if I had refused it was going to be considered as high treason."

"Good," said pastor Tshepang. "That's why you need to give him some time to comprehend and pray that he turns his back on the world and learn to focus on God. You should have it as something you expect from God. Pray for him so that he completely becomes the husband that you wanted him to be."

"You must go back to him, but do it after a week or ten days maybe he would have calmed down."

"I will go live with my mother for a while until I go visit him."

"Very good idea," said pastor Thabiso. "We pray to God that you will be safe in the name of Jesus and that God shall touch his heart and minister to him to repent from his sins."

"Amen!" She responded to the prayer.

"We will always be with you," said Pastor Tshepang.

"Thank you pastors for your support."

"Go well and don't miss this Sunday service."

"I won't miss it."

Secret agent Botha waited by secret agent Dumisane met outside the Gautrain station in Sandton. They decided to meet and talk about those pictures that exposed Siphokazi to the underworld while being secretly rewarded by the authorities. Who could have done such a terrible thing to their colleague?

"If they have photos of Siphokazi, then they also have photos of us."

Secret agent Botha smiled out the corner of his mouth and said, "I believe they've always known us Dumisane.

"Meaning those who facilitated everything because we just got rewarded."

"They can go to hell."

"We need to be prudent Botha."

"I know but..."

Suddenly an unidentified car stopped beside their car, and some crazy folks with uncovered faces mercilessly shot at them. Botha was aware of the danger and pushed Dumisane for his protection because he was an easy target, and that could end up deadly.

"Open the door," he shouted with his strong voice.

Secret agent Dumisane got the message and never requested why, he instantly opened the car door and rolled down like a soccer ball, followed by secret agent Botha who unfortunately received a bullet in his right shoulder. The assault happened at such a speed that they didn't have the time to see who wanted them dead on the spot.

Their assaulters were already gone, disappointed for they surely grasped that the target was missed. Screaming in pain, secret agent Dumisane quickly raised to attend to his colleague who was trying to stop the bleeding from his shoulder. So quickly he put him back in the car and drove to the Sandton clinic not far from the Gautrain station.

Once his colleague was attended to, he immediately called Siphokazi.

"Good afternoon, Dumisane."

"Sipho, we got attacked."

"Where?"

"In Sandton. Botha was shot in the right shoulder. Be very careful."

"Somebody influential and who used to eat along with them is taking revenge. You need to go back to the ministry of defence and ask for the photographer, maybe he took a bribe."

"It is a good idea Sipho, thank you."

After talking to her he went back to his colleague's room to see how he was doing and he saw Botha talking to one of the beautiful nurses that was taking care of him.

"I believe we should go to the department of defence and investigate," said Botha.

"That's what Siphokazi told me."

"You already called her? You finally asked her to marry you."

"Why?"

"Because you love her."

"But she doesn't Botha."

"Are you sure?"

"She still loves her rotten husband."

"Women, women. A rotten husband who will stay twenty-five years in prison and perhaps will get out of that prison worst than before. Why can't she move on with her life and leave such a waste of skin?"

"Ask her? Can you remember those assaulter's faces?"

"It was very quick; I didn't have time to see. Just to make sure my life was in danger."

"My life too."

"Of course. Please I want to go home now," he spoke nicely to the same nurse.

"The doctor said only tomorrow," she said kindly.

"Dumisane by tomorrow already let's get to the department of defence and get the name of the photographer and take him to our offices, he must tell us who bribed him."

On the following day, around nine in the morning, secret agent Dumisane very vigilantly came to pick up his colleague, Botha, who was already dressed and ready to leave the clinic. His right shoulder was still painful, and secret agent Dumisane realized that his colleague didn't sleep alone for his beloved wife joined him after he left.

"Good morning, madam Botha."

"Good morning Dumi, long time and whenever I see you it is always with bad news."

"It is because you don't come to our barbecues."

"So how is your shoulder?"

"He needs to rest for at least two weeks but he doesn't want to," said his wife.

"It isn't that painful as you think, let's not waste time we need to go to the department of defence."

"Please Dumisane talk to your colleague who's being stubborn, he's being unfair to me, and they could have killed him."

"But they didn't," said Botha.

"Botha maybe you need to rest as your wife is saying. I will go there and keep you updated before evening."

"Honey, I'm alright, it will be fine."

"Ok if you insist," she finally said and she kissed his forehead. "But be very careful because I still need you in my life."

"I will see you before sunset."

"Love you."

"Love you too," and she left.

"And don't worry about the car it is already home," bye Dumisane.

"Goodbye, Caroline."

Once in the department of defence the two secret agents went to the reception and asked for the organizer of the ceremony, but he was absent and then asked for the state photographer who fortunately was there but lost in the corridors of the administrative building.

"Let me give you his cell phone number or do you want me to call him."

"Please do so, and give us also his number," said Dumisane.

But Dumisane noticed that Botha was in pain.

"Maybe you need to rest with the help of some painkillers."

"I'm feeling dizzy."

"Your wife was right. Sit down for a while; let me talk to the photographer."

"He's coming down to reception," said the receptionist.

"Thank you very much," and he sat beside Botha who looked tired.

Suddenly secret agent Dumisane's cell phone rang.

"It's Keegan, hallo chief."

"Why didn't you report to work this morning?"

"We were at the hospital because Botha got shot."

"I know but you were supposed to first bring yourself here, where are you? I was expecting Botha to be resting at the clinic until he feels better but you left with him, who does he think he is?"

"Sorry chief," said secret agent Dumisane.

"Make sure you take him back to the clinic, the same one. And I want to see you here in the next two hours."

"Yes, chief. Keegan wants you back at the clinic while he wants to see me in the next two hours."

"I believe the photographer is there," said Botha.

"Yes, are you the photographer who took photos during the award ceremony?"

"Yes, I am."

"Wonderful," said Dumisane. "We work for the intelligence agency and you don't need to know our names, but we have a few questions to ask you."

"No problem, besides I remember you and you were amongst those…"

"Yes, those who got awarded."

"Yes, where is the lady?"

"She is not here," responded Botha in pain.

"Do you remember that we were only three to get awarded?" Demanded Dumisane.

"Yes of course."

"And who would have access to the photos taken?"

"Anyone working in the department, however so far this time just one person asked for them apart you."

"Really! Who is that person?" Demanded Botha.

"Mr Peter, you should know him."

"Peter!" Said Dumisane.

He looked at Botha greatly surprised at why would the number two of the intelligence agency asked for their photos.

"Thanks a lot," said Botha, "but don't tell anyone we had this conversation."

"I won't."

"Quickly let's do what chief Keegan ordered before he shouts on us exposing all his veins."

"Mr Peter asked for the pictures the photographer took of you at the ceremony?" Demanded Keegan surprised by the news. "Why?"

"Yes, chief and we need to know as quickly as possible if he's connected to the shooting."

"Of course and you need help. How is Botha?"

"Still in pain."

"He needs to rest for at least three days and you can then together attend to Mr Peter; you need Botha for his experience."

Chapter 18

She had just arrived at the premises of Malume (Pty) Ltd where a remarkable silence was reigning. Most of the offices were empty as the executives were not there, and already many of the staff were retrenched and waiting for their severance pay, and the final report from the South African Revenue Services. The only one helping her was Miss Lindiwe, her father's assistant who was helping with her father's files.

She went to the boardroom alone to look at all the photos that were on the wall explaining the history of the company. They were beautiful photos exposing a wealthy, aristocratic family that her father used to love. Nonetheless, that era was over now for the simple reason that the game may not be won all the time, as a consequence in the process he even lost his precious life. She got the idea to call secret agent Dumisane and get some news about the shooting.

"How are you Sipho?"

"I'm alright and you?"

"Fine, fine."

"And Botha?"

"Resting in the clinic and I'm waiting for him so that we can go after Mr Peter the number two of the intelligence."

"I don't understand."

"He's the only one who asked for our pictures."

"Ooh my God! So he's the one."

"We need proof. Just be careful where you're for they are looking for us."

"Thank you for letting me know."

"You're welcome."

She constantly made sure to carry her P38 pistol in case she was attacked because all the secret agents including her, who were involved in the arrest of the executives were in danger. She left the boardroom and went back into her office to find a file on her desk labelled SARS (South African Revenue Service). Her heartbeat grew faster for she was more concerned with the NGO, and the family mansion where her mother was living. She had a mother so in love with the gorgeous mansion, her father bought in her name many years ago.

How much money did Malume owe to the government? She had to be able to pay out severance to those retrenched, but the company had enough money for that, however, what was owed to the government was still unknown and had to be paid first.

"I just received it now," suddenly spoke Lindiwe who was behind her.

"Thank you, Lindiwe, I will take it from here."

"Madam, take it easy."

She sighed.

"Thank you; you're such a good friend Lindiwe."

The file was frightening and merciless as the amount indicated inside had to be paid within a reasonable period of time, but would the company bank account provide enough for what she had to pay? According to an internal audit, the company had a balance sheet showing a total of fixed and current assets amounting to a hundred and twenty million Rands excluding the not-for-profit organization and the family mansion, as well an actual cash bank balance of just seventy-five million Rand. According to Lindiwe; Malume including his executives were big spenders of the company money.

After thinking about all of that she decided to open the big scary envelope to discover what was inside. Before calling her chief financial officer who already gave her an amount estimation of what the company could owe SARS, a big amount of eighty million Rand accumulated over ten years, Siphokazi was ready to face the worst on her own.

With courage, she opened the big envelope had inside at the same time feeling for her mother who since the death of her husband was getting more and more easily broken. After opening it she right away went for the amount owed to the government. On the second page at the bottom was written in red; indicating a big infringement.

An amount of ninety million Rands that had to be paid within one month, and SARS wasn't the only creditor of the company. It was probable that most of the working force of Malume (Pty) Ltd including the chief financial officer would have to be retrenched, leaving her only with Lindiwe who possibly will use her experience to help her. Of course, the largest part of the assets of the organization had to be liquidated, but she was going to negotiate to pay the amount over three months to avoid losing too much at once as the bank also was claiming what was due to her. But would that be possible? She decided to call Lindiwe.

"Lindiwe would you come to my office, please."

"Coming, Siphokazi."

And once there she said to her, "Let's try this, use your experience and ask SARS to give us three months to pay the tax amount owed to them. Just try but I'm not sure, and please call Ashraf to come to my office."

Ashraf was the company's chief financial executive who has worked for the company for the last twelve years. About five minutes later Ashraf turned up a bit tired with his laptop in his left hand.

"Please come in and sit down Ashraf."

"Thank you."

"This is the file from SARS and we owe a lot, why? Ninety million Rands so I have requested Lindiwe to write to SARS to give us three months repayment period. Is it possible? You know we have other creditors."

"It is a good idea if we can afford to pay them something straight away."

"Like how much?"

"Thirty million or more because the amount is huge and by promising them within three months we must be able to honour during that period."

"What about your severances?"

"Let me talk to SARS, no need to write any letter, it won't work, I will personally go there and arrange for something."

"Please do so Ashraf, we don't have much time left."

"Give me until next Monday."

"All the best."

Secret agents Botha and Dumisane had just left Sandton clinic, heading to the John Foster police station in Johannesburg CBD. They called for some guidance from Lieutenant Keegan who was already waiting for them. Botha was much better and ready to go back into his duties and start going after Mr Peter's case.

Secret agent Dumisane's eyes were all over the place while driving to avoid a bad surprise from those who wished them dead. They were not going to give up until they were all buried and forgotten. Once at the office, they found Lieutenant Keegan seated on his desk patiently waiting for them.

"Finally, you are both here and please inform me before you expose yourself to death."

Tired and exhausted they both wanted to sit down.

"Don't sit down."

"Sorry," said Botha.

"How is your shoulder?"

"Much better, chief."

"And what is your plan for Mr Peter?"

"That's why we are here chief," said Dumisane. "We wanted to follow his moves and see what kind of people he meets."

"I believe he's involved but we need proof," said Botha.

"I believe too," said Keegan. "Ok go after him and bring good results."

"Thank you chief," said Botha.

Miss Morefi used to spy for Colonel Themba since Nthabiseng passed away and she was as subtle as Nthabiseng was. Colonel Themba was the master of discovering those kinds of people.

"How come you couldn't spot my wife as a threat to the company?" Said Colonel Themba to Ms Morefi.

"She is skilled and don't forget she's also an executive of the company. I possibly will have a problem approaching her."

"But no one shall lay a finger on my family, including you."

"But look at what she did to all of us."

"My family is what I am left with and she is my business; I will handle this and squeeze her in the corner until her only option will be to commit suicide."

"What about me now, Themba? You think I've never loved you. I know you won't raise your finger against her because you still love her. How can you forgive such a woman? You will be here for twenty-five long years and you dare to forgive her?"

"Siphokazi is my business; I will handle her my way. But I would like to reward you with a good amount of money for all the good services you've done for me, do you understand? And talk to the rest of the guys that I will sort them out very soon with what they deserve so that you can move on with your lives."

"It was a pleasure, my colonel, thank you for everything."

"You will thank me for the day you will receive your severance, and now get out of here and don't ever come back."

Morefi left the prison with some tears in her eyes for she, in actual fact, had fallen in love with a man who enjoyed her company like no other men in the past, and she hated Siphokazi for what she did to all of them. She stopped everything without them noticing the roaring lion that was among them ready to hit. But when driving she was followed without her noticing. She was not far from where she stayed in Soweto Diepkloof, and she suddenly received a phone call from someone. She checked the screen. It was Mr Peter of the national intelligence calling her.

The two secret agents saw her pulling into a petrol station to respond to the phone call for she never went to refill her tank.

"Hello, Mr Peter."

"Hello my Morefi, but why did we miss the two agents?" He asked, furiously.

"You know I'm not the shooter Peter and I believe we should stop with all of this."

"Stop! Why my dear?"

"Because I'm no longer interested and I would like to move on with my life. This game is getting too perilous."

"Colonel Themba deserves to spend the rest of his useless life in prison while hoping he dies there, he destroyed my life with your predecessor Nthabiseng who I killed with the blessing of Malume happily using one of you traitors. Listen I want his wife also dead, all of them."

"And how much do you have for me?"

"Now we can talk young lady. But I need more than that, kill also the other agents that your people missed. He brutally cut the connection. Ms Morefi sighed, turned on the engine and drove off, when unexpectedly an unknown car parked in front of hers. She saw two gentlemen coming out of it smiling at her, and she recognized them because she had their pictures with her in her bag. She identified who they were, beloved secret agents of the government.

"Would you step out of the car please," said secret agent Dumisane.

She obeyed without saying anything.

"You seem to know us," said secret agent Botha.

She nicely smiled at them while secret agent Botha noticed she had an incredible smile.

"Yes I know you," she said kindly, "and what can I do for you because I'm not a threat to the South African police force?"

"We know that's why we want to check who were you busy talking to," said Dumisane.

"Give me your phone," said Botha with his strong voice. "Dumisane while I'm checking her phone check her bag."

"You don't have the right to do so," she said trying to defend herself.

"Yes, we do," said secret agent Dumisane, "give me your bag or we take you right now to the police station."

She finally submitted and gave them what they wanted. While checking Dumisane was so surprised to discover their pictures in her purse, in an envelope and that terrified her, she had to justify that.

"So you were in conversation with another enemy of the state, Mr Peter."

"Botha, take her in her car and let's immediately go to the police station, this woman is dangerous."

The two secret agents handcuffed her and put her in the back seat of her car. They drove like racing cars, to the police station for she could have been followed or even the secret agents could've been followed by the hitmen, eager to finish off what they had difficulties to start with. Once at the police station, they were joined by Lieutenant Keegan in the interrogation room.

"Very interesting," said Keegan. "Carrying your pictures."

"Yes," said Botha.

"Who ordered the hit on us?" Asked Dumisane.

"Peter," she responded.

"Why does a young woman like you, with a bright future ahead get involved with such criminals?" Said Lieutenant Keegan, "And now we also identify you as a criminal."

She said nothing.

"Cooperating with us will help you to spend fewer years in jail," said secret agent Dumisane.

"I have no choice," she said.

"Thank you for appreciating," said Botha.

"Tell us where the shooters live, but we will proceed this way," said Dumisane. "Call for a very urgent meeting tonight, requesting also the presence of Mr Peter. And we shall arrest them at once and we shall let you free. What do you think about it?"

"It sounds good because Peter pisses me off, they all piss me off, and I want to move on with my life."

"Great, great," said secret agent Botha. "We will now give you your phone to call them while listening to you speaking to them. What do you think you should tell them?"

"They want their money."

"And Peter?" Asked Botha.

"A plan to kill all of you."

"Call them now," ordered secret agent Botha.

Ms Morefi sighed, and then dialled first the number of the leader of the hitmen located in Johannesburg CBD.

"Yes, Morefi."

"Tell everyone else to wait for me tonight for I've got some good news for you."

"We need our money Ms."

"I will bring the money and don't be late."

"Will tell all of them."

"Great."

"Well done," said Botha, now call Mr Peter.

"Can I drink some water, please? "

Botha first took her cell phone and went to get some water from the tap for her.

"Thank you," and she drank all of it at once.

"Now call Peter," said Dumisane.

Ms Morefi realized they were all in hot water and that there was nothing she could do to avoid the predicament to happen.

"Hallo Morefi! Are you ready to plot it well?"

"Yes but I need you to also talk to the guys tonight at their residence in town, I can't do it alone Peter, they want money to motivate them."

"How many of them are ready for the work?"

"They are six."

"I'm not sure but."

"If you don't make it I won't be there to encourage them."

"What time?"

"Half-past seven tonight."

"And then we can have all the night to enjoy, Themba is no longer around to spoil you with his money."

"Why not, Peter? I like it."

"See you then."

"Well done again," said Botha taking the phone from her.

"What about if he calls?"

"We are here together."

"But I need to change my clothes."

"You'll be out of here once all of them are in jail, my dear," said Dumisane. "See you tonight."

And they left her alone in the room with a policeman watching on her.

On Market Street; Johannesburg CBD at 19h 20:

Ready for one of the most dangerous assaults in the Johannesburg CBD, wearing bulletproof vests for their protection, armed with AK 47s and P38s, the two secret agents with Ms Morefi on their side followed by a calm police contingent, were going towards where Ms Morefi was directing them. Towards those expecting getting their pay.

They were on Market Street intending to reach the corner of Jeppe and Eloff Streets. And at that corner and on the third floor, flat number 305 was where all the villains were waiting for her, but she first needed to know if Mr Peter was already around for they were already on Ellof Street.

"Call Mr Peter and ask him if he's already there with them," said secret agent Dumisane.

"Hello, Peter! Are you already with them because I'm almost there?"

"Why are you late because I'm on the third floor?"

"It is fine I am parking now," and she hung up. "He must be with them as we speak."

Like a rocket, secret agent Botha accelerated the car, and they arrived there within two minutes, making sure to park behind the building according to Ms Morefi's advice. The plan was to let her knock at the door and speak to them so they recognized her voice, and then surprise all of them without any bloodshed, but anticipating the possibility of some reacting fiercely.

"Where is she?" Said one of them impatiently.

"I've just spoken to her, she was parking."

Suddenly someone knocked at the door followed by the voice of a woman and it was her voice.

"Please open. It is Morefi."

"Coming."

This time both secret agents were in front just slightly behind Ms Morefi, ready to execute the biggest shock, and once the door was opened they pushed her on the side to get her under the protection of a sergeant assigned to keep her safe with him. The assault was well calculated as the hitmen were all surprised by the secret agents. One of the hitmen panicked and screamed at the agents. He drew his gun and shot twice towards the agents.

"All of you on the floor," shouted Botha with his strong and terrorizing voice.

The burst viciously hit one of the policemen who was just behind secret agent Dumisane who was about to handcuff Mr Peter. Mr Peter was laying on the floor with both of his hands holding his head. Botha, without wasting time, spotted the shooter and rapidly intervened and shot him twice in his right shoulder, causing him to scream in such a way to create more panic in the building as the two shots already caused terrible insecurity in the residential building.

Overpowered by the intelligence and busy swearing, the hitmen were surprisingly surrounded by the plotting of their own Ms Morefi who was not even around. "Where is this traitor so that I can shoot her between her eyes for I have a bullet with her name on?" said one of the hitmen.

"Shut up," said secret agent Dumisane. "Everything you say here will be used against you in the court of law."

The intelligence handcuffed everyone who was there and once outside the flat, Mr Peter saw Ms Morefi handcuffed too and this was orchestrated to give them the impression that she was not involved in their arrest.

"You're here," said Mr Peter distraught.

"I'm sorry I was followed," she said with tears running down her face.

The third floor of the residential building was crowded and everyone seemed happy to see the hitmen arrested by the police. It looked as if everybody was afraid of them because they were spreading terror throughout the Johannesburg CBD. Once outside they were loaded into police vans towards John Foster police station in high spirits to have arrested those very strongly linked up to Malume Empire.

On the following morning, Colonel Themba was talking to some of Malume's executives in the prison yard, and most of them complained about the boring food that was given to them every day.

"We are here given that we are lawbreakers, and they want us to commit the fact to memory," he said.

"We have learned that your wife is the one who gave all of us over to the police," said one of the executives furiously.

"Who told you such a lie?" Responded Themba.

"Such a lie? Are you protecting that turncoat at this point?"

"Don't forget that you're talking about my wife."

"The executive laughed in mockery and then said, "You've never loved her as a man should, and that can explain why."

"Shut up!" The colonel shouted.

"Do you want me to shut up? I accept as true that you are both traitors and you deserve to die."

Subsequently, they all left except for one of them called Tladi known as the millionaire.

"They hate you, Themba," he said.

"And you?"

"I don't, but watch on what can come against you."

"I know Tladi," he said looking at the floor.

"I was about to resign from the company a week before we got all arrested."

"Really! Why?"

"But I was thinking about my safety and the one of my family because of people like you, Themba."

Themba looked at the sky, saying nothing.

"And it was a great idea; on the contrary, fear truly is the number one enemy of man. I was troubled by your evil abilities, but look at how you're nothing."

"Yours too, Tladi, although I've always enjoyed your company, conversely, do you know the person I hate the most among all of you?"

"Which one?"

"Malume."

"Malume! Why? Your beloved father-in-law made you a millionaire, and I suppose no one will know where those millions are."

"I hate him because he used me; he brought into play the uniform of a colonel to destroy him and his family."

"Be careful, Colonel," Tladi laughed, "Because here someone else shall use you again like what your father-in-law and wife did to all of us."

The colonel violently slapped him on the face; afterwards, Tladi touched his left cheek and left laughing. Right away the colonel realized that he was left alone and in danger inside a merciless dwelling. All the executives took wind of the traitor of all, Siphokazi his wife, and retribution was imminent against her person. A half a friend is a traitor.

One prison guard approached him.

"You have a visitor, and I saw you slapping someone."

"He insulted my mother, don't worry I have something for you."

Walking behind the warden, Themba was wondering who was the visitor he was about to meet. He didn't want his wife, the mother of his children to come again; on the other hand, if it was her then he was going to warn her of the threat she was facing. Once he arrived in front of the glass he found her moulded in what he used to call "the Madam of the man". She was beautiful and serene, and he felt great joy to see her once again, but he refused to smile at her.

"Good morning," she greeted smiling nicely at him.

"What are you doing here? Can't you get it Sipho, but let me warn you that all the executives know that you're the traitor walking free out there so you better be careful. They all hate me inside here because of what you did to the big family."

"Themba I was under obligation and you know I couldn't turn the government down, forgive me the way I have forgiven you Themba."

"But they won't, really, I hate your guts, including your fathers."

She remained silent, looking down.

"You're still my husband."

"Listen, woman, I'm going to die here, all my enemies are here. You better tell your mother the truth and go marry another man, a good man, a righteous one. Go and cry at your father's grave."

Calmly she stood up weeping and turned around walking slowly.

"Go!" He said softly.

"Why do you want me to go away? She said coming back to her seat. Do you know how much I have suffered in your hand? Egocentric man, you were selfish and enjoyed your millions with other women more than your wife and you dare to blame me for this."

"You're not allowed to shout here," said one of the wardens.

"Sorry," she apologized while wiping her tears.

Colonel Themba with his furious eyes dived in her eyes said, "You don't deserve a man like me Sipho, go away, go to your lawyer and bring some divorce papers I may sign and move on with your life."

Again she stood up calmly, and this time without looking behind she left the prison deceived and confused like never before.

Chapter 19

"Cruelty my daughter is a lamentable attribute, and your father had it, but I don't know why I kept loving him."

Siphokazi heard it from her mother as she entered the living room.

"Hello, Mum! Are you talking to me Mum?"

"Yes, I am and you look exhausted my daughter. Come I would like to show you something."

Siphokazi, curious, joined her mother.   She was busy enjoying ironing some of her clothes, and her daughter understood why, she just wanted to be busy. When she got closer she caught sight of three of her photos put on the stool beside her.

"Where did you get these pictures mum?" She asked surprised.

"Why are you not telling everything to your mother my daughter? Your mother-in-law is the one who brought them to me yesterday. You see my daughter you're also vicious as your father was when believing in something, but at least you believe in uprightness."

"Mum everybody is fighting me," she said crying.

"Don't cry, I'm not fighting you and I will never; I fought enough in my life; this is what God has given me."

"I'm sorry, Mum."

"Don't be," she said wiping her daughter's tears.

Her mother took her in her arms.

"I know you suffered a lot my daughter, and what you're going through now is the prize for turning your back on the world."

"Themba hates me, and he's pushing me to marry another man."

"You have to make your own decision as I did my daughter."

"I'm sorry mother. Father died because of what I did to all of you."

"You don't have to regret it, my daughter."

They were both crying consoling one another. Siphokazi sighed and said, "Marrying another man is not the solution mother."

"Then what are you going to do?"

"To just pray, plead for him every day; I'm still in love with him mother, and I know he still loves me. He's saying he doesn't deserve me and I'm welcome to bring him the divorce papers and move on with my life. And because of what I did mother, my father is no longer with us."

"You didn't kill your father, he did that to himself but I couldn't stop him. You cannot stop a man who believes in what he's doing. I am proud of you my daughter, just move on with your life, but be full of wisdom when walking around."

"Thank you Mum for your support."

"Just be careful my daughter."

One month later walking inside of the Mall Of Africa in Midrand, north of Johannesburg, Siphokazi was pleased to have solved the tax problem faced by the family; and changed her mobile phone number which helped her to stay away from what her past used to look like for she needed other surroundings to survive the disappointments she went through that were poisonous as a venomous black mamba snake.

Visiting the mall in the middle of the week to her was the best option for the mall was popular and very busy during weekends. She needed some clothes that could well suit her children and mother. It was more than a month that she stayed away from visiting her husband in prison. For her to remarry was like the cobra venom that doesn't pardon, in addition to that she also had a distrust of men, and for her to be able to trust another one than Themba so soon, especially after what her father had done to her family made her realize that putting your trust in the flesh is a very bad decision to take.

Walking along with his ex-fiancée Phumzile, secret agent Dumisane still working faithfully for his government saw a silhouette, at least two hundred meters away from where he was that looked exactly like Siphokazi browsing outside a shop. He was very much tempted to approach her, but refrained for her former colleague had never met his ex-fiancée, and still, he intended to marry Siphokazi one day. But he grieved over it because it was more than six weeks since they chatted and he missed her because the phone number he had for her was always going to voicemail. Nonetheless, he was happy to see her looking good and most importantly, alive.

He quickly went inside the shop to talk to his ex.

"Phumzile while you're buying your stuff I would like to talk to someone outside."

"Don't disappear," she said.

"Five minutes."

Running like a child after his mother, secret agent Dumisane was determined to not fail to spot her. But she wasn't where he saw her browsing so he decided to enter the shop and see if she was inside and she was.

"Siphooo!" He suddenly called so happily.

"Dumisane! What are you doing here my good friend? Nice to see you after so long."

Without saying anything he came and hugged her like never before. She welcomed the gesture by saying nothing and when he released her, she held both of his hands.

"I missed you so much Sipho; I thought maybe something wrong happened to you, and your number doesn't work."

"I know. I excluded myself from the people to relax and mostly forget Dumi."

After a few minutes, Phumzile appeared in the shop looking for Dumisane. She saw them talking so nicely to one another. When Siphokazi perceived her standing at the entrance of the boutique with her eyes on them, she realized that secret agent Dumisane was not alone.

"I think someone is looking for you Dumisane," she said pointing her finger towards where Phumzile was standing.

The secret agent turned around and saw that it was his ex-fiancée, and said, "Yes, Sipho let me introduce you to my ex-fiancée Phumzile, come to Phumzile, this is my former colleague Siphokazi."

With a smile, the two beautiful ladies looked at each other and greeted each other.

"We need to leave now," suddenly said Phumzile.

"Just two minutes, Phumzile."

"Please don't make me hang around," she said at the same time turning around to go out of the shop.

"A sticky ex-fiancée," noticed Siphokazi. "You never told me about her."

"It is not a good story to tell."

She just looked at him and turned around to leave.

"Go. She is waiting for you."

"But what about your new number, Siphokazi?"

She sighed first before saying, "My old number will restart working in a week's time."

"Please don't merely say that to calm me."

"Promise."

"You are still so beautiful my dear, Bye!"

"Goodbye Dumisane and she is good for you."

She smiled and continued browsing.

"She is more than a colleague," said Phumzile.

"She's a good person. "

"A good person, you mean a good woman right?"

Dumisane laughed.

"Yes, she's a good woman."

"But married, I saw the ring. Don't waste your time with such a person."

The secret agent sighed.

"You may be right Phumzile; she's married to a husband facing a heavy sentence of twenty-five years in jail."

"And because of that, you think she will stop loving her man?"

"I believe he doesn't deserve her."

"Oh, My poor Dumisane! So in love with the wind."

"This is what I hate about you," he said.

"No, I'm telling you the truth, she still loves her husband more than you."

"I need to hear that from her."

"Go ahead and you'll tell me what."

She sped up her pace, leaving the Mall Of Africa.

In the middle of the Namaqualand flowers in the Northern Cape with her children, Siphokazi despite everything was trying to put the family tragedy behind her and move on with her life. It was yet very hard to go back to visit her husband at the prison after what he harshly said to her that was so difficult to digest. There is a time for everything and he needed a lot of time to get healed of those wounds caused by her duplicity. Before leaving Johannesburg to Springbok she made sure to give her mother the personal contacts of secret agents Dumisane and Botha, just in case there was an accident.

It was still spring and the beautiful daisies of Namaqualand had spread over the ground like a carpet attracting so many local and international tourists. Many were coming to Springbok during spring intending to breathe the fresh air of the Namaqualand flowers. Siphokazi along with her children were enjoying far from Johannesburg. They were all happy in the middle of other happy people they had never met before.

The weather was hot and incredibly good for those in need of a suntan while at the same time visiting the carpet of flowers that were making them think about paradise. Her mother was the only one she told about travelling to the Northern Cape on vacation for a week and it was excellent, really the right moment. But sometimes she thought about Dumisane, the man who also knew a lot about her. He will always be good news to her, a caring man who never hesitated to tell them how much he loves her.

Isolated from all the executives, the decision in their meeting was taken to plot against the number one betrayer of Malume (Pty) Ltd.

"Our guys saw her in Springbok yesterday; I got the news yesterday night," said one of the executives.

"All my accounts in my name have been frozen by the government; however I'm left with those on my children's names, but not much for survival."

"The kidnapping will happen in two days, and they are closely following her every move, but she is not alone, with her kids."

"Themba should pay us not less than five million Rands, this bastard who was unable to stop what his wife has done to us."

"And he is a dead man if the plan fails, I promise you."

"What are you talking about, noticed one of the wardens who was coming towards them?"

"Just talking about our children, we miss them."

"It is time for supper."

"Do you see them?"

"They are now getting into our seven-seat taxi."

"Doesn't this hotel have a shuttle service?"

"Maybe they are all busy and it is good news for us. I believe they are going straight into the city to discover more about Springbok, the moment is favourable for the kidnapping, brothers."

"She has been here for five days, right?"

"Yep and she's ours, let go."

"What about the kids."

"Including them too."

The city centre was about twenty-five minutes away from where the hotel was, and with two days left she wanted to visit some of Springbok's malls and perhaps do some shopping. It was 11:00 a.m. and hot with few cars driving on the streets of Springbok, which was going to make the strike easier for the kidnappers The driver was one of them waiting for their signal. Siphokazi and her children didn't know anything and were enjoying the ride with a driver who was motivating them to also visit the West Coast National Park near Langebaan.

Without her fire-arm, Siphokazi felt released from the everyday pressure faced in Johannesburg. She needed some freedom to see the other side of a life she had never lived through before, and she noticed that even her children were enjoying the ride without asking about their father. It wasn't long when all of a sudden the unexpected happened along the quiet road.

A beautiful German brand new car went past them without anyone gazing in their direction, and that made Siphokazi feel uneasy because they looked suspicious and not trustworthy. She had studied about kidnappers and robbers' motives and behaviour, and what she spotted looked like one of them; however, the talkative driver behaved as if he saw nothing and continued distracting them with his stories, and more to the point he had many of them.

"Would you pull over for a while," she said to the driver to see what the German car was going to do.

"Are your children in need of a restroom?"

"Please just pull over," she repeated worriedly.

The driver without talking again pulled over, but it wasn't the only car following them because while Siphokazi was interested in watching the German car which was a reasonable distance from theirs that encouraged her, an extra car had just stopped behind theirs. Three armed men got out and, in the blink of an eye, encircled their car.

She was about to scream when one of the kidnappers laid his gun on her head and said, "Think about your children."

With the children holding their mother, they were quickly transferred to another car that took them to an unknown destination.

"Give me your cell phone," said one of the kidnappers.

She quickly gave without a word.

"Is it the only one you have?"

314

"Yes," she said protecting the children. "Where are you taking us? Who are you?"

"You'll shut your mouth lady."

All terrorized, she regretted going on vacation, but it was her mother only who knew about the trip, consequently, where did the leak come from?

"I have some money with me…"

"Shut up lady," he cut her off.

They went into a very fine-looking neighbourhood that looked just like some areas in Roodepoort while knowing well that her time to pay for her disloyalty has arrived. To her big surprise, the driver of the seven-seat car was following them behind with only him driving the car, meaning he was a fake taxi driver waiting for the misfortunate in their lives.

They entered a compound that had a tall wall around it, but nicely painted, with a tall and heavy gate that could only be opened electrically.

"Where are they taking us, mum?" Demanded her son Ntombisi.

With full of tears in her eyes, she didn't know what to say.

"Mum!"

"Yes, Ntombisi; I don't know."

"We told you to shut up," shouted one of the hijackers.

After parking the car they were aggressively taken into one of the rooms of the house that just had one single bed. They were all crying with no idea of what was going to happen to them.

"Mum, what do they want?"

She checked the door, but it was locked. Thousands of thoughts started running in her mind. Why did I travel, and who could be behind this?

"My children we've been kidnapped, I'm sure they need money."

"Are they going to kill us," said her second son.

"Don't talk like that my son."

It was approximately half-past five in the afternoon and Siphokazi had not called yet. Helena was used to chatting with her by that time since she left for Springbok on vacation. She allowed for another twenty minutes to pass, but there was still no call from her daughter, and that worried her. She decided to call instead of waiting for her daughter, but the call went straight to voicemail. She tried a few times but still in vain and that didn't seem like her daughter.

Without delay, she began looking for the hotel number where Siphokazi was staying. She dialled the fixed-line number a woman's voice answered.

"Claurodia Hotel reception, what can I do for you?"

"I am Helena, Siphokazi's mother who occupies room 125; I would like to speak to her."

"She has not been around with the children since 11 o'clock this morning around. Her room keys are still with us here."

"She is not back yet?"

"No, try her on her cell phone."

"She is not responding and I have the impression she is not safe."

"Do you want us to call the police madam?"

"Please do so, my daughter."

Helena remembered she should immediately in case of any problem contact the two secret agents Dumisane and Botha. She quickly looked around but found nothing; then she recollected that her daughter saved those numbers in her cell phone for her. Opening up her contacts list she found Botha's number that she dialled after calming herself down for panicking was not good for her health.

"Hello!" She heard a strong voice.

"Is it Botha? I am Siphokazi's mother."

"Siphokazi's mother! It is a pleasure talking to you, how can I help you, mama?"

"Siphokazi is not responding on her cell phone from Springbok where she went on vacation."

"Calm down, mum. Since when?"

"She always calls me before 11h30 but she hasn't today, and she isn't responding when trying to call her. And the last time she was seen with the children at the hotel was around eleven in the morning, and until now she isn't back. Maybe something wrong has happened to her."

"Thanks a lot for letting us know; I'm right now calling my colleague Dumisane to arrange a trip to the city. Do you have the name of the hotel?"

"Yes, Claurodia hotel."

"Don't worry about the telephone number, our system will provide us with it."

"Please speed up, sir."

"Everything will be fine, madam."

"Thank you."

Secret agent Botha phoned his colleague Dumisane who answered after calling three times.

"Botha, calling. Are you alright?"

"We have some problem with Siphokazi," he said.

"What! Something wrong happened to her?"

"According to her mother, Helena, she's reported missing with her children in Springbok."

"Oh no! Tell me you're kidding, I want to rest."

"She's missing; I've already called chief Keegan, and we have the green light to travel there."

"Where are you?"

"Let's do this, let's meet in one hour at OR Tambo airport." I'm tired."

"Do you still want to marry her or not?"

"I'm coming."

The two secret agents made sure to arrive in Springbok on that same night to lend a hand to their former colleague who was possibly at risk according to her mother who was greatly troubled by her silence.

"Do you still have her mother's cell number?"

"Yes, I saved it."

"Great."

Suddenly Dumisane's cell phone rang.

"Yes, chief."

"Have you already arrived?"

"Yes, chief."

"Stay at the same hotel she is and call the local police for assistance, they need to know that you're in the region."

"We're already on our way to the Claurodia Hotel."

"All the best," and the Lieutenant hanged up.

"I'm calling Sipho's mother to give us her daughter's number that we don't have."

"Do so, my friend."

It was eight o'clock in the evening and the prison was quiet with only the warden's footsteps being heard walking from corner to corner. Tladi, one of the executives, along with four others were on their turn cleaning the bathrooms of the penitentiary although to them it was mostly an opportunity to hear the news that one of them had concerning what they were busy with, was plotting against Colonel Themba.

"I am Mandla and I am a man of my word."

"You mean it is done," said Tladi.

"Yes, she is under our control and we are asking for a ransom of five million Rand."

"Well done," said one of the executives.

"Are you cleaning or busy chatting nonsense?" Grumbled the warden.

They quickly went back into cleaning the bathroom.

Silently sitting on the bed with her children, Siphokazi saw the door of the room being opened by two men followed by one lady elegantly dressed up but with a face expressing anger. When the children saw what was cropping up, they all quickly surrounded their helpless mother who still was saying nothing.

"I'm sure we look so miserable to you," said the lady.

319

She got nearer to Siphokazi and slapped her on the face, causing her to start bleeding through her nose. As the children were crying she glared at them.

"You shut up, shut up. I believe we can start our conversation now."

It was frightening and the only way to get out from this place alive was by cooperating for the hijackers were driven by evil motives to hurt, and there was no give and take.

"We need water," suddenly said Siphokazi.

"Bring them some water for we won't do well with dead bodies."

The lady took one of the chairs that were there and sat just in front of Siphokazi who was holding her children who were bound.

"We need some first-class money from you," she said, "And that's the only way to leave this place alive. And start thinking about who you should commission to bring the money within forty-eight hours, and no more."

"How much?"

"How much? You're getting it Siphokazi."

"Do you know my name?"

"Who doesn't know Malume; he's dead and left us poor."

She was violent and wicked, realized Siphokazi.

"And now we have the heiress who is busy enjoying what her father has left, isn't that right? We need five million in forty-eight hours if not one by one your children will start dying starting with the little girl until we get to you, so start thinking who to call to start making all the arrangements; I will be back in ten minutes."

The two men and the woman left the room at once.

"Mum, they want money."

"Yes and a lot of money my children, we are full of enemies but we are going to be fine, hold on."

The Claurodia hotel, what a beautiful accommodation it was, noticed the two secret agents once outside of the taxi. They saw three policemen entering their van ready to leave the premises and their presence could be connected to the disappearance of Siphokazi, as a result, Botha took the resolution to use his influence and ask them about the case, but Dumisane intervened.

"Don't do that we can end up looking suspicious to them, let them leave and we shall talk to them after any news from the receptionist."

"Great Dumi."

The two tireless secret agents entered the hotel and went straight to the reception area to discuss the matter with the male receptionist who was still busy talking to a customer. Dumisane let Botha handle the situation once the receptionist got free to talk to.

"Good evening," he spoke with his strong voice.

"Good evening sir," responded the receptionist with a smile. "We still have some available rooms on the second floor."

Dumisane was just beside him.

"Very good news said Botha; we're from South African intelligence."

They both showed their badges.

"Thank you, gentlemen, are you here for the lady called Siphokazi who disappeared this morning because the police just left?"

"Yes, of course."

"She's not back yet sirs, and we're dead worried about her and the children."

"Do you have some CCTV cameras out by the main entrance?" Demanded secret agent Dumisane.

"Yes, we do and the police will be here tomorrow morning to watch the video."

"Come on they had the whole day to watch the video, great!"Said secret agent Botha. "Then give us a room."

"Please not a double bed, but two separate beds, I don't want to feel his heavy breathing on my face."

The receptionist laughed and then said, "Are you paying cash or by debit card?"

"Just give us the receipt the government will pay," said, Botha.

"Oh sorry! We're not allowed."

"Ok, I'm paying," said Dumisane.

The two men went into the room followed by the lady carrying fast food in her hands.

"I believe you're hungry," she said with a sadistic smile. "But before eating, tell me who are you going to call to accelerate the process?"

"My mother," she responded.

"Your mother, I know her. Dial the number and after dialling immediately give me the phone."

322

Siphokazi took the phone and dialled the number, and instantaneously gave back the phone. Helena on the other side was resting on the couch in her lounge with her cell phone beside her responded to the nameless number.

"Hello!" She responded.

"Are you Helena?"

"Yes, I am."

"Someone would like to speak to you, quick," she said giving the phone to Siphokazi.

"Mum, it's me Sipho," she spoke with a shaky voice.

"Sipho! Helena called through her tears.

"Mum, they want us to pay an amount of five million Rands within forty-eight hours before releasing us."

"Are you with the children?"

They could all hear as they were on speakerphone.

"Yes, I am, mum."

"Quick!"

"But I don't have such an amount of money."

"Go to the office tomorrow morning mum and they will organize it."

And then the lady snatched the phone from Siphokazi's hand.

"Well done," she said, "Tomorrow morning again we're going to call."

"Eat your food now," said one of the men.

Realizing the unpleasant situation in which her daughter and grandchildren was in, Helena hastily called for secret agent Botha who was laid on the bed enjoying eating some muffins.

"It is Mama Helena," he said to a Dumisane who was half-sleep. Hello mama!"

"My daughter and grand-children have been kidnapped this morning, I've just spoken to her now and they are asking five million Rand before releasing them."

"Five million!" Exclaimed secret agent Botha.

"What!" Said secret agent Dumisane.

"Please do something in forty-eight hours."

"We're already in Springbok, what else did they say?"

"She said I should call the office tomorrow morning to organize the sum of money."

"Meaning they will call you tomorrow morning again to check, and please keep us updated."

"Please don't allow them to hurt my family."

"Be strong mum, they won't hurt them as long as they are in no doubt they will get their money."

Secret agent Botha sighed disappointedly.

"Indeed bad," said Dumisane.

"I'm tired."

"We're tired, tomorrow morning."

"Six a.m."

"Goodnight."

Among other prisoners, Tladi was trying to locate where Themba was, and he finally found him with some elder folks eating a bar of chocolate.

"Wow!" He said, "Chocolate following the rich man."

"I have one for you."

"Please let me have it; I haven't eaten one since I've been here dying slowly."

"Why Tladi? So ridiculous."

"I need to speak to you."

"I will excuse myself," said the elder. "And thank you for the chocolate."

They both retreated to talk.

"I will get straight to the point. Your wife has been kidnapped."

"She deserves it."

"That's all you have to say?"

"She betrayed her family and mostly her husband, what do I have to do with such a woman? Is it what you had to tell me?"

"But guess by whom?"

"I'm not interested and I don't even trust you Tladi; go rejoin those plotting against me. That woman yes she betrayed me, all of us because she became one of the executives, but be careful for she is the mother of my children."

Tladi left him without saying anything further and was busy enjoying the chocolate given to him by his former collaborator. Left alone, Themba recognized his enemies were closer to him than ever before, and he had to be watchful for hate was spreading out in people's hearts. In addition, the state of affairs was not in his favour for he was alone and lacked backup. But they all had a common regret, lamenting the death of the empire, and dying in jail like in a mousetrap.

He went to the tap that was closest to him to drink some water, and while drinking Themba felt a tap on his left shoulder, and when turning around it was yet again Tladi.

"You again, Tladi," he said.

"They also kidnapped your children."

Out of the blue Colonel Themba elbowed him in the face, causing blood to spurt from his nose. Tladi found himself rolling on the floor screaming for help, but Themba was not done with him for he deserved additional punishment for his provocations. He jumped on him while other prisoners were shouting encouragement to the fighters to carry on with hostility. He released a series of punches, causing more injuries to his face when he suddenly heard behind him a voice telling him to stop.

"Stop or we shoot you. "

He right away left him and put his hands up, however it was enough to isolate him for three days in a dark room of chastisement. All that happened with other executives watching the scene.

"Three days in that dark room will kill him," said one of the executives.

It was 5:30 in the morning, and Dumisane was already awakened and thinking about the woman he loved so much. Where was she with her children in this reputed town of Springbok? She had many enemies through what she did to the empire including all of those greedy executives right now in jail. On top of that, she inherited most of the leftover business which was worth millions of Rands so they were going to make sure she shares the residual.

"Botha," called secret agent Dumisane. "I need to tell you something."

"Come on it is not yet six in the morning; I put the alarm on."

"Who's going to help Mama Helena with such a big amount of money?"

"I never thought about it, that's genius from you."

"Botha, one of us should go back to Johannesburg to fetch that money."

"You go but let's first watch the CCTV video."

"Great!"

Two hours later in the CCTV room together with the police, the video showed the family going out of the building walking towards the main entrance where there was a white seven-seater car waiting for them. The picture was complete because it showed them entering the car.

"Can you move the picture to show the car registration number?" Said, Botha. "Thank you, that's it, yes the number is legible. We need to know the owner of this car."

A tall guy wearing sunglasses appeared in the CCTV room. He was confident and with the outlook of someone enjoying what he was doing in life. And he went straight to talk to the two secret agents who had completed viewing the video.

"I am detective Petersen," he said stretching out his arm to salute them.

"The two secret agents did the same."

"We are secret agents Botha and Dumisane," said Dumisane.

"You're in my town and we don't need your help," he suddenly said, holding eye contact.

"Those kidnapped are known to us, the lady used to be one of us," said Botha.

"Still, we don't need your assistance; we can very well take care of the situation without you going around our city. But what do you have in mind as you're already here?"

"They are asking for five million Rands," said Dumisane, "And we believe the money if it can be raised, will get here from Johannesburg."

"Five million Rands, that's a colossal amount of money. Who is this lady? A secret agent with such an amount of money?"

"She inherited a lot from her father; she is an executive now handling the whole business," said Botha.

"Then I will need you here, but don't do anything stupid because this is my town."

Both secret agents looked at each other.

"Talk to me before doing anything, and we're going to work perfectly well with each other."

"No problem," said Botha.

"So what's the camera show?"

Secret agent Dumisane explained everything to him without forgetting any detail.

"Meaning one of you should go and get the money in Johannesburg in case the payment happens here," he said.

"We also concluded that way," said Dumisane.

"Concerning the registration number; I will verify it and let you know, and this is my direct number on this card."

"Thank you, detective," said Botha after taking the card.

Bongani, Siphokazi's big brother was already in Johannesburg helping her mother to solve the terrible crisis in the family. As soon as heard, the night before he took a flight from Cape-Town to come and support his mother who was troubled by the whole thing. Not long ago it was the passing away of her beloved husband, and now it is her daughter and grand-children kidnapped in a town she has never set foot in, her entire life.

"So mama they want the money in thirty-six hours."

"Yes, I'm sure they shall call again to tell us how to get that money to them."

"Hopefully, the money is there, but that's all you have mum."

"This is what your father left in this house that nobody except me knew and I don't care my son, money is nothing. All of this is because of money and I don't want my child to die because of this filthy money."

"It's alright mum, it will be fine."

It was 10:30 when her cell phone rang, and it was again an unknown number.

"Hello!" She responded.

"Do you have the money?"

It was the same woman's voice.

"Yes, I have."

"Someone must bring that money here."

"Can I talk to my daughter?"

"They are all fine but listen old woman make sure that the police isn't with you and we only want you to bring that money to us here in Springbok. Some of us are already watching you.

Take the next flight that will land at Springbok is around four this afternoon and I will call you." And she hung up.

"Please God help me!"

"Do they want you to travel to Springbok with this money? Only you mother?"

"They are crazy but we can't say no, they will kill them."

After serious consideration, she called secret agent Botha to explain the whole complicated situation.

"Mum remain calm, look for a very strong bag that you'll use as a handbag to bring the money here, and once at the airport before going out of the airport call us, use the restroom to call us for once outside they will be watching on any suspect move."

"Thank you, I will do as you said."

"Did you hear that Dumisane?"

"No need to go to Johannesburg, smart from them."

"Let's wait until she calls, and detective Petersen, no feedback yet?"

"Nothing."

Chapter 20

While drinking some fresh wine from the Western Cape in the restaurant at the hotel, Dumisane saw detective Petersen coming into the hotel. Petersen saw the secret agents and came to them carrying a piece of paper. "Enjoying your vacation," he said.

"Your town is hot," said Botha.

"The white seven-seat car belongs to a certain man called Mandla."

"Mandla?" Repeated Dumisane.

"And the car comes from Johannesburg using a fake Northern Cape registration number. Probably to disorganize us."

"So let's hope we cross it on the way," said secret agent Dumisane.

"Yes, my guys are looking around, but is there any progress that you would like me to know."

"Yes," said secret agent Botha, who explained to him the whole scenario as clarified by the mother.

"Wicked people," said the detective. "I suggest we should dress up as cleaners and wait around the airport. Do you know the lady?"

"Yes, we know each other very well, however, what you said is a good idea," said Dumisane. "We should follow them in the airport and create a surprise attack."

"Let's get to the airport from quarter to three," said Botha.

"Let's meet here at two p.m. then."

"Great detective," said Dumisane, "We're making good progress."

Siphokazi and her children were seated on the bed saying nothing to each other, yet the children could notice that their mother was praying, and then suddenly her son Ntombisi remembered that he had his cell phone switched off in his bag.

"Mum, I have my cell phone," he all of a sudden said.

"What! Is it charged? That's great my son, give it, let me talk to your grandmother."

Her mother's cell phone rang twice before responding.

"Hello!" She said.

"Hello, mum it's me Siphokazi."

"Siphokazi! Are you fine? Please talk to me."

"I'm using Ntombisi's phone, give me again Dumisane's number so that I can call them and locate us."

"Ok! Here's the number."

"Thank you," she said after writing the number. And immediately she dialled and it was secret agent Botha responding on the other side.

"Botha speaking."

"Botha, it's me Sipho," she whispered behind her hand, hoping no one outside the room would be able to hear.

"Siphokazi!"

Dumisane was with Botha, and he got closer to the phone.

"Try to locate us; I'm using my son's cell phone."

"Take this number and call detective Petersen to locate you, we are also going to the police station to join him; take the number."

After taking the number she called the detective who was at the police station occupied preparing his guys to go to the airport. One sergeant sprinted to him.

"Sir, Petersen, there's a lady that would like to speak to you."

He immediately went to the radio control room to respond to the phone call.

"Detective Petersen."

"It is me Siphokazi and my children, who have been kidnapped, please try to locate where we are."

"We are already busy with that, twenty more seconds left to finalize it. Great, we got you."

"Thank you."

"Hang up and wait and make sure they don't find you with that phone."

And after finishing talking to her, he noticed that the two secret agents had arrived at the police station.

"Good job," said detective Petersen.

"Do you know where she is?" Demanded Dumisane.

"Yes fifteen minutes away from here, and a very quiet residential area with big houses, many rich people live there."

"So what are we waiting for?" Said, Botha.

Heavily armed and determined to put an end to the lawlessness, the two secret agents checked their watches; -

12:10 p.m. - and got into the back seats of the car that was transporting detective Petersen.

"I've observed your secret agent Dumisane and you look sad," said the detective.

"He's a man in love with the lady," responded Botha.

"Shame," said the detective.

"She's a very strong woman," said Dumisane, "And I do indeed have a crush on her, Botha's big mouth is right."

Detective Petersen laughed.

"I understand," he said, "we're almost there."

The street was deserted but beautiful, and the residence according to the GPS was two hundred meters away from where they were. Police vans were left at the back to avoid frightening the residents for most of the houses had cameras pointing towards their main entrances. They arrived at the tall gate of the house. Luckily for them, the gate was being opened and they seized their opportunity and rushed inside to take them by surprise. The car that was coming out had to reverse back in.

They were four grown men holding guns trying to escape by going back into the house and the detective followed by the two secret agents started shooting in the air.

"Stop running or we shoot you."

But they refused to halt and all went into the house. The trio led by detective Petersen was joined by other policemen. They walked to the door, Petersen pushed the door that was closed, but not locked and it opened. The house was big, beautiful but dangerous, and careful consideration before entering had to be applied to avoid any casualty.

"We're the police and we have already surrounded the house," said Petersen when he burst inside followed by those behind him ready to shoot at any threat.

"Where are they?" Said, Botha.

"Come out with your hands up," said the detective.

But there was no response. Sweating like never before they carried out checks on every room of the house without finding what they were looking for, Siphokazi and the kids were not at hand, and that could be very unsafe in case one of the outlaws informed those keeping them hostage. Upon entering one of the rooms, detective Petersen discovered a single bed; on which there was a paper with the police station's number.

"They were here," he suddenly said.

The two secret agents joined him to remark the same thing, and suddenly they heard three gunshots from outside, followed by a policeman saying "we got them." They quickly looked around to try to find any other evidence of the presence of the family in the house, and then left right away.

Once outside the house, they found the police with the four guys who ran into the house seated on the floor.

"They were trying to escape from the backyard," said the policeman.

"Great job," said the detective, "where are they?" He asked the four guys

"We don't know what you're talking about."

The slap landed on his face like lightning, causing an awful pain in his left eye.

"Where are they?" He repeated, but they said nothing.

"Shoot them," suddenly said Botha already pointing his firearm at them.

"Please don't shoot. They all left more than one hour ago."

Dumisane regretted the lost chance to shoot but kept his composure; he could with four bullets put them out of existence.

"To where?" Said Petersen.

"The airport, please don't shoot us."

"We are not going to shoot you but gladly keep you in jail for the rest of your miserable lives."

"And who is with them, and what car are they using?" Finally demanded Dumisane.

"They are with a lady with three children and four other guys."

"And the car?"

"A seven-seater white car."

"Did you try to call them?" Demanded the detective.

"We did not."

"Lock them up," ordered the detective.

The detective made sure to keep some police at the residence to thoroughly check the house and the surrounding areas, while Petersen and the two agents left to go to the airport where they will dress up, and start acting like cleaners.

It was 04:00 pm and Helena had just landed in what she thought was an oven ready to warm up some food. With a bag containing five million Rands in two hundred rand notes, courageously she began walking the tarmac of the airport towards the waiting bus That would take them to the airport terminal.

No one would imagine that she could carry with her such a significant amount of money, and she was frightened because it was huge. The money was put in a very expensive solid black bag that could attract anyone's attention, but at her age, many would avoid approaching her and asking. The good news was the police, except for the police working at the airport, were already there dressed like cleaners waiting for her to disembark.

The two secret agents were also waiting for her dressed like cleaners within the luggage area, for they wanted to see her coming. Talking to her could be dangerous too, but seeing her talking on her cell phone was possible because they had to locate her to take the cash.

All of a sudden they saw her, carrying the black bag and Dumisane noticed Siphokazi's beauty through her mother. They made sure she saw their helpful attendance, and when she saw them, secret agent Dumisane put his finger across his mouth to tell her not to talk to them, and her phone started ringing.

"Hello!" She responded.

"We know you are there," said a woman's voice that she recognized, "so follow everyone as they go outside, and once out of the building turn left and start walking until you see drop off number four, and once there you can wait for us, someone will pick you up there."

"Ok, I am coming there."

The whole area from inside the building up to the drop off zone was surrounded by the intelligence communicating effectively with one another.

"She has just finished talking on the phone, and is already beyond the luggage's area, heading towards where you are outside," said secret agent Dumisane to detective Petersen who was waiting outside as a respectful cleaner.

From where they were in the drop off zone, the lady accompanied by her four helpers saw a sixty-six-year-old lady carrying a black bag as agreed walking alone towards where their car was stationed, at drop off area number four. One of the men in the car jumped out, took the bag and left her there without knowing what else to do. The car without more ado sped away from the airport. Its occupants were unaware they are being followed by the intelligence ready to cause an ambush.

Detective Petersen, already joined by the two secret agents, caught a glimpse of what was taking place and waited until the white seven-seat car began being followed by another car. the driver of neither car didn't identify that the police was all over the area up to five kilometres away from the airport; they didn't know that their next minute was dangerous.

Driving fast with the black bag in his hand, he received a phone call.

"Hello!"

"Is the money in?"

"Yes madam."

"Great! We're just behind you."

"We can see you madam."

"Pull over and bring the bag to our car."

The driver pulled over and his colleague hastily brought the bag to her while expressing a smile that meant victory.

Holding their guns and ready for the assault against the kidnappers, detective Petersen gave the order to block the road in an area that will be difficult for them to escape. It was risky but worthwhile because they wouldn't have time to react effectively.

The car carrying the money followed by the seven-seat car with their boss inside was about to move off after a red light turned green, so it was the favourable moment chosen by the police to unleash the attack. The kidnappers saw two cars blocking them the way, so one of them shot twice towards one of the police's cars, breaking the windscreen, as a result, the reaction from the police was lethal. One of the police shot once, piercing the attacker's chest, the bullet ripped through his heart and he instantly died covered in blood. After that, the driver put his hands up when he saw what happened. However behind them, the driver of the white seven-seater car after witnessing what turned out, after following his boss order was about to overtake them and run away with the money, but they had no chance as the reply of the intelligence was well calculated.

A third police car blocked the road causing them to react brutally, and the shooting restarted as the kidnappers tried to break away from the police invasion, and they managed to grievously wound some policemen that were in their range. Noticing, secret agents Dumisane and Botha followed by detective Petersen jumped out of their car, rolling down like well-trained policemen resolved to end the kidnappers. They shot at the four kidnappers, who were shooting the police, killing them instantly.

Their boss was in the car in between the seats busy screaming and when the shooting stopped, she opened the car door and ran away carrying the bag full of money.

"You stop or we shoot you, lady," said detective Petersen.

She stopped fearful and sweating with her back to them. Detective Petersen quickly drew closer to her followed by one policeman aware of the situation. He took the bag and the policeman handcuffed her.

"You're under arrest and anything you'll say here will be used against you in a court of law."

"I hate you," she said to detective Petersen.

"Where are they?" He asked her.

"I don't know," she said very cross.

Without any more ado secret agent, Dumisane came with his gun, cocked it in front of her and held it to her head.

"Come on Dumisane; don't do that," said Botha.

"If you don't tell us where they are, I'll make sure right now that you're a dead person."

"Stop what you're doing," said Petersen.

"Lady do you want to die?" Said Botha, "Dumisane don't do that come on."

Dumisane was just in front of her sweating and expressing terror out of his face.

"Shoot then," said secret agent Botha, "Shoot!"

"Please don't shoot," she said closing her eyes, "We left them in our residence in the underground cage.

Immediately detective Petersen called one of his agents who were there to verify the underground area of the house.

"Look for the underground cage of the house they are in there."

"Going for it, chief."

Twenty-seven minutes later while entering the premises Dumisane saw Siphokazi with her children sitting on the floor outside. She was carrying her last born who was sleeping in her arms, and when she saw them she expressed her best smile of happiness that the secret agent knew and was grateful for.

When she glimpsed them coming towards her direction, she stood up to welcome them at the same time holding the child who was heavy; and Dumisane came straight to her and for about five seconds took her and the child in his arms.

"Thank you, Dumi," she said weeping in his arms.

"It is over now, Sipho, it is over, and you're all safe."

"But I don't see mum."

"The police are with her at the airport, and I'm sure she's by now at the hotel."

"I thought I was going to die with all my children."

And when she looked at one of the police cars, she saw their boss so ashamed of herself busy covering her face and looking down. She couldn't stand facing her.

Almost thirty minutes later Helena was holding a glass of water in the reception area of the Claurodia hotel, when she saw her daughter, Siphokazi, coming from the main entrance of the hotel with her three grandchildren, and what a moment it was for it changed the whole atmosphere. They were weeping in each other's arms like never before.

"Thank you Dumisane and Botha," said the mother.

After the hug, they spotted a tall and proud man stepping into the reception area coming towards them.

"I would like to introduce you to detective Petersen," said secret agent Botha, "I'm proud to have met him, it was nice working with you detective."

He came and saluted Helena, the children and their mother.

"Thank you very much, detective Petersen," said, Helena.

"You're welcome, that's why you must call me first before coming into my town," and he said laughing joined by the two members of the intelligence.

Two days later in the prison, Mandla with the rest of the executives was pacing up and down terribly irritated by the failed plot. Themba was victorious and still keeping those five million Rands for himself. What stood in their path was powerful with more determination than them. Siphokazi was just a fortunate woman with the Lord preserving her.

"My family was expecting a lot with that money," said Mandla irritated.

Tladi was silent and very observant and was laughing at them inside.

"Someone deserves to die and it is Themba," suddenly said Tladi.

"I'm with you," supported Mandla who was the most deceived of them all.

"Now he deserves to die," confirmed one of the executives, "I'm sure we are all going to die in this prison."

"We have been recompensed pitifully," said Mandla. "For what was my role in that company, the risk that I took to bring millions into our bank accounts, and he was unable to check on his wife, and busy sleeping with other women."

"We need to vote," said one of the executives.

"About what?"

"Who agrees with Themba's physical elimination? Enough with talking about what's behind us that we won't get anymore. Just lift up your hand."

Curiously all except Tladi lifted up their hands.

"What about you Tladi? You are the first one who said he must die," demanded Mandla. "He slapped you in public, going for the kill, did you forget about it?"

He finally lifted up his hand and said, "That's why I didn't lift up my hand, on the contrary, it is sad now that we've started killing one another, and after him who will be next? So how do we do that?"

"Beating him to death will be the best option for me, enough suffering for a traitor like him and his wife," said Mandla. "Tladi you know many people inside here, who can do the job?"

"With five hundred Rands we finish him."

And they all agreed to give the money until the amount was reached.

"Great!" said Tladi.

"We want the job done in twenty-four hours," said Mandla, "Good luck Tladi and don't come with excuses or you'll pay me back my money with interest."

"Trust me," said Tladi.

And he left them.

Going Into one of the restaurants in Rosebank, North of Johannesburg, secret agent Dumisane was holding Siphokazi's hand in order to help her enter the restaurant. There were some stairs before entering the restaurant and he absolutely wanted to give her a hand that she cordially accepted from the man who was always disposed to save her life, and after sitting down they ordered some drinks.

"This place is nice," noticed Siphokazi.

"Thanks a lot; I've been coming here for the last two years."

"The last two years and you never tell me."

"I was looking for the right moment like today, now."

"Yes it is worthwhile and I like the place, it is good for both of us."

He smiled.

"And how is your mother doing?"

"Stronger than ever, what happened has caused in her some sort of revival, to her it was like some kind of movie."

"That's good for her," he said laughing, "but what about you Sipho? Why are you still holding to that man? What he did is so heartbreaking and do you truly believe he will change? He won't forgive you, just marry me."

"Dumi," she called, "I know you're an exceptional man with a very good character, you! And I know that you love me, you want to make me happy and give me children, but I don't want to be the reason why you're not getting married, I saw Phumzile, she is the mother of your son and gorgeous."

"Yeah, Phumzile!" He said, "She's not like you but considerably in love with me; I'm not Sipho, you're the one that I love. I want to spend the rest of my life with someone like you."

"Let's order something to eat," she said.

"Why not," and he called the waiter who came with the menu.

"It is good that we speak this way; you're a good friend to me."

"More than a good friend Sipho, but a husband who will make you happy."

She stared at him with her best smile, and then moved her hand to hold his that Dumisane welcomed and then she said, "You're a good man."

He smiled when she said that with affection.

"I will pray that God meets the desires of your heart, for it is good you marry the one who will make you her King."

Something he never did in the past, he kissed her soft left hand. And she just looked without saying anything but taking good notes.

"Thank you Sipho and never hesitate to call me if you need anything, I will be there for you."

"Thank you, you're such a good friend, God bless."

The food came and they ate heartily.

Colonel Themba, after spending his three days in the isolated darkroom, was busy cleaning the toilets with another convict that he met for the first time. He knew that he wasn't safe in the prison. His former colleagues, the executives, were

345

putting the blame on him, the one who neglected to watch on his wife and bring to an end the embarrassment that finally ensured to them. For them, he was the cause of their sufferings.

While in one of the toilets he felt a light blow on his back, and when he turned around, he suddenly took two solid punches on his face and because of the impact, he violently hit his nape against the wall causing him to instantly lose consciousness. He came to seconds later and felt his body being pulled out of the toilet, and the beating carried on until he completely lost his mind, bleeding heavily and left there for dead.

The other convict who was cleaning the toilet hid in one of the cubicles when he saw the attack being carried out, he ran out of the toilet to rapidly call one of the wardens who was close to where the aggression happened.

"Please someone is bleeding to death in the toilet, he got brutally attacked."

The warden followed him and saw Colonel Themba who he knew very well in a terrible shape.

"But I know this guy, what happened?"

"He was busy cleaning one of those toilets when suddenly four guys assaulted him, so I hid terrified to receive the same treatment and there he is."

"We need to take him to the hospital, I don't want him to die here," said the warden. "Can you remember those guys? They didn't see you right."

"I didn't see them because I hid."

He went out and called more guards that came to take him to one of the rooms to wait for an ambulance.

"Check if he's breathing," said the warden to one of his colleagues.

"Yes, he's still breathing."

"Ok let's wait for the ambulance, but he lost a lot of blood."

Siphokazi pensive and somehow happy maybe because of the kindness of Dumisane, was determined to go to the prison to pay a visit to her husband. It had been more than a month now without seeing him, and she also wanted her children to know where their father was and make the journey together.

Dumisane is a gentleman who never tired to try to win my heart, she thought, to win the heart of a woman who is a mother of three children and deceived by a man like him, but it is good to be by his side, and enjoy the tenderness and caring feeling of a man in love. He didn't want to marry Phumzile simply because she is not like me, am I that queen of his heart that he absolutely wants? She shook her head and started her car.

Once she reached her destination during the visiting hour, she was already in front of the glass waiting for Themba to come but it was taking long, maybe he didn't want to come and see her. But she was ready to take it and move on with her life. She was beginning to think a lot about secret agent Dumisane who wanted her for himself and treat her as she desired to be treated. Finally, the warden came without him and she sadly understood that he rejected to come and see her.

"Your husband is not here with us," suddenly said the warden.

"He's not here?"She asked, surprised.

"They took him yesterday to the hospital after an assault, and he was not in good shape."

"Please where did you take him?" She said panicking.

"To Baragwanath hospital, but they won't allow you in to see him with what happened here."

She left her chair, opened up her purse to take her cell phone and called Dumisane.

"Hello, Sipho! How are you?"

"Please I need your help, please join me at the Baragwanath hospital, I need to see my husband who has been grievously wounded during an assault."

"Where are you?"

"I'm already at Baragwanath hospital," she lied "And they won't let me in unless I'm with someone like you, he's highly watched."

"Give me more or less thirty minutes and wait for me at the main entrance."

"Please come."

She hung up troubled, marched out of the prison building towards her car, started the car, and headed off in the direction of Baragwanath hospital. Tribulations were endless, and she could only face them through resiliency because no one was going to take her place and overcome all the broad range of problems sticking to her.

The hospital was about seven kilometres away from the prison, so she first calmed down and then continued to drive towards the hospital thinking about the worst that could take place in her life, and that was losing her beloved suffering husband. She knew she had enemies among the executives who were after the five million and failing to have that money could have been the primary reason for trying to kill him, but she knew that her husband was a strong man.

She parked the car in the parking and went straight to stand in front of the main entrance to hang around for secret agent Dumisane who was surely on his way. He was a man of his words and would do anything to please her. And twenty minutes later she saw him coming, and not alone, but with secret agent Botha.

"Thank you, thank you to see you," she said walking towards them to welcome her former colleagues.

"Hello, Siphokazi!" Greeted Botha.

"Do you know where he is?" Demanded Dumisane.

"I didn't dare ask yet," she responded.

"Ok, I know where they usually take them for security reasons, they won't mix the prisoners with the ordinary patients.

They entered the hall of the hospital and went straight to where the prisoners were usually taken The hospital was big, and they had to walk a long way to get to the prisoner's ward. They found it and went to reception.

"Good afternoon!" Gently greeted Dumisane.

"Good afternoon sir!"

"We are from South African intelligence."

"I know you," immediately said to the nurse, "Are you here to see a prisoner?"

"Yes, his name is Themba."

"Let me check on the list, yes he's here, but only two of you can go in, and you will find him on bed number seven on your left."

"Go in. I will wait for you here," said secret agent Botha.

"Do you really want me to come? "

"Yes, Dumisane."

The ward had many prisoners and also the presence of the police was remarkable. Siphokazi walked in the middle of those beds, counting them until bed number seven where her husband was laying, and it was painful but crucial. He was there seemingly asleep with plasters on both arms, and his face was swollen with a bandage down its left side.

With tears going down her face she suddenly heard.

"Why are you crying as if I was dead Sipho?"

"Themba," she called.

"Don't worry, I can see you; I am all swollen, they wanted to kill me."

"I'm sorry," she said.

"Who is that man?" He unexpectedly asked.

Secret agent Dumisane kept his distance in order to avoid eye contact with Themba.

"You're with those who helped you to arrest me? Get out of here."

"No! He just brought me here to help me to come in."

"Did you bring them here to laugh at me? I asked you to divorce me and move on with your life then you'll be able to forget about me."

Dumisane left the ward to rejoin secret agent Botha outside.

"I just came to see how you were doing, I'm from prison and I got rushed here."

Being able to see through one eye only, he saw her getting closer to him seeking for his hand to hold, and when she found it, she took it in her hand and started caressing it.

"How are my children?" He asked softly.

"They are fine but asking about you all the time."

"They also wanted to kill you but they couldn't, and that is why they came after me. What are you waiting for to bring the divorce papers? Tell my children that I'm in prison because of you." He released his hand from her hold, and then called one of the policemen with a hand gesture to say to him; please take this woman out of my sight.

"Themba why?" She cried out.

And he turned his face on the other side.

"Please madam," said the policeman, "It is good that you leave now because he must rest."

"I'm leaving thank you, goodbye Themba."

Once outside her friends were waiting for her, but feeling sorry for her.

"Are you done?" Asked secret agent Dumisane.

"Yes, I'm done," she said wiping her tears.

And they left the place without talking until they reached her car to let her go.

"Take it easy Sipho, and know that I'm always there for you."

"Thanks to both of you."

"Wipe your tears once for all and start a new life, and never apologize for the decision you took to assist your government because it was going to be you betraying your government by plotting against it."

And they hugged her and left.

Once in the house in Roodepoort her mother noticed that she had a tired face that has cried a lot.

"Where do you come from with such a face?"

"My face?"

"You've been crying, my daughter."

"Themba was beaten to death, Mum."

"He's dead?"

"In critical condition at the Baragwanath hospital."

"You still care for that man right?"

"I still do, Mum," she said caressing her right wrist.

"But know he's making sure you regret what you've done to him and your family."

"That's exactly what he's doing, pushing me to divorce him, torturing me."

"I know. You are a better version than what I am because there was a time I was about to leave your father but I just couldn't, maybe because he could replace me with any other woman, a young one maybe, but I still loved him. You on the contrary he's behind bars, and you still want to care for him until he goes out of prison. Is any guiltiness taking you in that direction?"

"I've always loved Themba, Mum."

"But you were about to divorce him? Remember."

"Yes I was but I knew I was unable to do such a thing; I already had the papers; I was strongly trying to get him to stop what he was busy with other than his own family, but he loved what he was doing and when the government reminded me about the statement of loyalty, I got stuck, Mum and it caused more sufferings."

"I am proud of you my daughter, but you need to put a cross on your pass and move on with your life."

"You're the one who told me that we get married for better and for worse."

"Then stop crying every time when you go to the prison to see him because your father was there caring for me, but Themba, my daughter, is not with you right now, and your father never pushed me to divorce him; he cherished me rather."

"Mum, if it was you in my shoes would you divorce him?"

"I wouldn't have divorced Malume if he still wanted me."

"Thank you, Mum, and I know Themba still loves me."

"Now my daughter is focused on those who are with her, and just pray for that stubborn man of yours that you don't want to divorce, take care of the family business and don't stumble, trust God as you've been, and watch on your kids."

"I will, Mum."

Chapter 21

Ten years later Ntombisi had just completed his matric and was ready to go to varsity, and his mother Siphokazi was proud of him. As a single mother, she survived to overcome most of the worries caused by his adolescence and managed to take her son to varsity, but that wasn't enough because despite the fact her children knew that their father was in jail, they still didn't know she was the facilitator used by the government, and that was a secret she had kept for a decade, but now she was about to expose it before they discovered the truth from someone else, from an enemy of the family.

Ntombisi had many of his father's attributes, very determined and disciplined, he was also handsome with many girls coming after him. Siphokazi never took that initiative to take them to see their father at the prison and they never asked about paying him a visit, but she wanted that close contact as quickly as possible for they had to face that reality. However, before that, she had to tell them the whole truth.

They were back into their house five years ago and life became more enjoyable with no threats from anyone to the family. Since seeing Themba in hospital, she never returned to prison to visit her husband or meet Dumisane and Botha. The business was doing fantastic as well as her mother, but her mother-in-law was not doing well; she was very sick with breast cancer. Ntombisi approached his mother."Mother, I need some money to go and see grandma."

"We do have enough petrol in the car, but you know I don't want you to drive long distances yet."

"Mother, I can do that."

"But I first need to speak to you my children, call your brother and sister."

And when they came, she took courage and engaged speaking to them.

"I wanted you to come with me and see your father in prison."

The kids looked at each other without saying anything.

"But before we do such a thing I have to tell you something I've never told before; I was used by the government to arrest your father."

"Really mother?" Replied Ntombisi.

"Yes, but I had no choice because I was working for the intelligence; she said wiping some tears from her eyes. I used to be a secret agent or an undercover agent, and the government knew that your father was my husband and he was wanted, and if I had refused it was going to be considered as high treason from me to my government."

After saying that she waited for the reaction of their children, especially from her firstborn who again looked at his siblings.

"Mum, you did what you had to do, dad was a bad man," said Ntombisi. "And you still love him in spite of what he has done to you and us."

With tears in her eyes, she left her seat to come and hugged all her children.

"Thank you for understanding me, but I need you to come with me to see him?"

"After how long mum?" Asked her second son.

"Ten years now and since he knows the truth he has always rejected me, and even asked me to divorce him, but I wouldn't."

"We are ready to go and see him, Mother," said Ntombisi. "But I'm disappointed in my dad, he's cruel."

"Don't talk like that my son, learn to forgive. Tomorrow morning we go to Soweto."

And Ntombisi left.

Johannesburg was shining The following morning, and Siphokazi with her children went to Southgate Mall to buy some groceries in the hope that their father maybe was going to accept. To her great surprise while in the mall, she met secret agent Dumisane with Phumzile accompanied by one boy and a girl who she believed were their children. Without refraining, she went, followed by her children to surprise him. He seemed happy.

"Good morning, secret agent," she said from behind him.

"Sipho!" He called turning around delighted.

"That's me," she said.

"What a surprise after so many years," and he hugged her and gave a handshake to the kids.

"Yes, ten years," she said. "Ntombisi this is secret agent Dumisane, we used to be colleagues and work for the government."

"Nice meeting you sir," said Ntombisi.

Phumzile was not far, and she also joined them.

"Ah, Sipho! You know Phumzile; she is my wife now and our two children."

"Congratulations, you never invited me to your wedding."

"I couldn't get you; I did my best but you were not around."

"I'm very happy for you, and how is Botha doing?"

"He's doing well and we all have been promoted to a mentorship position and paying well."

"I'm missing you guys; I have to go now," she said.

"It was nice meeting you again," said Phumzile.

"Bye!"

"Bye Siphokazi," he said watching her leave with her children.

Driving to the prison despite it being close to the mall took them about twenty minutes because of the traffic.

"We have arrived," said their mother.

"Dad is inside here?" Said Ntombisi.

"Yes."

Once inside the visitor's room waiting for her husband to come the beating of her heart accelerated since she didn't know what to expect from Themba after all those years without seeing her. How he was going to react once he sees his children visiting him for the first time ever in the prison. After about ten minutes, there he was looking fine, but a bit older and when he saw his children with their mother, he was very surprised and started crying.

"Ooh my God!" He said wiping his tears, "Why did you do this to me Sipho, they are so beautiful."

"Hello, papa!" Greeted his firstborn.

Siphokazi also with tears in her eyes moved a little bit to allow her children to speak to their father.

"I love you, my children," he said touching the glass that was separating them with his hands. "How is school?"

"I'm starting varsity in January," said Ntombisi.

"I'm in grade eleven dad," said their second son.

"And you, my daughter? Look at how beautiful you are."

"I'm in grade four."

"Mum did very well to bring you along," and after saying that he looked at her but slowly, she looked down the floor with a smile that he remembered very well.

"Thank you, Siphokazi," he said, "Did your mum tell you everything?"

"Yes she did," said Ntombisi.

"That I'm in jail because of her."

The children said nothing to that.

"They know everything Themba that I am the traitor," she said, looking at him in the eye.

"Please don't start fighting," said Ntombisi.

"You're welcome to come and see me anytime," he said to his children.

"We will, Dad," said the children all together.

Siphokazi again saw some tears going down his face, and then left them without adding any other word, but wiping his tears.

"Let go of my children, it is very difficult for your father."

"It was nice to see dad mum," said her daughter.

"Yes, I was also happy to see him again after so many years."

Three years later at the Johannesburg hospital, Siphokazi turned up with her mother Helena to hearten their in-laws who were waiting for some feedback from one of the doctors who was busy attending to the case of mama Themba, her husband's mother. The spreading of her breast cancer had reached the final stage, and there was no hope of recovery according to one of the doctors a week ago.

Siphokazi took some distance. After what happened with her husband and Malume (Pty) Ltd, and the rumours about being the author of their nightmares. Her mother was the one closest to her family-in-law encouraging them while waiting for the feedback from the doctor. She struggled with cancer for more than five years, and even cutting her breast was not enough to stop the spreading of the disease in her body. Only prayers could save her.

From where she was she saw the family going inside the ward surely where her mother-in-law was, and after five minutes, she called her mother who told her that they gathered around her mother-in-law who, with difficulty, could speak to them and that she would like her to come and see her final moment. So she took courage and came where they were standing just behind her mother who was talking to mama Themba.

"Where is Siphokazi?" Demanded mama Themba.

"She is here with me."

"Come, come my daughter."

"Hello, mama!"

"I'm happy to see you today my daughter; I know you still love my son and you're still his wife, at least he won't be left alone, and know that I've never had a problem with you."

Siphokazi was listening weeping for she was being forgiven by her mother-in-law who was dying.

"Thank you, Mama Themba; I promise I will wait for him until he gets out of prison."

"I'm proud of you. My son wouldn't listen."

After saying those words, Siphokazi got closer to her and kissed her forehead, and then left with her mother. Two days later they took delivery of the news that she breathed her last in the morning and in the presence of her family and that the funeral will be held on Saturday. Very heartbreaking news. Siphokazi decided herself as his wife to take the matter to her husband at the prison. Besides he already knew that his mother was not doing well at all, so he expected some bad news like that one.

Mama Helena also was for the very first time decided to pay a visit to her son-in-law who she had last seen thirteen years ago at the terrible event of his arrest. It was time to see him, she said to her daughter.

"It will be painful to see Themba because he was always with your father," she said to her daughter who was driving the car.

"I'm sure he's going to appreciate your visit."

"I hope so my daughter."

Once there and already seated in front of the glass waiting for Themba to appear, the warden came to inform them that

360

they still had to wait for another ten minutes because of some event hosted by the department of correctional services. About ten minutes later there he was holding with him a cold drink, and also seeming blissful. And when he saw his mother-in-law after so many years, he cried aloud.

"Mama Helena, how are you?"

"Themba I'm fine," she responded.

But he never said anything to his wife, his attention was focused on his mother-in-law.

"How are you, Themba?"

"I'm alright Sipho, and you?"

She first looked at her mother who gave her a sign of the head to go ahead with the news.

"Is there a problem?" He demanded suddenly worried.

"We came to announce to you that mama Themba is no more," said Siphokazi.

With a grimace on his face, he looked down and then covered his face with his hands for a while until tears filled up his eyes.

"And I can't even bury her, stuck in this prison."

"The burial will be held this coming Saturday, Themba," said mama Helena. "And receive our deepest condolences, this is everyone's final destination, my son."

"Thank you, mama Helena and yourself how are you doing after what happened? So sorry for what happened to Malume."

"Time heals my son, and we've learned to live without him, and you do the same until the day you will leave this prison, but don't leave this place without having forgiven your surrounding, do you understand?"

"Yes, Mama Helena," he said looking down regretting the death of his beloved mother.

"We were all there at the hospital before your mother breathed her last, and she had a very good conversation with your wife, and she left us in peace."

"Thank you very much for coming to tell me the sad news; I know you'll bury my mother with honour, and don't forget to bring me some pictures."

"We will my son."

"It is time said the warden, everyone out."

"Bye Themba!"

"Bye!"

After the funeral and nine years later and still in the city of Johannesburg, Mama Helena, now in her early eighties, had been suffering from chronic severe blood pressure for two years. Her doctor had difficulties controlling it. She was sometimes stressed out and missing a lot, the man who died many years ago that she had always loved and never forgotten. However, she was happy to have lived many years and to have seen the coming of many grandchildren. She was grateful to God for the favour, but she was no longer feeling as alright as she used to, and that's why for the second time Siphokazi had to move to Roodepoort to stay there with her.

"Mum, I still believe I should take you to my place just to change the environment."

"Why do you want to take me away from Malume?" She replied.

"Please, Mum, just for two weeks."

"There's no need for something like that, I'm fine here."

"I'm going to work and leave you with Nsiki; Nsiki please come," she called.

Nsiki was their faithful servant who spent more than twenty years working for the family and was in her early sixties and had become a friend of the family.

"I'm going, and take care of mum as usual."

"I will madam, do you want me to bring you something to drink or eat, Mama Helena?"

"Not now, Nsiki."

"Goodbye, Mum."

A week later in the premises of the not-for-profit organization in Roodepoort, Helena was also in the boardroom listening to what the executives under her daughter Siphokazi were deciding on the company going forwards. She was happy that two of her daughters, Siphokazi and Anele, joined the force, working together for the advancement of the organization that had a very good reputation and was receiving donations from all over the world for their involvement in taking care of mothers and children living with HIV combined with the maintenance of public schools in the townships.

Siphokazi was passionate about the project and was receiving many tenders from the government that she was dealing with much care to bring accomplishment. After the board meeting, which they all enjoyed, her little sister Anele took their mother home as she was feeling tired. Soon after Siphokazi received a phone call from Anele

"Sipho, mum is not alright, and I'm taking her to the clinic."

"I will meet you in the next thirty minutes," she responded.

The clinic was about seven kilometres away from their home but getting there was going to be slow because of the traffic.

"Please don't take me to the clinic," suddenly said mama Helena.

"Why mum?"

"Anele I'm tired, I want to die peacefully in my house."

"It will be fine, Mum."

"Take me to my bed, I want to rest."

Anele immediately called her big sister again.

"Sipho, mother doesn't want to go to the hospital. She said she wants to die peacefully in her house."

"I'm on my way Anele, and please call the rest of the family."

Bongani was in his office in Cape Town when he received a phone call from his little sister Anele.

"Good day, Anele! "

"You need to come to Johannesburg, mum is not doing well, and she doesn't want to go to the hospital and wants to die peacefully in her house."

"Where is she? I want to talk to her."

"She is lying down on her bed, let me go to her."

After a few seconds, she reached her mother who was with Nsiki their servant.

"Mum, Bongani wants to speak to you."

"Hello, mum!"

"Hello, my son!"

"Mum, you need to be taken to the hospital, and you'll be fine."

"I don't want to, I'm tired and I don't want to die in the hospital."

"I'm taking the next flight mum."

"You don't have to my son," she said.

And he cut the communication. A few minutes later Siphokazi entered with the family medical doctor and went straight into the room where her mother was. She was found sleeping with Anele sited aside her.

"How is she doing?" She asked.

"She is very tired."

Without wasting time the doctor took her blood pressure together with her temperature, and they were both high.

"Your mother needs to go to the hospital."

"But she doesn't want to," said Anele.

"Give her an extra 5mg Amlopidine to lower her blood pressure, and allow her to rest. Also, use a cloth soaked in lukewarm water to reduce her temperature."

"Where are her medications?" Demanded Siphokazi.

"I have them," said Anele, "Mum wake up to drink your medications."

"Is she regularly taking her medications?" Asked the family doctor.

"Yes she does," said Siphokazi. "I make sure before leaving to the office that she takes them."

"She needs some rest and after that, she will be fine, but she must stop stressing."

"We're struggling with that doctor."

It was eight in the evening when Bongani arrived from Cape-Town to the family's house. He found his mother with the rest of the family assembled in the TV room, watching some TV. But his mother was weak and still sleeping.

"How is she doing?" He suddenly asked.

"Bongani!" Called Anele, "There you are."

"Mama is not alright Bongani," said Siphokazi, "And she is categorically refusing to go to the hospital."

He sighed and said, "She is tired to go to the hospital; I will stay with you for a week and watch on her, she must go to the hospital."

"Let's hope so."

And suddenly she woke up.

"Bongani my son, you're here," she said happy to see him.

"Hello, mum! What is this story that you're refusing to go to the hospital; we don't want you to die."

"Who said that I'm going to die?"

"You said it."

"I hate the hospital and you're spending a lot of money for nothing, I'm old my children, and I'm fine here."

"Mum, you're under medical aid so you don't have to worry about the money. How do you feel?" He asked.

"Much better since you're here," she said smiling nicely.

"I'm here for a week and make sure you're fine, if not I personally will take you to the hospital you like it or not."

Five days later while in her office, Siphokazi received a call from her big brother, Bongani, informing her about the health condition of their mother that wasn't alright at all, and that he had already called the family medical doctor.

"I'm on my way," she said, and Anele also joined her.

Once home, they straight away rushed into her bedroom with the hope to see her well again, but they found the family doctor in attendance with very little to say.

"Your mother is dying," he said.

"I love you, my children," she said.

"Mum!" Called Siphokazi with tears in her eyes.

"I'm happy to see you around me in my final hours."

"Don't talk like that," said Anele weeping already.

Bongani the big brother was quiet with his arms crossed against his chest observing what was happening, and he had already spoken to his mother before their arrival.

"Be strong, my children," and she breathed her last.

The doctor came to Bongani.

"Close your mother's eyes."

"I can't," and they all started crying.

The doctor came and closed their mother's eyes.

"Be strong, family," he said, "I will come to the funeral."

Two days later Siphokazi went to give the information about the death of Helena to her husband. She wouldn't like him to discover her death after coming out of the prison, and it was also a means for her to pull him closer to her life; she wished for him to still be part of the family in spite of all those years gone, and above all making sure that she wins back the broken heart of her husband.

Again Themba faced the woman to whom he still had to admit the many sins of his youth, and after twenty-two years, she still looked attractive to him. He was sixty-three years old and she was fifty-eight and appeared so beautiful while busy talking to him.

"Mama Helena is no more, Themba," she said.

"Another tragedy," he said, "what went wrong with her?"

"Her blood pressure was very high, and she was also stressing a lot."

"She was also old, thank you for the news, and how are the children?"

"They are excited to see you in three years' time coming out of this place."

Themba looked at her and realized in his heart that she was an adoring wife that he abused for so many years and surely needed his compassion right now.

"Tell my children that I love them, and I'm also eager to see them in three years if I don't die here because many are not making it."

"You won't die, remember you're a soldier," she said looking down towards her hands that she was caressing, and when she lifted up her head he was gone.

She smiled and sighed, maybe he didn't want her to see him crying. Yes for many years it had been a conflict between emotion and reason, and she knew how proud he was, however she believed she was getting where she wanted him to be, and that was to admit his wrongdoing and forgive her in order to gain his freedom. For her, it was a sense of purpose to pull off in the life of her husband who was egocentric.

The warden who was advanced in age kindly came to her after seeing that and said to her, "I've seen you coming here for many years; do you really still love this man?"

Siphokazi laughed and said, "What did you notice?"

"He's a very lucky man, all these years; those who were arrested with him; I remember I was here when they brought them into this prison are all dead except him and one other.

"Really!" She said amazed.

"I believe it is because of your prayers, you're a good woman."

"Thank you," she said smiling at him, and she left the premises.

After many praises and worships songs to the Lord, Mama Helena Nhlakanipho was in all dignity buried in the Tembisa Township by the side of her husband, Malume.

Two years later when Siphokazi turned sixty, her son Ntombisi prompted her to take early retirement for he was an excellent manager and totally loyal to the company. He was the opposite of his father in relation to business choices, and she was considering retiring once the family accepted him as the next C.E.O of the company for he also had a masters in business administration.

On that same day, Pastor Thabiso was with delight walking in the corridors of the prison of Soweto. Three years ago he received a license from the department of correctional services to get as close as possible to those whose transgressions have locked them far from the community, and he had worked hard to get hold of it. For him it was like accomplishing the last phase of what God had put in his heart to achieve, ministering to prisoners in their prison cells. But it was risky and he was always accompanied by two well-armed wardens ready to protect him in case of an attack against his person, for the prison was most of the time an unsafe place.

Ministering to them was a moment of great joy for he knew what to tell them, and many repented their sins crying like babies waiting for their mothers to arrive. While walking on that day in one of those gloomy corridors he turned his head towards one of the cells on his right, his eyes fell on Colonel Themba's eyes who was very surprised to see him in such a place.

"Pastor Thabiso!"Themba called shocked, "What are you doing here?"

"Colonel Themba," but he never said it loudly.

"Please don't call me colonel here; besides, I've been downgraded a long time ago."

Pastor Thabiso looked at the two wardens to let them know to open the cell door.

"I will minister to him," he said.

After opening the door, he entered without them as they realized they had known each other for a very long time, but they were still there watching carefully for the rule was to be inside with the minister. But Themba was ashamed of himself; it was already known that he was living a double life that finally got him exposed.

"I'm very happy to see you after so many years, Themba and we are no longer young."

"Of course, pastor," he said laughing, "but what are you doing here? This is not a good place for a servant of God like you."

"Souls outreach. I love that, don't forget I'm a slave of our Lord Jesus Christ. He died for the unrighteous, and he sent me to you today because he loves you, furthermore He wants you to come back to him today. Don't forget that our Lord God is gracious and merciful, and wants to restore you emotionally. I know you've been through so much. On the other hand, you have a beautiful and wonderful wife who once said to me while crying that she loves you so much to dare divorce you, and this is the grace of the Lord."

Themba began weeping.

"That woman has suffered a lot, pastor; I've been the cause of much havoc; I am to blame for what happened to my family, and I even had the guts to blame her for her loyalty towards our government I used to work for and misrepresented. May God forgive me?"

"I'm so glad that you have already reconsidered and repented of your sins before God. Next time when she comes to visit be the one to let her know and in your own time pray to God, and he will guide your heart."

"I will, and thank you for coming to me pastor because I needed these words."

Thank God for his mercy, but know that even if I see your wife at our assembly; I won't tell her anything of what we've spoken about, you must do that and bring peace in your family, and relationship with our creator."

"I will pastor Thabiso."

Holding his Bible and determined to be a blessing in his community, pastor Thabiso was not done yet but enjoying continuing walking in what he called the journey of the Lord.

371

There were two months left of life in the Soweto prison, and Themba was expecting his wife Siphokazi's last visit before leaving the prison. But she was still not coming, and because of irritation and disappointment, he had lost all the contacts he used to have of the family. Tladi and he were the only ones alive among the executives of Malume (Pty) Ltd and we're very excited to get their freedom back and rejoin the family members they've missed for so many years.

He increasingly missed and she was worth a public apology, further, he was dying to do so. He became conscious of turning her into the scapegoat of the family while he was the main author of all the family unit's miseries. While eating like other prisoners, Tladi sat near him with his plate and started eating.

"Do you know where you're going after this prison?" asked Tladi.

"I have faith in going back to my family."

"You have faith," he said. "My wife left me fifteen years ago to marry another man, even my siblings stopped visiting me ten years ago, and all my children have forgotten that they have a father."

"That's bad, comrade, really sorry that you're facing such a situation."

"I'm sixty-seven years old and what do you want me to do in a big city like Johannesburg?"

"I believe the government will grant you some money that you'll start getting every month as a senior citizen."

"A senior citizen with a criminal record. It is better I die here."

"Don't talk like that Tladi, after all these years and die now when you're about to leave this miserable place."

"But I don't have a place to go."

"I believe we're going out on the same day."

Without saying more he ate his food, and after finishing he suddenly stood up and left. Themba was surprised to see him leaving without saying something. He left his empty plate and followed him.

"Don't be paranoiac Tladi. I will see if I can find you some money."

"It is not about money, but being alone. Unlike you, your wife never divorced you and you know where you're going, what about me?"

"Don't do anything stupid Tladi."

"I am ignored by the whole community, even by my own family and children, besides they all are delinquents by now."

Out of the blue Tladi picked up a big stone that was on his right-hand side and violently hit the warden who was busy watching the detainees eating.

"Stop!" screamed Themba, but it was too late because the warden fell on the floor with his face bleeding heavily.

"I don't care; I don't want to leave this place, and I don't care."

Themba could not stop the aggression for he did it very quickly for a man of his age. After that, he sat on the floor waiting to be taken wherever they would, and see his days of existence in the prison increase. On the following day, Themba heard from one of the wardens that he was transferred to Cape-

Town prison where he will spend another five years for his intentions were to commit very serious injuries to the warden.

Chapter 22

Still on his prison journey, Themba spent time thinking more and more about what freedom will bring into his life once released. Twenty-five years have been a very long journey in the prison and they changed his life; a change for the better. Life out there was no longer as it was twenty-five years ago. Even his children were no longer used to having a father by their side, and he was more confused about how to treat his wife as a husband should for it was many years without living with a woman.

He was in his early forties when he got imprisoned and now he was sixty-six, an old man but still full of life, and while in prison he succeeded with difficulties to restrain from drugs and even managed to stop smoking cigarettes. Time and again because of the level of stress he was tempted to become a slave to those things, but declining the use of them was just a sign of hope. But he acknowledged that what encouraged him to hold on was his wife's attitude throughout all those years, she was able to return love for hatred, and she persevered until she won back his unforgiving heart, and due to that, he missed her.

In three days time, the gate of freedom will be unwrapped for him to find again that lost freedom that should have been protected like an egg on the plate. Since the last time his wife came with the news about the death of Helena his mother-in-law, she came once again with the children, and that was it. Hence it was five months already without seeing them. But he was determined, no matter what, to move on with his life and die in dignity. He deserved what happened to him, and he had only himself to blame for losing many precious years of his life without his family beside him.

Forgiving her after so many years in the presence of God, gave him a renewed respect for life. No longer would he be focussed on making vast quantities of money and wasting it. He realised what his wife and children truly needed. Through forgiveness, he learned that protecting them should be his number one priority. Through forgiveness, he learnt to trust God and accept Him as the author of faith.

A week ago full of excitement as her husband was about to be freed, Siphokazi made sure to call the prison and ask for the day and time of his released, and also prayed so much that nothing wrong happened to him. She was still in doubt that he was going to come out of there as a transformed man able to put his past behind him and move on with his life. She definitely wished for them to bury one another or be buried by their children on the same day and hour.

Her children experienced the presence of a happy mother in front of them, They were very pleased for her for they saw their mother suffering because of a man full of derailed aspirations that could have jeopardized their future. She had made sure to discontinue the state of affairs by taking courage to do the unthinkable and save her family. All those wiped tears were not in vain and now there was brightness at the end of the road.

Ntombisi was now the president and C.E.O of the organization, while she just remained a member of the board of directors watching from afar as he was doing a great job, bringing new ideas that we're attracting more donations into the NGO, and she was satisfied with how efficient he was.

Now what she needed was the return of the gentleman of her life she has never ceased to love. She was already feeling his presence as she regularly held his clothes, putting them together for him to find them just ready.

If truth be told there is nothing impossible for those who believe and are determined to see their dreams coming to pass. Faith to see him again walking the corridors of his house was high and she trusted in God to make it happen for the sake of His love for humanity. Once when praying, she reminded God, saying, "you gave me this man so that I can help him, however, look at what he is today, but I still love him the same way I loved him at the beginning, and you are going to help me to carry on."

On the morning of his release from the prison, the day appeared different and unique for Themba as many of his prison mates came to congratulate him and say goodbye. Dressed like never before in his twenty-five years of prison, he somehow was disorientated not knowing exactly what was waiting for him just after he gets beyond the big gate that was about to be opened.

He was surprised to get out of the prison wearing the same clothes he got arrested with twenty-five years, and they fitted him exactly.

"Your wife never brought new clothes," said one of the wardens to him, "Why? Did she change her mind?"

He was a provocative warden sent to them ten years ago by the government.

"You can't trust women; they are not that strong for crazy guys like you. My advice is, if you carry on with that craziness and you come back to us, you belong here."

Themba determined to never come back smiled and said, "I was once a child and I am no more."

"What's that mean?" He asked.

"I've grown up."

The warden looked at him while shaking his head, and a third warden joined them with a document that he gave to Themba, and together they started walking towards the big gate that slowly was being opened. The hour and minute had arrived for his release, and he could start seeing freedom as he was getting closer to it until he completely found himself beyond the walls of the penitentiary. Suddenly he heard a big bang coming from behind him, and it was the giant gate landing on the floor abandoning him once again to the world.

When he paid more attention to those in front of him, Themba with pleasure noticed what made him cry. There, in his support, was his wife Siphokazi and his children, who at first he didn't recognize all waiting to take him home. First of all his children walking calmly came to him, leaving Siphokazi behind, for she didn't know how he was going to react after what she did to the family. But she enjoyed watching her children embracing their father with joy, for finally, he was back in their lives, and she made sure that it happened that way.

After the embrace with his children, he focused his attention on her for she was beautifully standing there waiting for him to welcome her. But she suddenly remembered the shock she caused to the whole cartel and mostly him. He looked down with her eyes on him and in a hesitating move, she turned around and started walking away with the children watching the scene when she suddenly heard him calling her.

"Siphokazi!" And she stopped, turned around to look at his eyes, "I'm nothing without you."

With her hands on her chest, she began walking fast towards him realizing she had been forgiven by the one she has always loved. Once in front of him, crying, she made sure to be in his arms that she had missed so much for the last twenty-five years, shedding tears like never before; truly the eagle has renewed its wings for a new life.

"I'm nothing without you Siphokazi; I love you so much and forgive me for the miseries, for all I've made you endure."

"I've forgiven you more than twenty-five years ago, and I'm happy that you're back into life."

Once at home and in that same house after many years of prison, Themba finally began to live a normal life of a father with his children, and of a husband, with his wife. On that Sunday morning, pastors Thabiso and Tshepang were happy to see them together as a winning family that God had elevated to His standard.

"Do you remember this song?" She asked him.

"After twenty-five years, you're still singing this song. Really God never changes."

THE END

About The Author

Born in Brussels, in the Kingdom of Belgium, originally from the Democratic Republic of the Congo and ethnic luba and now of South African nationality.

This is his first novel written in the hope to see a better drug-free society and at the same time raising awareness of rhino poaching activities that have to be stopped.

www.ingramcontent.com/pod-product-compliance
Lightning Source LLC
Chambersburg PA
CBHW021132260626
47169CB00005B/1569